THE CUMBERLAND MOUNTAIN SERIES

Ae fond kiss

LOVE BLOSSOMS IN TENNESSEE

JOAN DONALDSON

Black Rose Writing | Texas

ISBN: 978-1-68513-542-3
PUBLISHED BY BLACK ROSE WRITING
www.blackrosewriting.com

Printed in the United States of America
Suggested Retail Price (SRP) $20.95

Ae Fond Kiss is printed in Minion Pro

*As a planet-friendly publisher, Black Rose Writing does its best to eliminate unnecessary waste to reduce paper usage and energy costs, while never compromising the reading experience. As a result, the final word count vs. page count may not meet common expectations.

PRAISE FOR
AE FOND KISS

"This endearing tale will enchant readers of all ages as the beautiful but heartbroken Lizzie falls in love with William, a Cincinnati heir who loves her but keeps a dark secret to himself. Donaldson's well written prose makes the couple's struggles and delights feel real, and I lived every moment with them."
–Louella Bryant, author of *Sheltering Angel*

"Joan Donaldson's masterful use of lyrical prose takes readers on a journey filled with unexpected surprises. William and Lizzie's journey resonates with readers as they overcome past errors and transition from sorrow to optimism, finding a new opportunity for love."
–Suzanne Jenkins, *USA Today* Bestselling Author of the *Pam of Babylon Series*

"Join Lizzie and William as they navigate the unfamiliar path of grief and new life, answering God's call on them individually and as a pair. Author Joan Donaldson has done a wonderful job of bringing this time frame to life."
–Donna Schlachter, author of contemporary and historical books

For Jim and Pib,
Scots Wae Hae

Ae

fond

kiss

CHAPTER ONE

The sweeping theatre of hanging woods,
The incessant roar of headlong tumbling floods.
–Robert Burns

Steam billowed, and the train whistle shrieked, as the locomotive pulled away from Sedgemore. Lizzie ducked her head from the flying cinders and waved good-by to her sister, Viney, and her elderly father. Watching the caboose round the curve and vanish, Lizzie wished for a train or a ship, or whatever vehicle could transport her to her beloved George. But no trains rolled to heaven. No ships sailed through the clouds to that better place. Better for whom? Lizzie dug the toe of her boot into the soil. Not for her. Not for George.

She trudged back to her buggy, passing an older lady who argued with a young gentleman. He wore a black frock coat, top hat, and a silk blue cravat. His fashionable clothing showed the pair visited the mountains for the pure air. New settlers seeking work at Rugby arrived in slouch hats, sturdy woolen pants, and muslin shirts.

"I'm sorry, Mother." A slight beard hazed the man's chin and his chestnut-colored hair peeked out beneath his hat, curling around his collar. "Someone from the settlement was supposed to meet us."

Dressed in dark brown silk, the woman reminded Lizzie of a puffball mushroom with an excuse for a waist. A black velvet bonnet shielded the woman's face, but anger flowed from her voice.

"This is ridiculous. Your father owns most of that hotel." She stamped her umbrella on the wooden platform. "You must telegraph him immediately."

When working as a maid at the Tabard Inn, Lizzie had discovered ways to defuse irritated guests by saying a few light words, by offering to fetch tea, or some other diversion. She had grown weary of wealthy people who believed the world existed to serve them. Yet, her Aunt Alta's voice whispered to show hospitality to these strangers. As Lizzie stepped towards the newcomers, darker clouds sank between the mountains and flung rain at the scattered white clapboard houses. The woman scowled and raised her umbrella.

"May I help you?" Lizzie extended her hand. "I'm Elizabeth Walker of Rugby."

"I am pleased to meet you." The woman's gloved hand touched Lizzie's.

"My pleasure." The man bowed slightly. "I am William MacLeod, and this is my mother, Mrs. Alasdair MacLeod. We've traveled from Cincinnati, and our transportation has not appeared."

Mr. William MacLeod's fingers belonged to an artist, slim and tapered as if they should hold a paintbrush or move across piano keys, and like a splendid horseman, he held himself upright. His accent hinted at Scottish origins, while his square jaw and long nose reminded Lizzie of her brother Jacob.

"I parked my buggy yonder, if you would like to ride with me." Lizzie looked away from his blue eyes so like her late fiancé's.

"Thank you, ma'am," Mr. MacLeod said. "We would be beholden to your kindness. Let me tell the stationmaster to send our luggage on the next wagon." He strode toward the ticket window while Lizzie guided his mother across the road.

"You are a widow, I assume?" Mrs. MacLeod asked.

"I'm Miss Walker, ma'am. My fiancé died a year ago, a month before our wedding. So, I feel like a widow."

Those first months, Lizzie had beaten her fists against her pillows, squashing her face into them, screaming her protests. Her sobs had awakened her during the nights, and she lay pondering how to end her life. Viney had sensed her despair and lived with Lizzie at the Tabard Inn until the darkest moments had lifted, but they still hovered in the shadows.

"My sweet daughter, Rose, died a year ago in May, so I understand your heartache," Mrs. MacLeod said. "She was only twenty, about your age."

"I'm sorry, ma'am. So young to die." Lizzie bit her lower lip. If she could fly to heaven, Viney and Jacob would miss her, but they would cope. Seeing as her daddy had wandered off for nineteen years, he hadn't cared what happened to his offspring.

"But you are much too pretty not to wed." Mrs. MacLeod brushed moisture off her skirts.

"Yes, ma'am." What a bold woman, as bad as Viney in giving unsolicited advice. Lizzie assisted Mrs. MacLeod on to the buggy seat as William MacLeod strode toward them.

"Let me fetch the reins." He undid the knot and climbed up next to Lizzie. "Would you like me to drive?" Rain drummed against the buggy's leather roof. The scent of Bay Rum drifted from Mr. MacLeod's frock coat. Lizzie held her breath; George had worn the same fragrance.

"Yes, please. Would you prefer sitting in the middle?" Lizzie stood up. Even though she settled near the edge of the seat, Mrs. MacLeod's wide rear end claimed more than her third. Lizzie's knees brushed against William's and her insides cringed, remembering how she had used that ploy to entice men. As the buggy rattled down the pike, Mr. MacLeod's gloved fingers tugged the reins a bit to the right so that they would avoid a pothole.

"You like horses?" Lizzie asked. Most wealthy visitors could ride, but few could drive a team. William MacLeod handled the reins as if he had spent hours working horses.

"I love horses. My father is from Scotland and gave me a Shetland pony when I was four. By the time I turned eight, I had learned to jump and race. He also had a small cart built and taught me how to drive. I wish I had been born on a Kentucky horse farm. Do you ride?"

"Yes. My late fiancé and I rode." Lizzie stared at the sheets of rain, recalling the afternoon when she and George had ridden along the ridge. Pausing by a spring for a drink, George had cupped her chin in his hands and had asked her to become his wife.

"Miss Walker lost her intended last summer." Mrs. MacLeod patted Lizzie's shoulder. "Perhaps we should speak of other things. I assume you are one of the young ladies who helped settle Rugby. Where did you originate from?"

"No, ma'am. I was born in a log cabin on this ridge and worked as a maid at the Tabard Inn before it burned." Lizzie enjoyed watching Mrs. MacLeod's face flush as she realized Lizzie was a poor highlander. She had learned pretty ways from the English folk, and because George had bequeathed her a tidy sum, she could live as a gentlewoman. But she would have preferred a wedding band on her finger and waking up next to George.

"But you have met Mr. Hughes?" William MacLeod asked. "I read *The Rugbian* newspaper. My father is also curious about this classless experiment."

"Yes, I am friends with his mother, Madam Hughes, and his niece, Emily, but Mr. Hughes is currently touring England soliciting support for the colony. He will return in the fall."

Mr. MacLeod seemed an odd gentleman. Few of the summer guests cared about Mr. Hughes' dream of a utopia for young farmers. Most of the affluent visitors from Knoxville or Chattanooga flaunted their social status and spent their days playing tennis and swimming in the river, before changing their attire for the evening events. Lizzie had yearned for those same pleasures, but she now scorned the aimless desire for entertainment. A restlessness teased her as she pondered how to fill her lonely days. A gust of wind shook the buggy as it rounded a bend in the road, and overhead, a squirrel jumped from one limb to another.

"There's a bad pothole up ahead." Perhaps she should take the reins, since she knew the best route through the swale.

"Hold on," William MacLeod said, as they approached an expanding puddle.

"Veer, a little to the left. It's not as deep there." But she had spoken too late.

Bessie plowed straight into the quagmire, and the wheels sprayed water into everyone's laps. As the buggy sank deeper into the mud, Bessie strained in her harness, and Mr. MacLeod jerked the reins. A slight red spread up his neck. Bessie's sides heaved, and the smell of wet horsehair floated into the buggy.

"I'm so sorry. I should have warned you sooner." She should have snatched the reins, but such behavior would have humiliated him. Yet, instead of sputtering some nonsense and blaming the mud hole, William MacLeod stared at his gloved hands. His mother glared at him and shook her head.

"I'm sorry, Mother. What do you suggest, Miss Walker? I don't approve of whipping a horse."

Rain riffled the surface of the flood covering the road; even during dry times, the site remained soggy because of water seeping out of the overhanging rocks. The settlement was about three miles farther, and Lizzie doubted that Mrs. MacLeod could walk a hundred feet in her fine kid boots. Nor would the woman want to arrive in Rugby, soaked and bedraggled.

"I would never whip a horse. If my sister were here, she would push the buggy while I led Bessie." Lizzie glanced at William Macleod. "Are you willing to muddy your boots?"

"I have another solution." He shrugged off his jacket, removed his boots and socks, and rolled up his pants' legs, exposing calves covered with red hair. "Mother, I'll carry you to that overhang."

"This is ridiculous! You should have been more careful!" Mrs. MacLeod said. "What would our friends think! I'm not a sack of potatoes."

Lizzie cringed. William's mother should thank her son for taking care of her. Most young gentlemen would have demanded that someone from the settlement rescue them.

While Mr. MacLeod slogged through the mud, Lizzie stripped off her boots and stockings and jumped down. The water rose to her calves, soaking not only her skirt but her drawers and petticoats, and their weight dragged against her legs. She plodded to Bessie and gripped the halter.

"I hope there's a good laundress in Rugby." William MacLeod set his shoulder against the back of the buggy. "Now," he shouted and heaved.

"Come on, girl," Lizzie called. Bessie's ears went back, and she shuddered, trying to step forward, but the weight of the buggy anchored it in the mud. A gust of wind rattled the tree branches and a cluster of oak leaves fluttered to the earth. William MacLeod waded toward Lizzie with his shirt plastered to his chest. She blushed, wondering if her clothing revealed more than a proper lady should expose.

"You may not understand, but I've never had such a grand adventure. I've envied the young men who have settled here. I'm bored sitting in an office each day." He slicked his wet hair away from his face as rain dripped off his nose. "Perhaps if we stuck branches behind the wheels, then you and I could pry them from the mud as Mother leads the horse."

"Do you think she would do that?" Lizzie frowned. Mrs. MacLeod appeared to be the type of woman who expected others to serve and protect her from harsh conditions.

"We'll find out." He spoke to his mother, and her eyes widened as her lips formed a pout.

While Lizzie searched the underbrush for fallen branches, William MacLeod guided his mother to Bessie. Lizzie wanted to laugh at how the storm was teaching Mrs. MacLeod the rigors of the mountains and Rugby's free-spirited ways. The woman would not forget this welcome.

"Here." Lizzie handed two stout sticks to William MacLeod. "You probably know the best way." She fought against her soaked clothing, as Lizzie joined him behind the buggy and gripped a branch.

"Remember, we are using the principle of leverage to lift the wheels. We will push downward."

Lizzie had hated school and had no idea what leverage was. She had never understood how studying math or anything else would help her catch a husband. The only addition she had cared about was adding another fellow's name to the list of boys whom she had kissed. Brushing away those memories, Lizzie gripped the coarse bark.

"Now!" William shouted.

As Mrs. MacLeod pulled on Bessie's bridle, Lizzie and William pressed against their branches. Great sucking sounds rose from the mud as the wheels inched forward. He dropped his stick and rammed his shoulder against the buggy.

"Push!" he said.

With both palms on the buggy, Lizzie heaved. Dirty water flew into her eyes, and grit coated her lips. The wheels jerked free, and she toppled into the puddle, but muscular arms scooped her up.

"Please, put me down." Lizzie squirmed in William MacLeod's grip. She had vowed never to flirt again, nor to encourage suitors. What would his mother think of them?

.   .   .

"When in difficult circumstances, we should forget formalities, Miss Elizabeth. Please, call me, William. After all, isn't that the spirit of Hughes' community? Equality between men and women?"

He deposited Lizzie near the buggy, and she climbed up beside his mother. William slapped the reins and the horse plodded forward. Sitting on his well-padded chair in his walnut paneled office, reviewing invoices, and writing bank drafts, hadn't prepared William for avoiding the perils lurking along mountain roads. Miss Lizzie must think him a fool. Any fellow would have known to drive around and not through the mud hole. He had ruined her clothing, irritated her pride, and humiliated his mother.

But balls and formal dinner parties hadn't introduced him to a beauty who would wade in the mud and push a buggy to freedom. With black curls framing her face, and those deep brown eyes, Miss Lizzie could have stepped from a crofter's cottage in the Scottish Highlands. Despite the dark mourning dress, the lass displayed delightful curves. As he held her, the scent of rosewater had drifted from her hair, so like his sister's perfume.

With her lips pressed into a thin line, his mother disapproved of his behavior, but over the past year, when had his mother praised his conduct? Rain beat against the buggy roof, and William clucked to the horse. The sooner they arrived, the quicker they could bathe and don dry clothing.

Silence sifted over them. Mrs. MacLeod and Lizzie shivered and wrung water from their soaked skirts. When they entered the village, William studied the sawmills, cabins, clapboard homes, and the boardinghouses. The settlement matched the descriptions and etchings in the newspaper. What a pity Mr. Hughes was away. William longed to chat with him concerning his ideas about working with one's hands. What factors had created such a visionary.

"The houses look alike," Mrs. MacLeod said.

"Yes, I read how Mr. Hughes employed the architect, Andrew Jackson Downing, to create simple designs that were beautiful and functional," William said.

He inhaled the clean air, so different from the smog blanketing the Ohio River where his family's mills operated. He recognized Mr. Hughes' home, Kingstone Lisle, looking splendid with brown trim to offset the gold board-and-batten siding. Pink and red hollyhocks marched along the picket fence, and mounds of herbs grew in a kitchen garden. From inside Christ's Church, someone played the piano and sang *Guide Me Thou O Great Jehovah*. Come Sunday, he would worship in the charming gray building. He should have planned to spend the summer here, away from the heat radiating off Cincinnati's brick walls and noisy streets. Away from the pain of passing Rose's room, still arranged as if his sister would fling off her bedcovers and greet him with a kiss on his cheek.

Breakfast was dull without Rose. His mother ate in bed. From behind his newspaper, his father nodded at him. William sipped his coffee, heaped strawberry jam on his toast, and wished he could listen to his mother and Rose argue about how to help Cincinnati's poor. His mother had sided with the good works of her charity groups while Rose had espoused the virtues of the Social Progressive movement rippling across America. She had longed to ride a mule into Eastern Kentucky and teach school. If their debate lasted all day, then he would find Rose waiting for him. She would drag him into the library, asking him to convince their mother to permit Rose more freedom.

The buggy rolled by the commissary. A rough-looking man dressed in ripped trousers and a stained white shirt sat on its porch, leaning his chair against the wall. He tipped his hat, revealing unkempt black hair. "Hey Lizzie! Always did like seeing your hair down." He jumped to the ground.

William's eyes narrowed, and he frowned. Who was this bold fellow?

• • •

Lizzie slumped, so the sides of the buggy top would hide her from her former beau as he jogged down the street. Of all the times, why did Lucas loiter in town? From the look of his pants, Lucas should be home mending his clothes. No, he had planned on her, his wife, to tend to those tasks. He was like a tick, digging into her flesh, refusing to let go.

"Ain't a prettier sight in all of Tennessee," Lucas said.

Mrs. MacLeod scowled, and Lizzie sank further back into the corner of the buggy, wishing a blast of rain would send Lucas back to his farm. Or that he would leave Rugby and move to Knoxville and work in a mill.

"Where are you staying?" Lizzie turned to block Mrs. MacLeod's view of Lucas.

"We reserved rooms at Mrs. Carroll's boardinghouse. Do you know of it?" William asked.

"Yes, that's where I live. At the next corner, turn left, and then drive one more block. Her place is the large gray house with the wraparound porch."

"Whoa." William pulled up near a graveled path. He held his mother's umbrella over her head and conducted her inside. Lizzie stepped down and grimaced as Lucas' boots splashed through the nearby puddles.

"Want me to take your horse to the carriage house?" Lucas reached for Bessie's bridle. His eyes moved over Lizzie's soggy clothing, and her cheeks blazed. "Missed you, Lizzie. How about I come by tomorrow night? Who's the rich fellow driving your rig? Another Englishman come to tell us how to live."

"They are visitors who needed a ride, and they are no concern of yours. Please remove your hand from my horse." From the corner of her eye, she spied Tom emerging from the stables. "Mrs. Carroll's hired hand will care for her." Lizzie turned, but Lucas' boot clamped down on the hem of her skirt.

"I thought they taught ladies to say good-by to a gentleman." Lucas grabbed Lizzie's wrist. "Course, no matter how fine you act; we know what you really are."

"Let me go." Lizzie pulled away, hating how he referred to their past tryst. His tongue still bragged to men about having her. Fool, the more Lucas plagued her, the more she detested him. She stomped up the boardinghouse steps and stared at William's knees. One more step, and she faced him.

"Was that man bothering you, Miss Elizabeth?" he asked. "I came to see if you needed help." He offered his arm.

Her legs shook, but Lizzie straightened her spine. "Thank you." She accepted his elbow, eager to shun Lucas, for dry clothing, and the warmth of Mrs. Carroll's hearth.

CHAPTER TWO

The woods, wild scatter'd, clothe their ample sides.
–Robert Burns

Apricot brushed the eastern sky, and a low mist swirled through Rugby, foretelling a clear day. In dark trousers, suspenders and a cream-colored shirt sprinkled with tiny navy twigs, William stood on the boardinghouse's porch. Mourning doves cooed in the nearby dogwood trees, and the scent of wood smoke and frying sausage drifted from the open kitchen windows. The beauty of the mountains matched the articles he had read in *The Rugbian,* and the tranquility soothed the endless aching for his sister.

With his hands behind his back, William strolled the path leading to the main village. Rose would have loved such a soft morning. Dew sparkled on the red geraniums tucked into pots and moisture dripped from heart-shaped redbud leaves. His sister would have slipped her arm through his and urged him to seek more adventures, like the one at the mudhole. Unlike Rose, he would not need to travel with a chaperone. Month after month, she had tossed out ideas. They should sail to Scotland and find the remnants of their clan. She should disguise herself as a man and they would work on a riverboat floating down the Mississippi. He had laughed and walked to his family's mills, preparing to replicate his father's life and marry the woman his mother chose, until he had read about Rugby. The newspaper accounts hinted at opportunities like those Rose had desired. In front of him, boots crunched the gravel.

"Mr. William MacLeod? Amos Hill, here." A tall, thin man in worn woolen trousers, a linen shirt, and a gray woolen waistcoat offered his hand. "You look like your father."

"Pleased to meet you, sir." William shook Mr. Hill's calloused hand.

"Please forgive me. I was confused about the date of your arrival."

"You are forgiven, sir. A kind Miss Elizabeth Walker brought us in her buggy."

"Ah, Lizzie! She's a dear girl and a friend of my family. Out for a morning constitutional?"

"I wanted to see the village before workers arrived. I needed some quiet to think. You heard about my sister's death?" William glanced at Mr. Hill's kind face.

"Yes, your father wrote to me. I'm so sorry. Please accept my condolences."

"Thank you, sir. Rose would have loved this settlement. She yearned for greater equality for women. To be free from the expectations of society."

"What about you?" Mr. Hill nodded at a fork in the path.

"It's so peaceful here. The last year has been hard and left me with many questions." William wanted to jump and swing from a low tree branch. Or grab Miss Lizzie's hand, climb a mountain and enjoy a picnic. What provoked such thoughts?

"Questions can nudge us towards our dreams. Perhaps you feel a desire to linger and to experience more of Rugby?" Mr. Hill plucked a leaf from an oak tree where a robin sang.

"Yes. I would like that, but I can't." William longed to shake off his responsibilities and turn into a settler for even one week. He wanted to be part of this revolutionary experiment that could make his life more meaningful.

"I suppose your father needs your help with the business." Mr. Hill glanced at William.

"Yes. But summers are slow at the mill."

"If I offered you a temporary position, might that make a difference? You could be the answer to my morning prayers."

"What sort of position?" William stuffed his hands in his pockets. After the mistakes of last year, he doubted if he was the answer to anyone's prayers. Yet, a bubble of hope floated inside him.

"The schoolmaster we hired decided at the last minute to remain in Boston. Because the colony's children come from families who live in the hills and from English settlers, our board believes we must hire a gentleman to teach them."

"I've never taught." Nor did he have any practical skills other than brushing his horse, a task William performed because he enjoyed it.

"But you've kept accounts, read books, and written letters?" Mr. Hill laid a hand on William's shoulder. "And you like children?"

"I've spent little time with children." He should like them, but teaching them? William rubbed his palms against his trousers. Yet if he stayed for the summer, he could become better acquainted with Miss Lizzie.

"What do you say? It's only for eight weeks. Perhaps Lizzie could assist you. She needs a task, something meaningful to cheer her." Mr. Hill offered his hand.

"Splendid idea. Yes, I would like that." William shook Mr. Hill's hand.

"Thank you so much. I hated to cancel the term, and I'll telegraph your father about our decision. Lizzie can show you to the schoolhouse, and here's the key. Ring the bell at nine. I need to travel to Cincinnati for a couple of days and will check in when I return."

"Thank you, sir." William turned and strode back to the boardinghouse.

Such a wonderful opportunity to listen to Miss Lizzie reading to the children, while enjoying her profile and voice. He would invite her on carriage rides, or they could play tennis. In the evenings, they could attend the lectures and theatricals. Perhaps at the end of the term, she might choose to leave behind her mourning clothing. William's steps slowed.

But Miss Lizzie might not want to help him. She must have duties and obligations to perform. Yet without her, he would fail as a schoolmaster because he had never sat in a classroom. His father had hired a tutor for him and Rose, who had guided their education in the quiet of their library. No boarding school rumpus. No pranks and bullying. He had endured a term at St. Xavier College before leaving to work with his father. A college professor was not a good model for how teachers controlled their young students.

Upon entering the boardinghouse dining room, William pushed in his mother's chair, and took the seat opposite Lizzie. A visiting family assembled at the other end of the long table. For a flick of a bee's wing, William watched how the young mother urged her son and daughter to sit up straight and keep their elbows off the table. No harsh words, but she spoke with a loving authority.

"The mountain air agrees with you?" Lifting an eyebrow, Lizzie buttered a biscuit and spread peach jam on it.

"Oh yes. Rugby is more beautiful than I dreamed. I ran into Mr. Hill. The schoolmaster canceled at the last minute, so he suggested I teach the summer term. And I accepted." William spooned grits onto his plate.

"How could you?" Mrs. MacLeod set down her teacup. "A schoolteacher? What about your responsibilities back home?"

"Before we left, Father and I talked about his large investments in the Tabard's rebuilding. If I stay, then I can monitor the project." William remained silent about his desire to spend more time with Lizzie.

"But I could never tell our friends that you were teaching." Mrs. MacLeod stiffened her shoulders and shoved aside her plate.

"You can explain that I am looking after Father's business affairs. They would understand that." William dipped his fork into the grits. "Or tell them that I am fulfilling my sister's dream."

"Please don't speak of Rose that way." Mrs. MacLeod's voice quivered.

"I'm sorry, Mother. But serving here would honor Rose's desire to teach. For some odd reason, I feel closer to her, here." William drank his tea. His sister would have worked in the fields, weeding the crops, and picking tomatoes. He would do all those things for her, with Miss Lizzie's help.

·   ·   ·

Lizzie lowered her eyes, not wanting to take part in the squabble. William's decision seemed odd for a gentleman. Perhaps his confession was sincere, and he wanted to experience Rugby's social equalities. But she doubted William could handle the pranks created by the mountain boys and girls to test a flatlander. And he would have to convince the local students to accept the English settlers' children. There had to be someone from the settlement who understood her people and was more suitable for the position.

"Who will escort me back to Cincinnati?" Mrs. MacLeod stood. "I only plan to spend a few days and need to return for the Garden Club's Summer Benefit."

"Mr. Hill plans to travel to Cincinnati, perhaps he can escort you."

Mrs. MacLeod huffed. "I will inform your father that Mr. Hill must find a replacement for you. I should have left you in Cincinnati." Mrs. MacLeod swished out of the room.

With her napkin, Lizzie dabbed butter off her fingers. Without his frock coat and cravat, William resembled a newly arrived settler. But his palms lacked callouses or nicks inflicted by briars or the misplaced blow of a hammer, nor had sunlight tanned his face and neck. For all his enthusiasm, how long would William last in Rugby? If her sister had stayed, she and Viney would have flopped onto her bed and discussed the handsome stranger, wagering when William would flee. Lizzie forked a bite of scrambled eggs.

"Miss Elizabeth, Mr. Hill suggested you should assist me. Would you help me, please?" William asked.

She shook her head. "I'm not qualified. Besides, I'm having a cottage built and must oversee the work."

Lizzie stirred milk into her tea and watched the white swirl through the amber brew. Since George had died, many fine gentlemen had arrived in Rugby and had asked her to walk out with them, but she had murmured excuses. William's request was the oddest because he offered a job and not entertainment.

"I seldom read books. I can't remember what eight times nine is. You should ask my friend, Emily Hughes, Mr. Hughes' niece. She is well educated."

The kitchen door swung open. Mrs. Carroll placed the dirty dishes from the departed family onto a tray. Her auburn hair glistened in the sunlight and a white apron covered her dark blue calico dress. An impish grin tugged at her lips.

"'Tis true you're not skilled in mathematics, but you have a knack for explaining things. Away with you, Lizzie, you need something like this to cheer you. Plus, Emily is caring for her grandmother." Mrs. Carroll lifted the tray and stepped back into the kitchen.

Lizzie had forgotten how Emily's grandmother had fallen and broken her wrist. In her bossy way, Viney had told her to stop weeping at George's grave. That she should fill her time with something better. Lizzie placed her fork and knife at the edge of her plate.

"You will understand the mountain children better than me or Miss Hughes, whose grandmother needs her." William poured each of them another cup of tea. "Please? For a couple of days? Having you in the room will give me courage."

"Me?" Lizzie frowned. How could a mountain girl provide courage for a wealthy gentleman? The local folks would joke about her because they knew how she had frittered away her school days. Citing her silly flirtations, they might object to her presence, as many parents believed only men should teach school. Yet from how vigorously William stirred his tea, he was nervous.

"Yes, you. You encouraged me to push a buggy out of the mud instead of waiting for servants. That small victory inspired me to accept this challenge."

The local children deserved a city-educated schoolmaster who could teach them about the world off the ridge. Maybe if she had studied with someone like William, she might have paid better attention during class. No, she and the other girls would have whispered about his good looks. Yet, William must have a fiancé, and the young lady would not approve of her working with a betrothed man. From the way William fiddled with his napkin, he needed reassuring words.

"Let me fetch my bonnet. I'll help for today." Lizzie would have to speak with Emily about sharing this position.

CHAPTER THREE

Gin a body meet a body,
Coming through the rye,
Gin a body kiss a body,
Need a body cry?
–Robert Burns

Lizzie gazed up at the schoolhouse's second story, admiring the row of sparkling windows. William turned an iron key in the lock, pushed open a tall glass door, and they entered a room on the first floor smelling of fresh pine lumber. Crates of books stood beneath a long blackboard, and a map of the United States decorated another wall. Sunlight poured in through high, narrow windows. What a rich opportunity for the students compared to the log cabin school she had attended with one windowlight, torn textbooks, cracked slates, and a fireplace that smoked. The lack of supplies hadn't bothered her brother and sister, who had pestered the teacher with questions.

"If you didn't train to teach, why did you take this position? Why didn't you send for a schoolmaster from Cincinnati?" Lizzie stared at the map and located Jamestown, Tennessee. She lived near that dot in the long rectangle.

William raised a couple of sashes, propping them open with pieces of wood, and a breeze riffled through the room. A flock of bluebirds chortled as they flitted across the schoolyard.

"From the day my sister Rose could read her Bible, those passages about rich people bothered her. Rose lamented how our family only gave food baskets to the poor at Christmas time, but we showed no other charity throughout the year. She begged our parents to allow her to teach at a local school for immigrants, but they refused. Unlike Rose, I frittered away my time riding, shooting, and attending the next dinner party."

Lizzie ran one finger along the windowsill. Her past had mirrored William's description. Fine dresses, petticoat flounces edged in Belgium lace, a gold brooch studded with rubies; George's gifts and wealth had drawn her to him. Her kisses had encouraged his wandering hands, but her love had deepened when George had risked losing his inheritance if he married her. Thankfully, his father had agreed for George to manage his offices in Boston where folks would accept an American wife. Even as his fever burned and sweat ran down his face, Lizzie and George had dreamed of having a family, and how they would spend their summers in Rugby.

"I want to give Rose's love to these children." He moved a stack of books from one corner of his desk to the other side. "I owe her that much."

Why did William need to repay his sister for something? Out of love and respect, Lizzie honored George and kept his memory alive. She cherished her mourning brooch, its center woven from a lock of George's hair and encircled by pearls. Most nights, she ached to feel his arms around her. Most mornings, she lingered in bed, summoning the strength to dress herself. From William's comments and expression, the same numbness crippled him. The person she owed a debt to was Viney, for risking her life when the Tabard burned.

"If you can speak about it, how did your sister die?" Lizzie picked up a stack of slates and set one upon each desk.

"The doctors said pneumonia, but I think from despair. My parents didn't approve of her progressive ideas and refused to change their attitude about the proper roles for young women." William stared out the window. "Or about men."

"I'm sorry. Folks on the ridge also cling to traditions." Although Mr. Hughes had introduced the notion of equality between men and women, the mountaineers scoffed at the sight of the settlement's men laboring in the tomato canning factory. "Women's work," they muttered. Those men would object to her presence in the classroom.

Shouting flew through the open door as two dozen children ran into the school. The boys claimed desks on one side of the room and girls on the other. Contrary to what flatlanders said about mountaineers being shiftless, most of the students wore clean clothing, but being mid-June, they went barefoot. Pinafores covered the girls' frocks, and the boys dressed in chambray shirts and woolen pants. The boys needed more soap for their necks, but the girls' faces shone. The English children huddled in the doorway. Apprehension hovered in their expressions as their eyes darted about the room. She had experienced those emotions when she had arrived to work at the Tabard Inn. Lizzie motioned to them and grasped the hand of the youngest.

"Come join us. We're so glad you're here. Let me help you find seats."

"Good morning, students," William said. "I am your new teacher, Mr. MacLeod, and most of you know Miss Walker, who is assisting me today. First, we must learn what grades you are in."

"We call her Miz Lizzie," Betsy said. "My Daddy's building her a cottage, sir."

"Betsy, please raise your hand and ask for permission to speak," Lizzie said. "Why don't you girls explain to me where you left off in your studies while the boys talk with Mr. MacLeod. Betsy, you're first."

The fifteen-year-old's bosom filled out a red calico dress in the same way Lizzie's had at her age. Her brown hair hung in two braids tied with red yarn, and a few short curls framed her face. But her thin wrists and legs hinted at limited food.

"I can read good but can't cipher much. I came to meet boys and am glad you're here. My mama says you know how to catch fellers better than a frog snatches flies. Can you learn me your tricks?"

Red flushed her cheeks, and Lizzie prayed the past would not haunt her until her hair turned gray. "We'll talk about boys *after* school. That goes for all of you. Where did you leave off in your reader?"

Lizzie recorded each of the girls' accomplishments and wrote suggestions for how to help them in various subjects. Most of the local children had attended school for a few months each year, while the settlers had completed their respective grade levels. Integrating these students into one community would be a challenge, and Lizzie hoped Mr. Hill would have some ideas.

Betsy and her friends sat in the back of the room, but their gaze followed William as he spoke with the boys. Somehow, Lizzie must persuade them to care more about earning an education than finding a man. But why should they listen to *her*? She squatted near a tiny English girl with blonde hair the same color as George's.

"What's your name, honey?" Lizzie looked into eyes as blue as a June morning.

"Charlotte. My brother calls me Lottie." The little girl pointed at a boy dressed in a muslin shirt and dark blue wool trousers. "Sometimes he calls me a stinker."

"That's not nice, and I'm sure you aren't one." But the moniker was better than what folks called Lizzie. "What grade are you in?"

"First. I've never been to school before. But my mama taught me how to write my name and how to count to twenty."

"That's wonderful. I'm sure you will do well." Lizzie patted Lottie's shoulder and moved to the next young girl who came from Boston. Having these foreigners in the school would teach the mountain children about the world off the ridge, but she doubted if their parents would accept the outsiders' opinions.

•   •   •

William tucked Betsy's comments into his memory, along with the sight of Miss Lizzie's flaming cheeks. Her subdued manners and dark clothing hid any hint of past flirtatious ways. Perhaps that part of her had vanished when her fiancé died, just as something had drained from him when he threw shovelfuls of dirt onto Rose's coffin. The hollow thump of the wood, and the scent of lily-of-the-valley flowers still floated through his dreams. In the protection of his bedroom, William gave himself permission to sob until his cheeks burned from his salty tears.

After he handed out textbooks, the littlest students and even the girls settled into their work. But the older boys nudged each other, and although he sent stern looks their way, his stomach cringed. During his student years, William had drawn in his copybook and cheated in math. Why should he bother to study when he would inherit his father' mills and bank accounts? He frowned again at the boys who smirked and shuffled their feet. When Miss Lizzie bent over a crate for an armload of books, someone whistled. She jerked up.

"Who did that? Who whistled?" William glared at the boys, and the back of his neck reddened.

Not one of them spoke; they would never snitch on their friends. A couple of the older girls tittered, but when William stared at them, they looked down at their slates. Surely, a girl wouldn't have made a rude jest. William strode around the schoolroom, studying each boy's face, as defiance glinted in their eyes.

"Who whistled?" William had vowed not to use the leather strap stored in a desk drawer, but if he didn't gain control of the students today, he might as well pack his trunk. His mother would gloat over his failure and remind him to accept his place in society and at the mills. He stopped by Miss Lizzie's side.

"Best leave off," she said. "Move on with lessons so they forget about this."

"It's not correct for them to treat you with disrespect." His hands gripped the edge of his desk. "Believe me, leaving this sort of behavior unchecked leads to greater troubles."

William turned away from Miss Lizzie's stare. She had comprehended the meaning behind his statement. Whatever she had done in her youth couldn't compare with his selfish mistakes. Perhaps teaching these young men would atone for his past sins.

"Why don't you distract the boys," she said, "And I'll work with the girls."

"Upper-class boys, come to the front of the room, please." William paced. "Time for some mental arithmetic. To clear your minds."

. . .

Lizzie stiffened her shoulders as a chill rippled down her back. By evening, everyone on the ridge would hear how a student had whistled at Lizzie Walker's rear end. For the next week, the tale would expand as folks embellished it, girls and boys would act it out, and the men sitting at the commissary would hoot over it, especially Lucas. His little sister sat next to Betsy, and she would bring home the tale. What Lizzie had feared had occurred in the first hour of school, but she refused to cry. Now William should understand why she wasn't suitable to help him. Yet, his defense of her honor sparked hope that her former lack of character would not harm their friendship.

As Lizzie helped Rebecca sound out c-a-t and r-a-t, she watched William. He would place a hand on a boy's shoulder, say something, and move on to the next student. But instead of warming to William's attentions, the boys bristled, and their faces hardened. At what point would their disdain transform into meanness? She deserved the boys' scorn, but William displayed the proper breeding of a gentleman and scholar. The rascals should be thankful for his efforts.

As the last child dashed away from the school, William slumped into a chair. Lizzie leaned against the doorframe, watching the pinafores and petticoats fly down the path. Although William hadn't solved the mystery of the whistler, she had her opinion about the culprit. Even if she spoke to the student's mother, the woman wouldn't listen. Like the other mountain women, she would shake her head and remind Lizzie how she deserved the catcalls. If George had lived, Lizzie could have lost her past on the brick streets of Boston.

"Tired?" Lizzie took a wet rag and washed the blackboard. William needed to sit on the boardinghouse porch with a cup of tea and a plate of cookies. Her fingers yearned to pick up her smooth steel lace needles and fall into the rhythm of creating her favorite edging while chatting with William. Sharing a peaceful moment would be better than sitting by herself reading a copy of Harper's Magazine.

. . .

"I'm exhausted. My brain is fuzzy from keeping an eye on everyone while teaching a handful. Thank you for helping me." William closed his eyes and chided himself for not working with Lizzie as she tidied the room.

"I enjoyed it. It's good to have the English and Yankee children mingle with the highlanders. Hopefully, they can help the settlement make friends with the mountain folk."

"Yes." William rubbed his temples. The noble man who had bragged about honoring his sister's wishes had hated each minute of teaching, while the humble mountain lass had decided she liked it. What he wanted to do was down a shot of whiskey and return to the serenity of his office. But his pride, yes, his manly pride, refused to give his mother the victory. Nor would he allow those pesky boys to drive him off the mountain and away from Lizzie. His half-closed eyes followed Lizzie as she ran the rag from the top of the blackboard to the bottom. With each lifting of her arms, he understood why a boy had whistled.

Hadn't he pinched the rear ends of the chambermaids bending over to clean the fireplaces? He had stood at the bottom of the stairs watching their well-turned ankles move down the steps. When a new maid had passed by him, he had brushed shoulders, relishing her blush. Some had smiled at him and offered a kiss while others had fled. When Lizzie had worked as a maid at the former Tabard Inn, had she endured men like himself strutting around, expecting more than cream and sugar in their tea? William forced his eyes away from Lizzie and focused on his hands.

"Do you have any ideas how to encourage the boys to study? And the girls, to stop whispering?" If he wanted to stay, he must manage this brood.

"Perhaps the oldest could tutor the younger ones, and you should give the boys small jobs. That way, they won't have to sit for long spells. A break in the morning would perk them up. You need to devise a plan to bring food for some of them."

"Food?" During the noon dinner hour, he had hidden in the schoolroom, citing a need to organize the afternoon lessons. Every child had held a dinner pail while marching out the door.

"Yes, some of them had only a chunk of cornbread or a cup of milk. Soup beans would put flesh on them and help them learn. One little girl was too tired to play." Lizzie rung out the rag.

"How sad." He had never eaten soup beans. Heaping platters of baked ham, fried chicken, or roast beef had graced his family's table during dinner time. Bowls filled with green beans, glistening with melted butter, potatoes whipped with cream, and warm rolls had traveled to his plate. Dishes of pickled beets, chow-chow, and dill pickles added zest to the meal. He had been grateful for the walk back to his office, and sometimes after closing the heavy door, stole a quick nap.

"What do you suggest?" William pushed in his chair.

"I don't know. We can discuss it with Mrs. Carroll, and she might have some good ideas."

After locking the schoolhouse door, William looked towards the echoing beat of hammers. "Would you please accompany me to the Tabard's construction site? I'm supposed to monitor the progress for my father." He offered his arm, but Lizzie hesitated.

"It's such a lovely afternoon, and a walk would clear our heads. Please?"

"I suppose so." Lizzie exhaled and accepted his arm.

CHAPTER FOUR

Dare to be honest and fear no labor.
–Robert Burns

"Let's take the deer trail. It's faster." Lizzie nodded at the faint path threading through a small grove of trees and dotted with honeysuckle bushes. A flock of crows cawed as they flew over the treetops. Lizzie linked elbows with William.

Today had provided enough grist for the gossips, and their tongues would flap even faster if they spied William escorting her through town. His request for advice had shocked her, and his sincerity was endearing. Although grief still shadowed her days, Lizzie had missed hearing a deep voice discussing settlement news or commenting on a book. George had explained about his family's mills in London and, like William, had asked for her opinion about matters concerning the laborers. As their love had matured, George had resisted his lust and tempered hers. Finally, he had slipped a ring with a glittering emerald onto her finger, vowing to cherish her as his wife. When fleeing the flaming Tabard, Lizzie had lost both the ring and her locket with George's tiny portrait.

Lizzie matched her stride to William's as her skirts swished against the ferns. Perhaps because they had faced a classroom together, sharing a walk felt comfortable. But would George feel betrayed? Hammers pounded, and saws sounded, as they neared the site of the first Tabard. Men swarmed on the scaffolding as they nailed up clapboard siding to the three-story skeleton. Rafters for a mansard roof topped the structure.

Even though the scent of pine drifted from the newly cut lumber, ashes and smoke still swirled in Lizzie's heart and she blanched. She had avoided this grim place and could not banish the memories. Viney had raced through the flames to save her and had burned her hands; scars etched her sister's palms and during cold weather her fingers ached. As selfish as Lizzie was, she should have died.

"I'm sorry. I see that coming here bothers you," William said. "Mr. Hill told me how you barely escaped the fire."

"He said that out of kindness. I lay in my trunk, longing to die, but Viney came to rescue me." Now, William would know what sort of person she was.

"Do not condemn yourself. The death of a loved one can play tricks with our minds, and many of us make decisions we regret." William looked across the landscape. "After I speak with Mr. Hill, might we stroll through the village? I would love to see where you are building your cottage."

Lizzie stared at her boots. She and George had selected their home site and if she shared their special place with William, his presence might dim the memories of her beloved. Yet, she was weary of describing her cottage to Mrs. Carroll. Lizzie straightened her shoulders; she refused to allow loneliness to dictate her days.

"Yes, you may come. You'll meet Betsy's father, Nate, who is building it."

Lizzie stood back when William and Mr. Hill bent over a drawing. William ran one of his long fingers along the lines. How would it feel to slip her fingers between his? She closed her eyes; those thoughts must disappear. While they worked together, she and William could only show friendship. After the men finished chatting, William and Lizzie ambled the path to her new home. Lizzie gasped at the sight of Lucas sitting with Nate on a stack of lumber, talking and drinking. Nate jumped up.

"Fine day isn't it, Miss Elizabeth?" Nate said. "Your house is coming right along."

Lucas stood up and whistled. "Wish I'd been there to see you bent over those books."

Lizzie hated how gossip could slither faster than a rattlesnake across the ridge. In former times, she would have relished being the topic of folks' conversation, but she had hoped her mourning attire would protect her from wagging tongues. Poor William, within twenty-four hours, his classroom helper had become the subject of the gossips. Lucas narrowed his eyes and glared at William.

"Might have to drop by the school some time."

"I am afraid your presence would disrupt the lessons," William said. "Maybe at the end of the term, we can organize a public recitation." Shoulders tense, William placed his hand on her elbow as if to protect her.

Lizzie knew that Lucas lacked self-control, she must extinguish this confrontation before it escalated into a brawl. "It doesn't appear much has changed in the cottage since last week."

"Well, Miss Lizzie, that rain set us back a bit. Then my helper broke his arm, so I hired on Lucas. We could work on Sundays." Nate pushed back his hat.

"That won't be necessary." Lizzie pressed her lips together. The cheek of that man. Folks would frown at a schoolteacher whose workers didn't keep the Sabbath.

• • •

William strolled through the half-built cottage, examining the work. Had the Tabard's construction not been behind schedule, he would have sent over a couple of his carpenters. Whoever this Lucas character was, his presence irked Miss Lizzie. The fellow either didn't comprehend her feelings or didn't care, and he should apologize for his crude statements. Lizzie may have been born on the ridge, but they should honor her as a young lady.

Despite not being a builder or an architect, William recognized how the walls weren't plumb, and noticed several two-by-fours had cracked and the stone foundation leaned to the north. He wouldn't allow these men to take advantage of Lizzie, who had neither father nor husband to assist her. William pointed at a board.

"Who inspected the lumber? Several boards are warped, and you should have rejected them."

Nate spat at a patch of clover. "Can't look at every board. We're using plenty of nails."

"So, I see." William frowned. "Miss Elizabeth, if you like, I could oversee the progress of your cottage."

From her frown, Lizzie doubted his ability to manage these mountain men. But he had supervised the mill bosses who had fled Ireland or Germany or places beyond. If his mill workers hadn't produced enough stockings for the week, he had called in the bosses and discussed the difficulties. Broken machinery? Lack of repairmen? Because William had listened to their broken English and thick accents, the men had respected him. Sometimes their ideas hadn't resolved the problems, but other times the men had created workable and safe solutions. Nate and Lucas resembled the older boys in the school; perhaps by overseeing these mountain men, the boys would come to respect him.

"Thank you, but Mr. Hill is supposed to be watching over my cottage," Lizzie said.

"Between the new interns and the construction of the Tabard, Mr. Hill is overwhelmed," William said. "So, please allow me to help you."

He hated how Lucas glared at him, and Nate smirked. Even if he never earned the men's respect, they must learn how to answer to a superior. He stuffed his hands into his pockets to avoid touching her arm. How William wished to place his hand on her shoulder, but he wouldn't repeat that mistake. For Rose, he would change.

. . .

Lizzie looked away from William. If she gave him this authority, would he think she was encouraging his attentions? Nate and Lucas saw him as a city dandy who had never held a hammer and they would find ways to torment him. Still, she hated how Nate had cheated her, and would continue doing so. Lizzie knew what would change his behavior, a peck on Nate's cheek, and the swish of her hips to move her bustle. Whiskey and women drove Nate, and his eyes had followed her ever since the day she had pinned up her hair. But that flirt had perished when George had declared his love.

"Thank you. I would appreciate your help." There, she had accepted his favor and hoped that William wouldn't ask for a payment for his troubles. Yet, a man who taught to honor his sister must have a wholesome heart.

William pulled out a small notebook, drew a sketch, wrote a bit, and pointed out what needed to be corrected. Lucas glanced at her, and Lizzie wanted to smack him, but wouldn't the ridge enjoy that tidbit? Sometimes she wondered if she could create a better life in some other town, but then she couldn't visit George's grave. Nate muttered something, and William shook his head.

"If by Friday I still find this mess, I will fire you. Lizzie will not pay you for what you should have built soundly the first time."

William slid his notebook in his frockcoat pocket, exuding the confidence of a business owner who expected to be obeyed without raising his voice. Yet from Nate's surly expression, William had riled him. At first, Nate would agree and appear obedient, and Lucas would follow Nate like a gosling behind a gander. But like a copperhead resting beneath a burdock leaf, Nate would strike. Lizzie would have to warn William.

Lizzie accepted his arm, and they ambled a tree-lined road leading to the boardinghouse. A squirrel scolded them, and a cardinal flitted from tree to tree. Closer to the village, daisies bloomed along the side of the road. Lizzie removed her arm from William's. Perhaps she shouldn't return to the school. Although she had relished seeing the small ones' eyes brighten as they learned their letters, she didn't want to cause more trouble for him.

"William, the older boys could concentrate better if I wasn't in the classroom. And the older girls are not much different. They only want my advice on how to catch a husband."

"I am sorry for what happened today, but the girls need your influence. Please stay, I don't think I can manage without you."

"Thank you," Lizzie said. William's gentle voice warmed her like standing in front of a fireplace on a raw day. Not since George had died had someone needed her or praised her. Mrs. Carroll thanked her for helping in the kitchen, but any woman could have chopped onions or shaped dinner rolls. William needed what she could offer the children.

.   .   .

Think. He had to say something to convince Lizzie to remain in the classroom. William feared standing in front of those many pairs of eyes, wondering what mischief he would have to endure. Like wolves, the students smelled the terror lurking behind his stern countenance. Lizzie had understood to ignore the whistler and proceed with lessons. Although she didn't believe it, Lizzie had better teaching skills than he did. He ran a finger along the little notebook in his pocket, and an idea wiggled into William's brain.

"Last night at dinner, you mentioned how you enjoy designing and sewing your clothing. Would you be willing to give sewing lessons to the girls so they could understand how arithmetic works in daily life? You could show them *Godey's Lady Book* and explain how to draft patterns."

Lizzie shook her head. "Most of those girls learned to sew before they came to school."

"But the girls admire your clothing. Working and learning together, might help the settlers' daughters get to know the local young women."

"That's true. I asked the English girls to join us at the noon break, but they kept to themselves. But I doubt if the mountain families could afford the cloth for stylish dresses."

"Then I will purchase the fabric as a gift."

"That would be kind, but they would look at the gift as charity. And no one on the ridge accepts charity."

"We'll have the girls earn it by doing chores around the schoolhouse, sweeping, washing the blackboard and such. The girls would study harder if they could look forward to sewing with you. Please say yes."

William paused on the boardinghouse porch. He needed Lizzie's emotional support to face those boys and longed for the opportunity to share more time together. Yet despite Lizzie's calm demeanor and proper deportment, heartache lingered in her eyes. Mr. Hill had prophesied correctly; Lizzie needed this distraction to pull her from her grief.

"Perhaps their mothers could barter any extra vegetables for the yard goods, then you could give those items to Mrs. Carroll as part of your rent." Lizzie gazed out over the gardens.

"Brilliant idea! Shall we go buy the fabric?" William offered his arm.

•   •   •

"Yes," Lizzie said. When he grinned, William's dimple deepened, prompting her lips to curve. He must have been so adorable as a little boy. What brought such thoughts to her mind?

"I bet your smile wheedled extra cookies and cake from your cook."

"Of course. And after a long ride on my favorite stallion, I consumed slices of apple pie smothered with a warm, rich custard. A growing fellow is always hungry. The commissary is to the right, correct?" William stuck his hands in his pockets.

"To the right, after we reach the main road." Lizzie lengthened her steps to keep up with William. Somehow, he had comprehended her love of soft wools, and even simple calicoes. Some women hungered for taffy or fudge, but she longed to rub her face against a bolt of silk and dream what to sew from it.

"Forgive me." William slowed down. "I'm excited that you will continue to teach. The sewing lessons will honor Mr. Hughes' dream of the mountain families finding a better way of life."

"I think it would be more helpful if you thought how the lessons would bring more beauty into their rugged lives. My people have shown the settlers that they are not interested in a different way to live. In fact, you must act as if they are doing you a favor to let their daughters participate."

"Thank you for explaining that detail. I assumed the highlanders wanted us here."

"Some welcomed the settlers, while others wished they would take their silly ideas and go away. Even my own sister tried to drive the Englishmen away by releasing sacks of serpents at the opening ceremonies at the Tabard. And she sabotaged the wagons bought to transport the visitors to Rugby."

"But I am not an Englishman. I'm a fellow American." William shook his head.

"True, but you weren't born on this mountain. To my people, you are a foreigner with outlandish ideas."

"Did your sister ever change her opinion?"

"Yes, because she fell in love with an Englishman. She loved the new library and how Mr. Hughes encouraged equality between men and women. He also hopes that one day Negros will become part of Rugby."

"Interesting. I read he wanted people of other races to join in his utopia." William opened the door to the commissary; every eye turned to look at them.

Lizzie squared her shoulders and strode to the bolts of calico stacked on a back shelf. If she was going to teach, then folks needed to grow accustomed to seeing her with William. Two women looked away and started fingering the woolens, while several men wandered into the area selling bolts, nuts, and nails. A new clerk at the counter nodded at Lizzie.

"May I help you?" she asked, stepping towards William.

"I would like several pairs of scissors and packets of pins, plus a good hammer, please."

What did William need a hammer for? Lizzie ran her fingers over a lavender silk that she could sew into a lovely new gown for when she entered half-mourning. She could knit a wide lace collar for the frock. But why dress up if George could no longer escort her into the Tabard ballroom? The woolens would make an excellent riding skirt and jacket, but George couldn't ride with her, chasing her down some wooded lane. Lizzie slid the bolts back onto the shelf. After selecting four different flowered calicos in dark red, blue, brown, and gray, she paused by a bolt of muslin. From watching the girls play tag, most of them needed new underclothing more than a special frock for Sundays. How she would persuade the parents to accept new petticoats and drawers, she didn't know, but Lizzie would try.

.   .   .

With one eye on Lizzie, William prowled the hardware aisle, lifting various hammers, checking the price of a pound of nails. He wrote down a few figures to ensure he could quote the correct facts to Nate, who probably had overcharged Lizzie for supplies. He walked to a display of rope and pictured the bare schoolyard. William signaled to a clerk.

"Please choose the correct thickness and cut enough rope for three or four swings. You probably can guess how long they should be. And add a couple of two by eights to my bill." He ambled over to Lizzie as she pondered a bolt of lawn sprigged with pink roses.

"It would make a charming summer dress." William loved how she gazed at the cloth with yearning. Her expression revealed her love for fabric and for beauty. "You've been in mourning for almost a year."

"Yes." Lizzie placed the bolt of lawn back onto the shelf.

"But you aren't ready to enter half-mourning."

"Not yet. Someday."

William picked up the bolts of calico. Although certain fragrances and songs had sliced open his heart with memories of Rose, riding his favorite horse had nudged him out of the deepest shadows. Bent low over Robbie's neck, galloping over pastures and down country roads, a power would explode inside him. Riding had propelled him back into life. He had to find a way to help Lizzie shed her grief before she would consider a courtship. She was a flower petal drifting on a pond. They walked to the counter as the wall clock chimed four.

"Good gravy, I promised mother that we would share tea. She leaves tomorrow."

"You go on. I'll have them deliver the packages. Did you choose a hammer?" Lizzie glanced at William.

"Yes, I left it with the clerk. Thank you."

William turned onto the road to the boarding house and ran. His mother would complain about his lack of manners. She would warn him about spending too much time with a woman beneath his station. But in less than twenty-four hours, she would ride away. William paused at the foyer, caught his breath, and walked into the parlor.

"You are five minutes late." Mrs. MacLeod lifted the teapot and poured two cups. "Sit, please."

"I'm sorry, mother." William slid onto a straight-back chair and picked up his cup and saucer. Anger simmered in his mother's eyes, along with the weariness, resulting from sleeplessness. So many nights, he had arrived home in the wee hours and overheard her sobs while his father snored. Instead of grieving together, the three of them struggled alone. "Please forgive me."

She nodded and offered a plate of small sandwiches. "Hopefully, a day of teaching school brought you to your senses?" His mother studied his face. "I can't imagine you having the patience with those ruffians." She sniffed. "I doubt if they bathe once a month."

No matter William's age, his mother didn't understand the importance of saying something encouraging to him as a person. She could have started with an unbiased question, such as, *how was your day*? William ran his tongue along his teeth, willing his expression to appear calm. He would not rise to her goading even though he wanted to describe the well-scrubbed appearances of his students.

"It went well." He bit into a sandwich of soft cheese sprinkled with chopped thyme. "Tasty. Mrs. Carroll is a wonderful cook."

"Yes. And Miss Elizabeth? How did she manage?" Mrs. MacLeod sipped her tea.

"She's a better teacher than I am. Kind and thoughtful with the children." William stuffed the other praises into a corner of his brain. Too many compliments would ignite his mother.

"Perhaps you should turn the school over to her and return to your duties."

Blast it all! "No, I need to stay. I gave Mr. Hill my word, and because of the many students, it works best to have two teachers."

"Don't forget, this adventure is *only* for eight weeks. No dallying with Miss Elizabeth. Hopefully, you learned something from your mistake. Come fall, you must select a wife from our respectable friends and produce a legal heir. Your father and I are not so young."

"I will try." After attending numerous dinner parties and balls, none of the young socialites compared to Miss Elizabeth. She was kind, industrious, and loved children, and he wanted a wife like her.

"Watch yourself, William." Mrs. MacLeod rose.

"Mother, don't you think it is time for you to pack up Rose's frocks and give some of them away?" William stood.

His mother's chin quivered. "Who would want them? They're no longer fashionable."

"Both the local young women and the new settlers would enjoy them."

His mother's eyes narrowed. "I must rest before the dinner bell. Please ask Mrs. Carroll to send someone to pack my trunk."

"I think the only person here who could help is Miss Elizabeth."

"Then send for her and remember that she *is* a servant."

William gritted his teeth and walked to the kitchen. His father had encouraged this holiday, hoping that his wife would come to appreciate his investments in Rugby. Now, his mother would tell his father how foolish he had been for spending his money on the settlement and blame the poor man for William's choice to remain behind. He pushed open the kitchen door.

"Mrs. Carroll, my mother would like a servant to pack her trunk, please."

Mrs. Carroll held up her flour covered hands. "I suppose she wants a maid to arrive within the next ten minutes?"

"Yes, or sooner." If his mother had access to a bell pull within this home, the bell would ring endlessly.

.   .   .

Lizzie removed Mrs. MacLeod's black dress from the wardrobe and examined the flounces and boned bodice before folding the soft silk and slipping it into the trunk. She tucked in the extra drawers, chemises, and petticoats sewn from fine linen and edged with crocheted Irish lace. While working at the Tabard, she had fingered the same exquisite Irish lace that decorated tablecloths. By the glow of a hearth, the Irish women had gripped their thin bone crochet hooks, creating a web of delicate stitches that formed roses and leaves. Lizzie laid a set of lawn hankies on top of the clothing.

George had presented her with a similar set of hankies, edged with tatted lace and with clusters of blue forget-me-nots embroidered in the corners. Like everything in her trousseau, they had perished when the Tabard burned. The lone survivor had hidden in her pocket, stained, and smelling of smoke. Lizzie had washed and pressed it so many times that the lawn had shredded in spots. Each morning after she laced her corset, she slipped the small square beneath her chemise, and it rested over her heart.

"Is there anything else you want to add, ma'am?" She gazed at Mrs. MacLeod's grim face. Grief resided in her tight jaw and stiff neck. How tragic the woman hadn't attempted to find comfort in the beauty and peace of the mountains.

"I would like to add that my son will soon announce his engagement to the daughter of my best friend. So don't try to lure him away from her."

Back straight as a fire poker, Mrs. MacLeod tapped her fingers on the arm of her chair. No polite chit-chat from her lips before leaping into her thoughts and expressing her authority. Although William hadn't mentioned a sweetheart, Lizzie had assumed he cherished affections for a young lady. Yet, Mrs. MacLeod's words pinched Lizzie's heart. An engaged man should not be alone with a single woman in a classroom.

"Congratulations. The young lady will be a wonderful addition to your family." Lizzie buried her fists inside the folds of her skirt.

"Remember this as you assist William. He is spoken for."

"Thank you for telling me. If we are finished, I best go."

Lizzie tossed aside her boots and collapsed onto her bed. What a twisted sort of day. Tiring, but also revealing. How had she gone from wayward student and town flirt to a teacher's assistant? She had enjoyed telling the girls stories during the dinner break as the smallest ones cuddled next to her. If she and George had wed, she might be snuggling a baby with his father's blue eyes. Tears blurred her vision. They would have welcomed a flock of children.

The supper bell chimed, but Lizzie buttoned up her nightgown and slipped between the sheets. She didn't want to sit across from Mrs. MacLeod and endure her glares. Tomorrow, she would eat. Lizzie yawned. Hopefully, the sight of the calico would excite the girls and they could wheedle their parents into accepting William's generosity.

CHAPTER FIVE

Sing on sweet thrush,
-Robert Burns

The rattle of buggy wheels drowned out the soft cooing of a morning dove. Lizzie rolled onto her side and peeked out the window, which faced the front porch. In the early dawn light, Mrs. MacLeod's trunk stood next to her and William. Mr. Hill jumped down and loaded her trunk.

"Yes, mother. Have a pleasant trip." William kissed Mrs. MacLeod's cheek, helped her into the buggy, and waved as it rolled toward the pike.

Had Mrs. MacLeod told the truth about a wealthy young lady marrying her son, or had she made the statement to ensure Lizzie's indifference to William? Thank goodness the woman could no longer scowl at her during meals, but Lizzie would be careful not to encourage William's affections. No longer would she be the flirt responsible for breaking up couples.

Lizzie snuggled under a blue and white quilt and smooshed the pillow. Now that his mother had departed, would William act like the other gentlemen set loose from their parents? Many young settlers shed their well-mannered images and turned to moonshine, late night gambling, and if they could find a willing local girl, a romp in a hayloft.

The fragrance of coffee, bacon, and biscuits drifted from the kitchen. Lizzie hadn't been hungry for a year, but she understood the blessing of Mrs. Carroll's cooking. Some students would arrive with empty bellies, and Lizzie needed to solve that problem. She slid out of bed and opened the wardrobe.

Black skirts and drab gray shirtwaists. Surely her students would find her clothing depressing, yet Lizzie hoped they would see her as the widow she imagined herself. For a moment, Lizzie recalled the smooth silk against her cheek and the pleasing shade of lavender. Perhaps she was ready for half-mourning and should sew a lavender shirtwaist for next Sunday. She hadn't walked into a church since George's funeral, but a schoolteacher should set a proper example by attending services. William might also come to Christ Church with her.

"It's me, Emily." Her friend knocked on Lizzie's door. "May I enter?"

"Certainly." Lizzie opened the door. In one hand she held a hairbrush and a mirror in the other. "How's your grandmother?"

Emily took the brush and stroked Lizzie's hair. "She is on the mend, but needs help with dressing, and in other ways."

"So, you wouldn't consider becoming the classroom helper?"

"I'm sorry, but no. Grandmother needs me. I wish I had your hair. It's so thick and beautiful."

"You make me miss Viney; she liked to brush my hair." Lizzie rested her head against the back of the chair.

"I wanted to show my doily to you. I made a couple of mistakes and had to rip it apart." Emily set down the hairbrush and drew her knitting out of a drawstring wool bag.

"Now the thread is droopy and grubby." Lizzie twisted her hair and stuck pins into a bun.

"Yes. I'm better at taking photographs than knitting lace. But I'll keep trying."

"Good. You'll catch on. Would you consider taking a photograph of our students?"

"And then you could introduce me to the handsome new schoolmaster." Emily winked at Lizzie.

"I would be glad to do that." Lizzie's stomach pinched her, but she chided herself.

"I'll come by soon." Emily tucked her knitting into her bag and dashed off.

Lizzie sank onto her bed; her resolve to eat breakfast had evaporated. She had no claim on William, but she had cherished how they had shared the past couple of days and looked forward to teaching with him. She could tell Emily that William was engaged, but something in Mrs. MacLeod's speech had felt insincere, as if the woman projected her opinions upon her son.

.   .   .

As his mother's carriage rolled away, William stretched his arms above his head. Freedom from the mill and his mother had erased the tension in his neck and shoulders. Now and then, his mother had stayed with her sister in Kentucky and had left William and his father home for a week, but never had she given him two months of liberty. His poor father would receive Mother's full attention, but he would calm his nerves by playing his bagpipes, which he had hidden in his office at the mill. The noise of the machinery drowned out the music blasted by the instrument and his wife never visited the mill. William wanted to turn cartwheels, to leap and dance, to shout like a banshee.

But he strode into the dining room, nodded at the visiting family, and chose a seat. He heaped several fried eggs, sausage patties, biscuits, and sausage gravy onto his plate and reached for the jam pot. His mouth salivated when Mrs. Carroll carried in a large bowl of strawberries and set it on the table.

"I picked them at dawn," Mrs. Carroll said.

"Thank you. You should have asked me to help. Have you seen Miss Elizabeth? I thought she'd be here," William asked.

"That one needs to eat more." Mrs. Carroll's Irish accent clung to her words. "I thought after her friend Emily stopped by that Lizzie would come to breakfast, perhaps you should fetch her. 'Tis the third door down the east hall."

"Yes." William had watched to see where Lizzie resided. He marched to her door and knocked on it. Staying in her room wouldn't heal Lizzie's grief, and he needed her help.

"Lizzie, it's me, William. You skipped dinner, so please come to breakfast. You need sustenance."

Lizzie cracked the door. "I'll be there, soon."

"Lovely, I'll pour you a cup of tea." If anyone should hide this morning, it should be him. He hoped Lizzie would have some good ideas on how to manage those boys.

When she entered the dining room, William pushed in her chair and slid a platter with eggs towards her.

"Have you any thoughts about how I could win the boys' respect?"

Lizzie sipped her tea. "I have a few ideas that might work."

An hour later, William gripped the edge of his desk and gazed out at the rows of faces. See them as individuals, and not as a swarm of hornets, he told himself. Except for the settler's offspring, most of the youth were thin, tanned, and wore patched but clean clothing. They probably dreamed about the same things he had at that age. No, some of those expressions showed hunger, others a wariness or anger. He had ranted at his parents when they denied him some bobble, but he had never known the hard life these young folks lived. And the settler's children had experienced moving and entering a strange world where not everyone welcomed them. Perhaps if he concentrated on their faces, he could learn their names and more about each child.

"Would the older girls and boys please come to my desk." William motioned them forward with his hand. "Instead of starting with your lessons, for the first half-hour of the morning, each of you will tutor a younger child in reading."

"But then how can we complete our work, sir?" Silas asked.

"We won't have enough time, sir," Victoria said.

"By helping, you will understand the joy of tutoring a younger person, and you will learn to work more efficiently." William read the names of the students he had matched with the older ones. "If you need help, please signal to Miss Lizzie, and she will guide you."

"Third grade readers, please come forward," William said.

Every ten minutes, he glanced at the tutors and students, as Lizzie milled about them, answering questions. While walking to the school, they had discussed this plan, which appeared to be working. Lizzie needed to realize her gift for encouraging and managing the children. William looked at the wall clock.

"Older students, please return to your seats. Thank you for assisting with the younger ones. Fifth grade readers, rise."

Ellie Jo screamed and pointed. The other girls shrieked and ran to the front of the room. A huge, black spider scurried down the center aisle, turned, and aimed for the flock of girls who clutched Lizzie. Five-year-old Charlotte clawed her way up Lizzie's skirt and into her arms. The boys slumped in their seats, laughing, and calling out, "Sissies."

A cruel prank. William hated spiders, but fury rippled through him. These boys would not interrupt the lessons. Picking up the thick dictionary, he ran towards the palm-size beast and slammed the book down. Spider parts splattered the floor, and the girls screamed louder.

"Clean it up, Silas," William said.

"Why me, sir?"

"If you know the culprit, tell him to do it. There's a rag by the blackboard."

Two more hours to endure before the dinner break. "Fifth grade readers, please."

. . .

After school let out, the six older girls sang *Barbara Allen* while they washed the blackboard, dusted the books, and swept the floor. Lizzie stood in the open doorway and watched William as he walked toward the Tabard with his jacket unbuttoned. Sunlight shone on his maroon and gray waistcoat, and she spied a silver derringer poking out of the jacket's pocket.

Last winter, Lizzie had pondered borrowing Jacob's gun and heading for the woods. One bullet, and her pain would cease. But if she had followed that notion, then each time Jacob lifted his gun, he would remember finding her. But if she owned a small pistol....

Footsteps patted the gravel, and a barefoot woman wearing a faded sunbonnet and carrying a basket rounded the corner. Lucas's mother. Lizzie wanted to scamper into the schoolhouse. How much did his mother know about her and Lucas?

"Miz Lizzie?" Sarah motioned to her. "Can you talk with me?"

"Certainly, is something amiss?"

"Oh no, my least one told me what you're doing. I wanted to thank you for having the girls earn their calico." She held out a spool of thread. "I traded eggs for it. So, I could tell my man that we weren't beholden to you or Master William."

"Thank you, Sarah. Please tell your husband that we have plenty of small jobs for the girls." Lizzie wrapped her fingers around the spool, knowing what Sarah had sacrificed would have provided more food for her children.

Sarah ducked her head. "Thank you." Her sunbonnet bobbed down the gravel walkway.

Her own mama had probably been like Sarah, barefoot and weary from hoeing corn. If Mr. Hughes hadn't created his utopia, Lizzie would have trodden the same path as Sarah; married at sixteen, with a passel of young ones before the age of twenty. Lizzie had longed to wed a wealthy man and leave the mountains, but she hadn't understood what life would be like off the ridge until George had explained about his family's different expectations. From his descriptions, Lizzie had realized that in England, folks would scorn her accent and odd highland ways. Now, she yearned for the highlanders to discover how Rugby could enrich their lives.

"We're all done." Betsy stood on the steps. "Can we start now?" She and the other girls pulled up benches and sat at a long rectangular table with the English girls at the other end. As the pendulum on the wall clock swung, the two cultures stared at each other. Lizzie yearned to make them count off so she could divide them into integrated pairs, but only time and sharing an experience would unite them.

"I know you have been sewing with your mamas for years, but sometimes it is nice to change your patterns, so the top of a sleeve will have more puff." Motioning to Betsy to stand up, Lizzie unfurled a tape and took the girl's measurements while the others giggled.

"You'uns won't be laughing when I wear my new dress," Betsy said. "At least I have something to measure. And you foreigners in your prissy clothes, don't think you're better than us."

"That's enough. Remember Betsy that no one here is a foreigner any longer. We are one group of female students."

Soon Betsy wouldn't need a bustle, and a corset would make the boys squirm more during church. How Lizzie had loved the power of seeing the lads' eyes follow her, and she had enjoyed the boys' sweet talk with her after the church service. .

After sketching a bodice, Lizzie cut out a muslin pattern, and draped it over Betsy who stood in her chemise, patched drawers, and limp petticoat. She needed undergarments more than a new frock. Lizzie explained each step about drafting and fitting patterns to the other girls, who wrote notes.

Betsy leaned over and asked, "Are the teacher's kisses better than Lucas'? Or that Mr. George's? God rest his soul. Silas said you could teach us lots about kissing. I want my kisses to make boys dizzy."

The girls tittered, and Lizzie blushed. Romance was a prevailing interest shared by both groups, and thoughts about kissing consumed the young folk. She scanned their faces, so innocent and full of dreams of how love would make their world complete. Although the girls had watched their mothers care for a dozen or more children, they didn't think of the future challenges that marriage would bring to their lives. She needed to convince them to work in Rugby for a little while and save up a nest egg for a future home.

"Kissing is a gift." Lizzie looked out the window toward the cemetery. "Keep your kisses in your heart until you find a man who will cherish you. And who doesn't lure you into kissing and maybe more." There. She had tried to warn these young women so they could avoid her mistakes.

"You wish you hadn't kissed those other fellows?" Betsy frowned.

"I wished I had waited for Mr. George." Head bowed; Lizzie pinned the muslin pattern to a length of blue calico.

"But my sister says she enjoys practicing any chance she can," Sue Ellen said. "Can't see no harm in that. When she weds, she'll keep her husband happy."

Lizzie squeezed her eyes closed. She had to find the right words to encourage these girls to take a year or two to experience life in the settlement.

"Enough talk of kissing. We'd better attend to our sewing."

. . .

A few days later, William and Mr. Hill toured the inside of the Tabard, inspecting the wallpaper sent from England and the wainscoting milled locally.

"When this new Tabard is completed, it will rival the inns of Virginia and North Carolina," Mr. Hill said. "Hopefully, it will draw visitors from across the Northeast and the South. Have you ordered the furniture for it?"

"Ah, no, sir. I hadn't thought that far ahead. Plus, teaching has taken much of my time."

"I think Mrs. Hill has a list of furniture factories and shops. And I suppose your mother could recommend a furniture business in Cincinnati. A quick weekend visit home might assuage her feelings and most women enjoy shopping for furniture and such."

"And such, sir?" William stared at a cumulous cloud shadowing the ridge.

"Mattresses, pillows, thick rugs, those things we will need to provide for our future guests. I'm sure your mother could offer sources for them."

"Yes, sir. I will write to her."

"Good lad." Mr. Hill walked towards his home and William headed to the stables.

For a moment, he stood in the entranceway breathing in the rich smells of straw, leather, and horses. His shoulders relaxed and his heartbeat slowed. Even when William's elderly body became too frail to ride, he would sit in his horse barn and savor the scent. He walked by the stalls and studied each horse, noticing how the animal looked at him or shied away.

"Can I help you, sir?" A stable hand pushed a wheelbarrow full of spent straw. The lad dusted his hands on the side of his trousers. "I'm Ryan, sir."

Another Irish man like those who worked in the mills. William shook Ryan's hand. "I'm William, the new schoolmaster from Cincinnati. Your accent sounds like you're from Donegal?"

"Right, sir. But lately from Boston. Mr. Walton offered me this position."

"Congratulations. I would like to go for a ride."

"Of course, sir. We lease the horses by the day or for a month."

"Which one would you recommend?"

"Some gentlemen like the gray gelding, while others prefer the Morgan stallion, sir."

"I'll ride the Morgan. What's his name?" William ran a hand over the horse, remembering a Morgan he had cherished, but the mare had died while giving birth.

"Chestnut, sir, because of his coloring."

"Please provide the tack, but I'd prefer to saddle him myself." William picked up a currycomb.

"Yes, sir." Ryan strode to the tack room.

William uttered soft words as he entered the stall, and Chestnut glanced at him. For a minute, he gazed at the Morgan, appreciating his muscular yet graceful build and his arching neck. "You are a handsome fellow. Can we be friends?"

William raised his hand and ran the curry comb down Chestnut's legs. The Morgan shifted his weight but didn't flatten his ears. William smiled and continued combing the horse's sides. He needed more friends, ones that didn't judge him or expect him to pay for the next rounds of whiskey. Friends who would appreciate his fascination with Rugby and his desire to own a horse farm. The gentlemen back home understood making an investment in breeding horses but would shake their heads at one of their social class managing a farm. William checked each of Chestnut's hooves for bits of gravel, but they were clean.

William sat tall in the saddle, clicked his tongue, and they trotted through the settlement. When the stallion had warmed up his muscles, William urged him into a gallop, and they raced down the lane with the wind tugging at his hair. No matter what society and his parents expected of their only heir, he refused to allow them to take away this freedom.

He wished Lizzie rode beside him, with her curls flowing down her back and her cheeks flushed pink. But instead of Lizzie, Mr. Hill's comments about seeking his mother's advice twisted his gut. The man probably was right. A brief visit would show his parents that he cared for them, and he needed a woman like his mother to help him select the right furnishings.

· · ·

Lizzie walked over to her cottage and found Nate sawing boards and nailing in window frames. A fresh stack of lumber shone in the sunlight, but Nate hadn't straightened the corner where the foundation wasn't level. What else had he refused to correct? She should have waited for William to return from his ride, but she didn't like being beholden to him. After all, eventually he would return to Cincinnati, and she would resume the responsibility of managing Nate.

"Glad to see you, Miss Lizzie," Nate called. "I need you to walk around inside and explain how you want this divided into rooms."

"Perhaps we should wait for William. He would have good ideas. I wanted to see if you had corrected your mistakes." Lizzie pointed to the corner.

Nate scowled. "We were doing fine before he came. Reckon I overlooked that one. Come on inside."

Knots tightened in Lizzie's stomach when Nate grabbed her elbow and escorted her into the cottage. Even the scent of freshly cut pine lumber couldn't soothe her nerves. Nate slid his arms around her waist, and she tried to pull free. His fingers gripped her ribs.

"Lizzie, Lizzie. You used to throw kisses to any fellow who would do your bidding."

Nate pinned Lizzie's arms to her sides and shoved her against a wall. "I could finish this here house faster if'n you'd spare me a few…." His lips covered hers.

Lizzie gagged. He smelled of sweat, and tobacco juice dribbled out of a corner of his mouth and onto her chin. She stomped on his toes, wrestled one arm free, and elbowed him in the gut. Nate gasped as she flailed him with her fists.

"How dare you! Think of your children!" She shoved him away. "You're fired."

"Oh no, I ain't. None of the other fellars will work for you, if'n I tell them to stay away." Nate glared down at Lizzie. "You think you're something, but Lucas still brags about his time with you. Reckon I deserve a piece, too, you slut."

"Get off my land!" Lizzie's cheeks burned and her legs shook. She had been a stupid girl who thought she could gain what she wanted with her charms. She would prove that she had changed.

Nate laughed. "Oh, you'll have me back if'n you want this house by Christmas." He picked up his tools and marched off.

Lizzie ran to the cemetery. She sank onto George's grave, pressed her forehead against her knees, and sobbed. She hated how Nate was right, and she was dependent upon him completing the cottage. If she and George had wed, then men like Nate and Lucas would leave her alone. The mountain women would forget her dalliances and accept her as a respectable wife. She loathed how the past stalked, taunted, and manipulated her. Some days, death appeared the only way to escape from the pain twisting her heart. At the sound of boots, her shoulders stiffened. Don't let it be Lucas, she prayed, but the scent of horses accompanied the boots.

"Miss Elizabeth?" William kneeled. "Is something amiss?"

Lizzie stared at George's tombstone. If she told him about Nate's advances, as a gentleman, William would believe he must confront him. Nate would seek revenge, perhaps by rallying the older boys to rebel in new ways or even something worse. Lizzie knew Nate would tell William about her salacious times with Lucas. She enjoyed William as a friend and didn't want to see disappointment in her fill his eyes. Tears blurred her vision as she stared at George's tombstone.

"Next month, it will be a year since George died."

"I understand." William nodded. "Last month, I marked the one-year anniversary of my sister's death by skipping work and going for a long ride." William pulled out a handkerchief and wiped his eyes. "I don't know what's wrong with me today. Grief has a way of striking when we are most vulnerable."

Tears trickled down her cheeks as Lizzie took one of William's hands and cradled it. If the gossips witnessed her gesture, they would shred her, but Lizzie didn't care. Anguish lined William's forehead and lingered in his eyes. The same expression that stared back from her mirror. When would their sorrows cease?

"I'm sorry. Folks say the first year is the hardest." How strange to hold William's hand and know his touch wouldn't lead to improper advances.

"It is. But we must try to celebrate our loved ones and the joy they gave us." William laid his other hand on hers. "They would want us to live full and happy lives."

"Yes. I guess it is easier to focus on the loss." Like a thick layer of gray clouds, the pain trapped her to this earth, making her yearn for the peace of heaven. Lizzie took out a black bordered hanky and dabbed at her tears.

A flock of crows cawed as they flew from an oak tree and headed toward Mr. Hill's farm. Coming from the grist mill, a farmer and his team drove by with a wagon loaded with bags of cornmeal. His voice floated by as he spoke to his team. Such common sights and sounds pricked her as folks tended to simple chores.

William wiped his eyes. "I've never cried with a woman. It's odd how grief has linked us. None of my friends back home have experienced the death of a sibling. They attend balls and dinner parties and wonder why I prefer to ride my horse."

"Some of my friends have lost a sibling or a parent, but not a fiancé."

Lizzie couldn't remember her mother's death, and before George had passed away, no other family member had died. Last fall, Aunt Alta had left this earth, but she had been seventy-eight years old. Lizzie still missed the woman who had mothered her.

．　．　．

The pressure of Lizzie's fingers lingered as she slid her hand away from his. Small, delicate, and soft, William wanted to raise it to his lips, inhale her rose perfume, and kiss her palm. But he mustn't act on his desires as tongues would flap about the schoolmaster making free with his assistant. And he had promised Rose. He pulled up some grass from around George's tombstone.

"I admire your faithfulness to George. Only a few young ladies I've met loved their husbands-to-be." Rose had explained how most girls rated their suitors by counting how many fine carriages the man owned, the number of servants the family employed, and how many rooms filled his house.

William hated being defined by the output of their factories, the size of their third-floor ballroom and extensive gardens. But his mother employed the same economic standard as she analyzed the debutantes, and how their dowry would increase his bank account. If his mother could, she would marry him off to a southern girl whose family farmed hundreds of acres.

"Once I fit that description, but love can transform a person." Lizzie gazed across the cemetery. "Having money is useful for building my cottage, but I'd rather have George."

"You'll always miss him, but one of these days, you will realize how you haven't thought about him. Trust me. One afternoon, I realized how memories of Rose hadn't interrupted my thoughts." Although Rose would have encouraged him to find meaning in life, guilt had berated him for being heartless.

"Now and then, that happens to me." Lizzie sniffled. "Then I feel wretched for not remembering some special detail."

"I had to struggle with those feelings about Rose and about...." William tossed his handful of grass beneath a rosebush. "When I couldn't remember the sound of Rose's voice, I hated how shallow I felt. So, I read her diaries hoping to find her spirit in the written words."

Those pages reminded him of Rose's passion to help the less fortunate and how she disdained her family's wealthy lifestyle. He had relived hearing her complaints about parading herself in front of young gentlemen who eyed her sweet curves and her family's fortune. William wished he had comprehended his sister's anguish and had convinced his parents to allow Rose to fulfill her dreams instead of their desires.

Now the same emptiness lingered inside him, begging him to fill the hole with something meaningful. If William could claim his students' respect, perhaps teaching would satisfy the emptiness, but if he failed, his mother would demand his return. After experiencing freedom at Rugby, he had to remain in the settlement and be near Lizzie.

"Why do you carry a pistol?" Lizzie nodded at the bulge in his pocket.

"Oh, I suppose from hearing the tales about mountain men who shoot strangers. Carrying a rifle would be too obvious, and I'm a better shot with a pistol. Does it make you uncomfortable?"

"No, but most settlers don't arrive with guns." Lizzie stood up.

"I'm not like most of them. I think it is near dinner time." William offered his elbow, and she linked hers with his. A kindness that he hoped would lead to a deeper connection.

William dipped his pen in his inkwell and stared at the faint lines he had penciled on to the sheet of linen paper.

Dear Mother and Father,

Progress is being made with the Tabard and the wainscoting around the interior looks lovely. Today, I talked a bit with Mr. Hill, who explained that we need to order furniture for the rooms and suites, plus mattresses, pillows, and linens. He will introduce me to a couple of carpenters who build furniture in the local style, but he also pointed out that I should order finer pieces from Cincinnati for the more elegant rooms. Mr. Hill thought that Mother would have good ideas about where to purchase items. I will visit soon and hope that you can please help me.

While teaching young people is a challenge, I enjoy seeing the world through their curious minds. The term is progressing well, and we plan to have an end of the summer program. I pray you are in good health.
    Love, William

William addressed and sealed the envelope, hoping that his letter would not cause more insults from his mother.

CHAPTER SIX

To see ourselves as others see us!
–Robert Burns

William folded the linen napkin and placed it in the lunch basket, along with the cutlery and china dishes. Mrs. Carroll understood a fellow's appetite and had packed a goodly amount of ham sandwiches, dill pickles, a dish of strawberries, and a half-dozen ginger cookies. Plus, the good woman had sent along a basket heaped with biscuits for the students. While Lizzie ate her repast with the girls, he needed a break from the older boys. Two weeks into the term, and the lads had completed a minimum of the assignments. The girls reminded him of a nest of baby birds, chirping and cheeping, and vying for his attention. The little ones had endeared themselves to his heart, as they were eager to please him and excited about learning to read. He looked forward to seeing their bright faces and listening to their droll comments. William rose and stretched. But he had promised Lizzie he would spend part of the noon break with the students and must emerge from his refuge.

Shouting rippled through the small clearing where the younger students chased each other. The English and highland girls had separated themselves, each group clustered on either side of Lizzie, who read to them from a book. Off to one corner, the older boys took turns pitching and hitting a ball. He would not join Lizzie, and seldom had William played baseball. Rose had enjoyed croquet, but he had preferred riding or a game of tennis now and then.

"Mr. MacLeod," Silas called. "Come pitch for us." The other boys paused and motioned for William to join them.

William scratched his neck where a mosquito had bitten him. He hadn't touched a baseball in years, but he might as well play. William accepted the homemade ball and faced the first student who held a thick stick. Underhand? Or overhand? He would pretend he was playing tennis. William tossed, and the ball fell to the side of the batter. He needed to throw it harder. Silas threw him the ball, and it stung William's palm. He pitched. The student whacked the ball and ran around the bases. William threw again, and the next batter knocked the ball towards the older girls.

"Joey wants to flirt!" Silas shouted as Joey ran to fetch the ball from Betsy's hand. "My turn."

When William was Joey's age, he had stolen moments with the girls eager to be kissed. He and his friends had stood at the dances, daring each other to entice a girl into the rose garden where they begged for a kiss. Their parents had taught their daughters strict social manners, but their inner desires had sought to hold a boy's hand or have him touch their cheeks. So, he and his friends had fulfilled the girls' longings, but William had never told his friends of the young woman who had finally claimed his heart.

He threw the ball; it sailed close to the schoolhouse and landed in the road. A few more pitches and he would end the noon break.

· · ·

The girls stared at Lizzie as she opened *Jane Eyre* and read aloud. She had borrowed the novel from Rugby's library, hoping if the older girls enjoyed the story, it would inspire them to read more books. Betsy leaned over Lizzie's shoulder and peered at the pages.

"Look at all them words. Is there kissing in that book? Will the girl get her man?" Betsy asked.

"I've been told that it's a love story where a poor girl falls in love with a rich man."

"Just like you did, Miz Lizzie!" Betsy rearranged her skirts.

"They find true love?" Rebecca asked. At fourteen, she was piecing a quilt and dreaming of marrying her beau.

"I think so, but I'm only half-way through the story." Lizzie inhaled. This discussion was not what she had envisioned when choosing the book.

"My mother loves that story," Victoria said in her English accent. "And she has read the other books by the Bronte sisters."

"How wonderful, but please don't tell us the ending, Victoria." Lizzie glanced back down at the page. "Now where did I leave off?"

A little girl screamed, and Lizzie and the other girls jumped up. William had fallen to his knees. She ran to him as he moaned and clutched his side. Great heavens, what had those boys done to him? She should have paid closer attention to their shenanigans.

"Victoria, please fetch the doctor." Lizzie kneeled next to William. "What happened, Silas?"

"He got in the way of the ball," Silas said.

"It hit him in the side," Joey said.

"William, where does it hurt?" Lizzie touched his shoulder. Got in the way of the ball. What a pile of horse poop. Another mean prank. She would deal with the boys later. The children stared at their teacher and a few of the youngest wept. While their compassion was sweet, William didn't need an audience.

"I can't breathe. My side." William groaned and cracked his eyes.

"We're fetching the doctor." Lizzie prayed Dr. O'Neill was in his office as she wiped William's sweaty forehead with her hanky. "Everyone, school is dismissed. Please go home. Silas, bring me a bucket of cool water."

For a heartbeat, her hand paused, as the image of her bathing George's feverish face filled her mind. William didn't suffer from cholera, yet the ball might have injured his lungs, like when a man punched another fellow. Lizzie dipped her hanky in the offered water and washed William's neck and wrists. A buggy rolled up and parked by the school. Dr. O'Neill ran over and squatted next to her.

"What happened?" He picked up William's wrist and took his pulse.

"A ball hit his side." Lizzie nodded at the culprit.

"Must have been a wicked hit." The doctor unbuttoned William's shirt and pressed his hands against William's left side.

William grimaced and squeezed his eyes. "Not so hard." He panted. "I still can't breathe."

"Cracked ribs. No time for modesty, Miss Elizabeth. I'll need your help." Dr. O'Neill raised William to a sitting position and offered him a sip of whiskey. "Please remove his shirt while I find some bandages."

Lizzie swallowed. An unmarried woman should not perform such a task, but this was an emergency. She eased the shirt over William's shoulders, lifting the left arm from a sleeve, and then the right. His muscles couldn't match her brother's, Jacob, who chopped wood and hoed corn, but William's flesh was firm and sprinkled with fine ruddy hair. William winced, and Lizzie scolded herself for finding pleasure in looking at his body.

"Take another sip of whiskey, William. Lizzie, please keep him upright." Dr. O'Neill unrolled a bandage.

Pressing herself against William's back, Lizzie's hands trembled as she gripped his shoulders. More than a year had passed since she had run her fingers over George's bare back, soothing his stiff muscles, memorizing his shoulder blades, and the hollows at the base of his spine. Despite her grief, holding William sparked a warmth for his gentle soul. He didn't deserve to be tormented by those boys. The doctor wrapped William's chest with a muslin bandage.

"How's the breathing?"

"Each breath hurts." William exhaled.

"That's normal with injured ribs, but can you breathe deeper?"

"Yes." William closed his eyes and sweat beaded on his forehead.

"Good. Let's see if you can stand." The doctor gave him his hands and helped him rise. "Walk a bit."

Doctor O'Neill stepped beside William, ready to catch him if he stumbled. Lizzie's eyes followed the motion of his hips. She mustn't allow her mind to wander, to dream of pressing her palms against William's chest. Then don't watch, silly goose. She stood up and brushed the dust off her skirt.

"Help me get him into my rig," Dr. O'Neill said. "Climb up."

Lizzie obeyed. With one foot on the mounting block, the doctor pushed William higher and into Lizzie's arms. He groaned as she guided him to the seat.

"Maybe it was worth it to crack a few ribs to share a hug." He inhaled and leaned back.

"You rogue." Lizzie shook her head. "You should put on your shirt."

"Drape it around his shoulders, along with this blanket." Dr. O'Neill picked up the reins.

"I'll close the schoolhouse." Lizzie hopped down and walked into the classroom.

As she packed up William's satchel, his spicey scent lingered in the leather strap, and she rubbed it against her cheek. Weeping together in the cemetery had offered her comfort, but today's encounter stirred her womanly sensibilities. Her year of mourning would end in a few weeks. No one could chide her for looking beyond George's grave, but considering William's lingering grief for Rose, he may not wish to accept her attentions. Lizzie would not flirt. But in small ways, she would show how their relationship could flourish into something more. As a robin sang outside a window, thousands of daisy petals fluttered inside her.

·   ·   ·

Cracked ribs. While William had observed other riders tumble from their horses and break bones, he hadn't comprehended their pain. He had assumed they were inferior horsemen, and such injuries came from their incompetence. What an arrogant bastard! Laid low by a baseball in front of the children; he deserved the humiliation. As the buggy struck a rock, William gritted his teeth and closed his eyes.

"Careful Nellie," Dr. O'Neill called.

Lizzie's touch still tingled where she had bathed his forehead and chest. William wished she had ridden in the buggy and hoped the doctor would suggest that Lizzie nurse him today. The glow of the whiskey romped through his mind. An afternoon together without interruptions. What a lovely thought. Perhaps she could bathe his forehead again and hold his hand.

"Whoa!" The doctor tugged on the reins as the buggy rolled next to the boardinghouse.

"Goodness!" Mrs. Carroll ran onto the porch. "William!"

"Nothing too serious, but he cracked a couple of ribs." Dr. O'Neill said. "The lad's sturdy and will mend soon. How much whiskey do you keep?" He eased William down from the buggy.

"Plenty. And all of it legal." Mrs. Carroll put one arm around William as the doctor placed his on the other side.

William exhaled. Each step jolted his ribs, and pain roared through him. Sweat ran down his neck as he shuffled along the hallway and reached his room. Dr. O'Neill assisted William onto his bed, and Mrs. Carroll closed the curtains. The doctor slipped off William's boots and trousers and covered him with a quilt.

"Here, lad." Dr. O'Neill pulled a vial from his waistcoat pocket and dribbled a liquid into William's mouth. "A bit of laudanum. Sleep well."

But he didn't want to sleep. He wanted to listen to Lizzie's voice and inhale her sweet perfume. But William's eyelids closed, and his breathing deepened.

●   ●   ●

Lizzie spread out arithmetic papers on the kitchen table and explained the baseball accident to Mrs. Carroll. The older woman sighed and shook her head as she kneaded dough for bread rolls.

"William still wants justice for the person who whistled, and those boys know it," Mrs. Carroll said. "He spoke about the topic last night, but he needs to let it go. Just ignore those boys and those fellows, Nate and Lucas." She dropped the dough into a buttered bowl and set a clean dish towel over it.

"The boys will keep up the pranks until William either explodes or resigns. And I fear what Nate may eventually do to William." Lizzie stared at a student's answer. Something didn't look right. What was nine times seven?

"I pray our young man can endure for four more weeks. Our children need an education." Mrs. Carroll stuck a log into the firebox of her stove. "I'm headed to the garden to pick some sage."

Lizzie scratched her head with her pencil. Why couldn't she remember how to solve x2+ y2=something? Flipping through the teacher's edition of *Ray's Arithmetic,* she searched for the answers for today's lessons. William had to return to teaching and save her from looking like a dunce. Yet, she needed to review these concepts that she should have learned years ago. Instead of scanning for the answers, Lizzie read how to find the solutions to each problem. Sighing, she closed the book. The next time she and William corrected papers, she would ask him to explain how to work these equations. She should study the different geometric formulas that the older students needed to learn for their homework.

With her knitting basket on her arm, Lizzie tip-toed into William's room and parted the curtain enough that a ray of sunlight illuminated her chair. She pulled out her needles and counted the stitches as she worked on a lace edging. Even if she never married, she would edge her pillowcases and sheets with the sawtooth points of Van Dyke lace. How fine to wake each morning to beautiful linens. Lizzie squeezed back tears. How much better it would be if George slept beside her.

She glanced at William's pistol sticking out of his waistcoat pocket. When he recovered, she would remind him of his offer to teach her how to shoot. She liked the idea of having the power of a weapon. After she moved into her cottage, she might need to defend herself from intruders or need to frighten away a bear.

William moaned. Lizzie set down her needles and ran a damp cloth over his forehead. While most mountain men sported strong and rugged bodies created by hard labor, William was handsome in a robust manner that displayed his hours of riding horses. He had not gone hungry like some of her folk, but neither had he indulged in rich food that gave a gentleman a pasty complexion. And those long fingers. William had mentioned how he enjoyed playing the piano, but planning lessons and correcting schoolwork offered few moments for music. Perhaps, with his limited mobility, William could take the time to provide the boardinghouse residents with music.

Had he learned to play the piano before Rose died, or afterwards to express his grief? Most visiting gentlemen Lizzie had met did not play an instrument, as usually the English women devoted their time to those accomplishments. But William stood apart from the other gentry who had come to Rugby. If George had lived, would he have developed his skills as a portrait painter? A dream, he had confided to Lizzie. William stirred and cracked his eyes.

"How are you feeling?" Lizzie clamped her fingers around her knitting needles to keep them from taking William's hand. His door stood open so anyone walking down the hall could look into the room.

"Like a horse kicked me. My head still feels fuzzy from the laudanum." William exhaled. "I think I will stick with willow tea for the pain. Thank you for taking care of me."

"You must heal and return to teaching those algebra problems. I'm not much better at editing their essays."

"You are wonderful with the younger students." William winced as he struggled to sit up.

"Should you do that?" Lizzie rose and propped two pillows behind his back.

"I can smell Mrs. Carroll's chicken potpie, and my stomach yearns for a large serving. I will need to sit up to consume it."

"As you wish." Lizzie smiled and headed to the kitchen. She filled two plates and placed them on a tray, along with glasses of lemonade and silverware. Serving William renewed a pleasure she had enjoyed when working at the first Tabard. She had loved watching a guest's delighted expression when she had set before him a plate of fresh green beans, mashed potatoes, and fried chicken. Or seeing a child's eyes widen when given a slice of chocolate cake.

Lizzie arranged the tray on William's lap and settled into a chair with her plate.

"Thank you. Your servant's heart is as lovely as you." William touched her arm. "I must find a way to repay you."

"Please, I am no one special. Any person would have also helped you." Lizzie bowed her head. No matter how many compliments William heaped on her, the student's whistle reminded her of her foolish past.

CHAPTER SEVEN

My heart's in the highlands
–Robert Burns

William leaned against the back of the settee with his legs extending across the velvet fabric. From the expression on Mr. Hill's face, he came with ideas, and William hoped they included Lizzie, who sat across from him.

"I'm sorry about this accident, and I canceled school for the rest of the week," Mr. Hill said. "Now is a good time to take a trip to Cincinnati and order the furniture."

"I should have the doctor's permission to travel." William's insides flinched. Staying with his lovely nurse, Lizzie, appealed to him more than a journey to encounter his mother.

"I spoke with the doctor this morning, and he agreed. I bought a ticket for this afternoon's train." Mr. Hill placed the pasteboard ticket on the small table by William's bed.

"Thank you for canceling school, Mr. Hill," Lizzie said. "I'm not ready to teach without William."

Lizzie needed to believe in herself. William had faith that she could handle the classroom even better than he could, but he understood her concern. A Bible verse Rose had quoted reminded him how when two people worked together, they had more strength than a single person. William hoped that described the growing relationship between himself and Lizzie.

"Well, it looks like I have little choice in the matter, so I had better pack my bags." William stood and grimaced. At least the train ride would allow him to sit for several hours and contemplate how to talk to his mother about the Inn.

· · ·

Lizzie tied the reins to the hitching post as William gingerly descended from her buggy. The locomotive belched smoke as men loaded on coal and water. During the trip to the station, she and William had chattered about the students and their parts in the end of the year program.

He took one of her hands. "I will miss you."

Lizzie's cheeks flushed. "I'll miss you, too, but you'll be back in five days."

"Until Monday." William squeezed her hand and boarded the train.

Lizzie waited until the locomotive's wheels rolled and waved goodbye. The last time she had watched a train carry away her loved ones, she had wanted her life to end. But William's faith in her had breathed hope into her heart, and watching her students learn new skills had given her joy. She untied the reins and spoke to Bessie.

"I need some female companionship. Let's go."

Her buggy rolled by the woods, crossed the bridge over the river, and rounded the hills before entering Rugby. Bessie trotted through the village and to Uffington House. After tying Bessie's reins to a hitching post, Lizzie strolled through the grape arbor leading to the low rectangular dwelling with twin dormers.

"Lizzie! Come in." Emily opened the door. "Granny will be delighted to see you. I am sorry about William's accident. I'll ask for tea."

"Thank you." Lizzie placed her bonnet on the hall tree. "I don't think the incident was an accident. Those older boys cultivate mischief, but they probably didn't think their trick would cause an injury."

Lizzie followed Emily into a small parlor with beige wallpaper printed with rambling vines and leaves. Madam Hughes sat in a wing-backed chair covered with blue velvet; her foot rested on a matching ottoman. After Lizzie inquired about Madam Hughes' health, she joined Emily on a settee. Soon, a maid placed a silver tray on a nearby low table.

"Thank you." Emily said. The maid nodded and left the room.

"Why do you think the lads plotted such a cruel trick?" Emily picked up the teapot and poured three cups.

"Because their parents don't like the settlement, and their sons act out their family's anger. I have a feeling because I fired him that Nate encouraged them."

"I see." Emily stirred cream and sugar into a cup, and Lizzie took it to Madam Hughes.

"What do you plan to do?" Madam Hughes asked.

"I don't know, ma'am. Nor does William have a plan." Lizzie sipped her tea, grateful for the brew that soothed her nerves.

"Animosity towards the settlement has abated to some extent," Madam Hughes said. "We must continue to respect our neighbors, so they realize how the school, the library, and the commissary can bring helpful changes to their lives."

"Yes, ma'am." Lizzie doubted that Madam Hughes understood the ways of the mountain folk. "Emily, could you please assist me on Saturday during the young ladies' sewing lesson? I thought the settlement girls would appreciate having a "foreigner" attend the session. I can't convince the two cultures to mingle."

"You should go, my dear. The maid can handle my needs for an hour or so," Madam Hughes said.

"I would love to, and I will bring my camera. Perhaps taking a few photos of the gathering will please your students."

"Thank you. I will see you at nine in the schoolhouse." Lizzie set down her teacup. She looked forward to having an ally when managing the two factions of girls.

That evening at dinner, Lizzie nibbled at her slice of ham and stared at William's empty chair. Other male boarders attempted to chatter with her, but she missed hearing William's voice and only responded in monosyllables. Without William, she didn't want to correct the stack of essays the students had written, nor did she want to stroll through the village and admire the gardens. Tomorrow, she would eat in the kitchen and avoid the gentlemen visitors who tried to flirt with her.

. . .

William thanked his family's carriage driver and walked up the steps to his parent's house. Odd how he thought of this place in that manner, but in a short time, Rugby had become his true home. When the butler opened the door, William greeted him, strolled down the hall, and peeked into his father's study.

"William! Thank you for sending the telegram about your visit. Take a chair. How are your ribs?"

"They ache. I'm drinking willow bark tea the midwife gave, and I'm not to lift anything heavy for a few weeks, sir."

"Midwife?" His father's eyes widened.

"She is the local herbal healer, and the doctor recommended her teas, which I prefer to laudanum. What did mother think of my letter?"

"She's eager to help and invited the finest furniture maker in Cincinnati to come for dinner, so you can discuss what the Tabard needs."

William's stomach lurched. "Yes, Mr. Underhill's company produces excellent work. I suppose his daughters are coming, too?"

"You know your mother." Mr. MacLeod rubbed his chin. "Sharing a meal doesn't mean that you plan to propose."

"I should think not. I best wash up and dress for dinner."

William nodded at a maid as he climbed the stairs. Inside his room, he untied his cravat and dropped it on a small table. He should have expected that his mother would parade the Underhill girls before him. Several times, his mother had vowed that he should marry Violet or Grace Underhill, either of whom would bring a sizeable dowry to their marriage. The young ladies were pretty, but they spoke about fittings for gowns, the next dinner party, and the spring teas. According to his mother, either sister could manage his future household, bear respectable children, and be an adoring wife.

• • •

William entered the dining room, helped seat Violet, the elder sister, and then pushed in the chair for Grace. His place card rested between the two young ladies, and he slid into his seat. Turning his head back and forth, he answered their questions.

"I heard that the mountain folk are shiftless and dirty." Violet dipped her spoon into the cream of potato soup.

"For the most part, the mountain women keep their families neat and tidy. I am amazed at how hard they work, weeding the garden, drying produce, sewing, and mending clothes." William eyed Violet's soft hands that had never pulled a blade of quack grass.

"Have you met Madam Hughes? I hear she is the queen of the settlement?" Grace buttered her dinner roll.

"Not yet, I've been too busy teaching. But the young woman who assists me in the classroom, Miss Walker, is a close friend of Madam Hughes and her granddaughter, Emily." From the corner of his eye, William caught his mother's frown while a hint of a smile turned up his father's mouth.

"You must be bored listening to the crickets, living without Cincinnati's concerts and theaters." Violet sliced her piece of ham.

His mother patted Violet's hand. "William has assured me that after he finishes the school term, he will return home. Then you must accompany him to the next concert."

William balled his hands into fists. "Actually, I enjoy Rugby's quiet moments. Miss Walker and I enjoy strolling through the village, gazing at the gardens. Or we sit on the boardinghouse porch and listen to Mrs. Carroll play her fiddle."

Mrs. MacLeod's cheeks blazed, and her eyes snapped. William straightened his shoulders. Perhaps his mother should not make statements without first asking his opinions about the subject.

"I'm here to purchase furniture for the new inn." William turned to Mr. Underhill. "Could I please visit your warehouses tomorrow morning about ten, sir?" Most likely, the sisters would sleep until noon and have brunch in bed, so they wouldn't pester him.

"This sounds agreeable to me," Mr. Underhill said. "I'll see you then."

•　•　•

The click of his bedroom door woke William. He stretched, relishing his full-size bed, the soft sheets scented with lavender water and the lightweight quilt. While he loved his accommodations at Mrs. Carroll's boardinghouse, the narrow bed prohibited a good stretch. His feet enjoyed the thick Persian rug before he slid into slippers. Steam rose from a pitcher of hot water that the maid had delivered along with a warm towel. After shaving, William opened his wardrobe and stared at the dozens of pressed shirts, trousers folded on hangers, and the shelf of polished boots.

While at Rugby, he hadn't missed having a large selection of clothing other than an extra pair of boots would be handy. He had never listened to Rose's lectures about materialism and how he should simplify his wardrobe, but she had been correct. Before he left, he would sort through his wardrobe and have his father donate the clothing. William tucked a cream shirt flecked with brown twigs into a pair of wool pants, grabbed socks, and a pair of boots. He tiptoed by his mother's bedroom door.

His father sat in the breakfast room and set down his newspaper, motioning to a platter of pancakes. "Living at Rugby has made you into an early riser."

"I always arrived at the mill on time." William stacked six pancakes on his plate and reached for the butter and maple syrup.

"But today is a Saturday following a late dinner party." His father sipped his tea. "I'm glad the settlement has cultivated this habit. Would you like to continue as the schoolmaster?"

"You would bless that decision?" William finished buttering his pancakes.

"If you felt that calling, yes. Remember, son, I sailed away from Scotland because I refused to become a farmer. By rights, I should have inherited the small croft, but the dream of glistening machinery and the clatter of looms pulled me towards America. I want you to have that same freedom to choose your future."

"And I have found it at Rugby. But what about mother?" William forked a piece of pancake in his mouth.

"She will not agree. You are our only child now, and she doesn't want to lose you. Nor do I."

"You must come visit Rugby when the Tabard is completed." William knew his father would enjoy ambling around the village and meeting Lizzie.

"If you aren't sure about a future teaching school, then please continue supervising the Tabard, at least until the grand opening. Then we can discuss if you should return to your position at the mill."

William set down his fork. "I've never managed an inn." Already a half-dozen questions tumbled in his brain.

"You've overseen mill workers, and your mother taught you how to host dinner parties. While you will need to learn new skills, I think you have the personality for the work."

"Thank you, father. I will do my best." William glanced up at his mother as she entered the dining room.

"Your best at what?" Mrs. MacLeod accepted a chair and poured a cup of tea.

"I'll explain later, my dear. You are up early," Mr. MacLeod said.

"I will accompany William in selecting furniture, as he knows nothing about how to decorate a room."

William stuffed more pancake into his mouth to avoid spewing out a caustic comment. His mother's words were true, but Mr. Underhill could offer advice. He didn't need her tagging along and expressing her opinions about every chair, bed, and wardrobe.

"I see." Mr. MacLeod gazed at William. "I would make this a family outing, but I promised our vicar that I would meet with him this morning. He mentioned needing donations for a pipe organ. Perhaps you would like to join me, my dear?"

"No, thank you, William needs me." Mrs. MacLeod nibbled a bite of pancake. "And I will ensure that he doesn't ride all over town with those broken ribs."

• • •

The coach driver assisted William's mother into the carriage, and William took the seat opposite her and gazed out the window. Soot streaked the sides of chimneys, bits of rubbish blew along the gutters, and the rattle of dozens of wheels from wagons and carriages hurt his ears. He longed for the trilling of wrens, the rustling of oak leaves, and the music of Mrs. Carroll practicing her violin. Their driver slapped the reins and soon parked the carriage outside the factory. Mr. Underhill opened the main doors.

"Welcome! I wasn't sure if you knew the way to my office, so I decided to greet you here. Would you like to leave your gloves and bonnet there?" Mr. Underhill escorted them down a hall painted cream and with dark wainscoting.

"Yes, please. That would be kind of you," Mrs. MacLeod said.

When William spied Violet standing in her father's office, his stomach clenched. The women had plotted this conspiracy, leaving him no choice but to listen to their unwanted advice.

"Hello, Violet, how good of you to meet us." Mrs. MacLeod placed her gloves on a small table.

"I am thrilled that you trust me to help with the furnishings." Violet kissed Mrs. MacLeod's cheek.

"Miss Violet." William shook her hand and turned to her father. "Mr. Underhill, I'm eager to see your furniture and hear your opinions on what would look best in the Tabard."

"This way, please. Do you know how many rooms will need a single bed, and will the inn have several suites for families or wealthier couples?"

The back of William's neck flushed as everyone looked at him. Blast it all. He knew the overall number of rooms in the inn, but he hadn't considered how some would be singles, while others would be suites with small parlors.

Mrs. MacLeod pulled a piece of paper from her reticule. "I knew you wouldn't think to bring that information, William, so I had your father telegram Mr. Hill. There will be eighty rooms and ten suites, plus the dining room will need several dozen tables and chairs."

"Thank you, mother." William pressed his lips into a thin line. He should have known that his mother would prove his inability to handle this matter without her help.

"Father, may I show William and his mother our barley-style furniture?" Violet asked.

"Yes, sweetheart. The walnut pieces are crafted in the manner of furniture built in England during the late seventeenth century."

Barley furniture? The twisted legs on a small table look like coiled serpents and the four spiraling bed posts appeared too fancy for the wilds of the Cumberland Mountains. While his mother's friends embraced ornate furniture, William doubted if they could understand that the Tabard required more practical pieces.

"Ah, these are lovely, but the Inn needs beds and chairs that reflect the simplicity of the settlement."

His mother and Violet looked at him as if he had spoken in Russian, and William glanced at Mr. Underhill for encouragement. "What do you think, sir?"

"How about these pieces?" Mr. Underhill led them to a different corner of the warehouse and pointed out the simple lines of several oak chairs and bedsteads.

William ran a hand over the oval nobs topping the two posts of an oak chair. "This would do well." He wished Lizzie were here and could express her thoughts about how these pieces would look in a dining room.

"Do you have a catalogue William could take back to Rugby?" Mrs. MacLeod asked.

"Yes, back in my office. I have several that William can take with him," Mr. Underhill said.

"I hope that someday, you will give me a tour of the settlement, William," Violet said. "I imagine the mountains are beautiful in the fall."

"I haven't experienced autumn at Rugby, yet." Never would William invite Violet to his refuge at Rugby, but the fear that his mother might bring the lass to the village settled around his heart.

. . .

Emily met Lizzie as she unlocked the schoolhouse doors and escorted her friend into the main room.

"We teach in here and the room across the hall is where we sew. I went to a crowded one-room log cabin school that met a few months of the year. This place is heavenly," Lizzie said.

"It's a lovely space. My uncle had described his design for the school the last time I saw him. I hear the girls."

Betsy ran through the doors and stared at Emily. "We've got company. Another foreigner."

"Although Emily immigrated from England, she now lives with her grandmother, Mrs. Hughes, and offered to help." Lizzie smiled at each girl as they walked into the room. The four settlement girls sat at one end of a table where Emily joined them, while Betsy and her mountain friends took the other end.

"Today, I'll teach how to sew a French seam which is stronger than a regular stitching. I use this technique when I am sewing fine cloth like a light muslin."

Lizzie's needle stitched a narrow seam, and then she flipped the two pieces of fabric. "Now I will sew a wider second seam that encloses my first stitches and will keep it from unraveling."

Lizzie had considered assigning the girls partners to force them to work together, but then their parents might pull their daughters from the class. She needed to discover a way to encourage these young ladies to see themselves as one group.

"Very nice, Betsy. You make neat, small stitches. Perhaps you could help Victoria with her sewing."

Betsy stared at Lizzie. "Her? You want me to help *her*?" She pointed at Victoria, whose cheeks turned red.

"Her name is Victoria, and if you were having problems, I would ask an older girl to help you." Lizzie wanted to toss a handful of scraps at Betsy.

"Come sit beside me. Let's see what you got." Betsy jerked her head to a vacant chair.

Victoria slid onto the seat and spread out her crumpled cloth. Tears sparkled in her eyes.

"No need for crying. You made the first seam too wide, so the second one is thick and lumpy. Next time, make the first one tiny, like Miss Lizzie showed us. Here, I'll start it for you."

Betsy turned the fabric and took several small stitches. "Now, you finish it."

Lizzie smiled. Of all the girls, extroverted Betsy might be the one who could bridge the gap between the two groups.

CHAPTER EIGHT

The heart that is generous and kind most resembles God.
–Robert Burns

A light fog drifted through the settlement as William and Lizzie walked to the schoolhouse. The clip-clop of horses sounded near the Tabard construction site, and the faint buzz of the sawmills droned. A rabbit darted across the path and scampered beneath a honeysuckle bush.

"Somehow, I must regain my authority over those boys." William slowed his gait. "Drat these ribs. They need to hurry and heal.".

"We could talk to Mr. Hill." Lizzie matched his stride.

"I thought of that, but I must solve the problem without him."

"Do you respect the boys?" Lizzie avoided stepping on a cluster of ants carrying a leaf.

"Well, I guess I don't." William knew their names because of scolding them. Perhaps like managing his workers, he needed to learn more about each boy's talents and weaknesses. Joining their ball game had proven dangerous and his mending ribs still limited his activities. Some lads made good tutors, but others talked more to the little ones than worked with them. They needed a manly challenge.

"The swings." William paused. "The boys could build the swings. I bought the supplies but haven't had time to make them. And then, this injury." William ignored the truth of how he had never held a saw or drilled holes into a board. But those boys had watched their fathers build sheds and even furniture.

"You could invite their fathers to work with them."

"No, the boys need to be in charge; they must see that I trust them. We can borrow tools from the Tabard, and Mr. Hill can stop by for a few minutes. They respect him."

"And you'll need a couple of sawhorses."

"Ah, what's that?" His limited experiences pummeled William. Gentlemen were so useless. Society folks needed to listen to Mr. Hughes and accept working with one's hands. If the Irish and other immigrants stopped coming to America, his kind would faint from hunger.

"Those things with four legs and a two-by-four on top. You set the ends of a board on them, and then cut it."

"Oh, yes. The carpenters use them at the Tabard, but I didn't know their name. What would I do without you?" William lifted her hand to his lips. "Thank you."

Lizzie pulled away. "Folks will complain about the teachers flirting."

William stuffed his hands into his pockets. But he wasn't flirting. He wanted to court Lizzie. He longed to purchase cloth for new shirtwaists and dresses, and combs for her hair, plus fill her arms with dozens of roses. But she wouldn't accept those sorts of gifts. He would have to find different ways to express his affections.

.   .   .

Lizzie wanted to lay her head onto the table and cry. Betsy had created a small bustle by stuffing a sack with straw and tying it to her waist. When it shifted to one side, she pulled the bustle back over her rear end and straw fluttered to the floor. Viney had often pestered Lizzie with the question, "Why do you think a big bottom will catch you a husband? That silly bustle makes it hard to sit." Her sister had seen through Lizzie's folly. Now Betsy mimicked the former Lizzie's vanity and the other mountain girls would soon follow Betsy's example.

Although William had warned the boys, they kept pointing to the straw gathering beneath Betsy's desk. Even the local girls, along with the English ones, whispered as Lizzie sat beside the lass, helping her solve an arithmetic problem.

"Betsy, why don't you come with me? I could hear you better if we worked alone."

They climbed the stairs to a room, and Betsy stared at the trail of straw following her. Lizzie wished she had brought along a broom and dustpan. Now, when the students took their noon break, they would laugh at the litter.

"They all think I'm a fool, don't they, Miss Lizzie?" Betsy wiped her eyes with her pinafore.

"Well, everyone may tease you today, but something else will occupy their minds tomorrow," Lizzie said, speaking as much to herself as to Betsy. "Please remove the bustle."

"I wanted to stick out, just like you, both in front and behind." Betsy hitched up her skirt and untied the floppy sugar sack. "Could you learn me how to sew one, Miss Lizzie? And one of them corsets, so my waist will be smaller?"

Lizzie closed her eyes and licked her lips. The last thing Betsy needed was a corset to whittle her waist and push up her bosom.

"Someday, I'll teach you how to sew those things, but for now, let's work on long division. In time, young men will come courting."

"Oh, they're buzzing around our front porch now, pining for when I turn sixteen. I begged Daddy to let me marry. I'm a whole year older than my mama was when he wed her."

"You should wait a few years. Trust me." But why should Betsy heed *her*? Lizzie had collected kisses like some women saved buttons. A shiver trickled down her back. If Mr. Hughes hadn't established Rugby, she would have married Lucas, and be sweeping a log cabin's dirt floor with a baby on her hip.

"Why? I know after the wedding comes babies, but I like babies. I'd have fewer clothes to wash if it was just me and my man and a baby. It takes Mama and me all day to wash for everyone."

Lizzie's cheeks flushed. While most mountain children lived in one-room cabins and could overhear their parent's nightly activities; the English women had taught Lizzie not to speak of such delicate subjects. Yet those foreign girls had gossiped about kissing boys as much as her local friends.

"Having your own infant is not the same as caring for a sibling. Eventually, you might have a dozen children. Please take some time before you marry. Try working here in Rugby, and meet different people, like I did."

"But those English boys don't give much respect to the mountain girls," Betsy said. "They expect us to dally with them in the hayloft, and then they head back to England. A couple of fellows left Jenny carrying a baby, and Mandy, too."

Lizzie couldn't point out how Lucas had behaved in the same way, or his sister would hear that tidbit. Betsy was right. No matter whether a boy came from the ridge or England, the girl bore the shame and the child. If Betsy became caught in that situation, Nate would make the fellow marry his daughter. Lizzie yearned to convince these girls to experience the new ideas offered by the settlement. Then they could choose what they wanted to do with their lives before they began bearing children and baking endless skillets of cornbread.

. . .

William gritted his teeth as he climbed onto the wagon seat. Mr. Hill slapped the reins, called to his team, and the wagon rolled toward the schoolhouse. A couple of carpenters nodded at the duo, but most kept hammering nails or sawing lumber. Standing on scaffolding, a trio of men painted the Inn's clapboard white, and it gleamed in the sunshine.

"How are your ribs?" Mr. Hill asked.

"Much better." William drew in a deep breath. "But sometimes, they still ache, sir."

"Bones need time to heal. Was your trip home profitable?"

"Yes, I visited a furniture warehouse and brought home a catalog to show you. I think you will like the oak bed sets."

"What did your mother think of it?"

"It wasn't fancy enough for her, sir."

"Then I will probably like it. I want to introduce you to a few men who make furniture. In the last Tabard, some rooms showed off our local talent such as Viney's coverlets. How are things at the school?"

While Mr. Hill navigated the short drive to the schoolhouse, William explained the boys' pranks, his struggles to discipline them, and his decision to show more respect for the students. Along the way, he recognized the mothers of several boys and girls and waved at them. Being Saturday, he also called out hello to the children playing in front yards or rolling hoops down the street. As a child, he would have enjoyed the freedom to race to a friend's house or to wander over and watch the Tabard being constructed. Girls might experience more restrictions, but Rugby was a boy's haven.

"Having the lads build the swings is a fine idea. Gives them responsibility." Mr. Hill stopped the wagon in front of the school where the older boys stood. "I'll stay for a while. After all, I'm the head of the school board."

"Should I stay?" William ran his fingers through his hair. He needed to check on Lizzie's cottage.

"Talk to the lads and then leave. On Monday, you can thank them." Mr. Hill lifted a sawhorse off the wagon and grinned. "Go over next week's lesson plans with Lizzie."

William stepped down from the wagon and walked to the boys. Instead of looking sullen, their expressions showed curiosity and excitement.

"Thank you for coming and please thank your parents for allowing you to leave behind your chores. I'm sure some of you have made swings for your siblings and know more than I do about building them."

The boys chuckled, and Silas rolled his eyes. "Probably do, teacher."

Silas should have called him Mister MacLeod, but William steadied his gaze. "So, I trust you to build these swings. Mr. Hill plans to get you started and then you are on your own."

"All right, lads, let's get to work," Mr. Hill said.

William strolled down the lane toward Lizzie's cottage. A small flock of chick-a-dees flitted behind trees calling "See me!" By the picket fence enclosing the garden at Newbury House, a climbing red rose perfumed the air. William bent down a rose cane and sniffed. As lovely as his sister. His heart ached from the longing to talk to Rose about Lizzie, about the students, and Rugby. If his sister had lived, he would urge her to visit, but she could no longer share her laughter with him. Closing his eyes, William envisioned Rose, with her wispy blonde hair and dimpled smile, and the determined glint in her hazel eyes. Even on the night when his sister entered society as a debutant, slogans from the Progressive Movement peppered her conversations. Rose would have defended Lizzie to their mother.

At the cottage site, William frowned at the limited progress and berated himself for not inspecting the construction sooner. Nate hadn't hung the windows or built the chimney or finished the interior walls. At this rate, Lizzie wouldn't move in before Christmas. Despite his ribs, they should ride out and speak with Nate, so he would work faster. William strode to the boardinghouse and found Lizzie in the garden.

"How would you like to ride to where that Nate fellow lives? He hasn't accomplished as much. I want to speak to him."

Lizzie avoided his gaze and plucked beans from a plant. "What about your ribs? Should you be riding? I need to finish picking and preparing these."

"I'll help you finish. My ribs be danged, and we'll take it slowly." Something troubled her. Had that Lucas fellow pestered Lizzie? He should occupy his time working on her cottage.

"I haven't ridden in a year." Lizzie dusted bits of grass off her skirt. "My riding habit burned, and I saw no need to replace it."

"I think your attire would suit. Come, please. Do you want to ride Bessie, or we can find you another mount?"

"Tom said Bessie threw a shoe, and the blacksmith can't see her until later this week."

.   .   .

If Lizzie told William how she had fired Nate, he would want to know why. William would assume that he could hire a different carpenter to finish her cottage. Then she would have to explain why no other man would accept the job. Nate would return when he felt like working again. Lizzie paused at the stable door and inhaled the soothing scent of horses and hay.

She had shunned riding because of the pain of remembering George helping her into the saddle. Or how she had admired George's firm thighs as he rode ahead of her. Perhaps William was right, and she should recall the glad times when she and George had cantered down trails. One evening, they had paused by a spring to water their horses. George had kneeled, staring up with his warm blue eyes and had slipped a ring studded with sapphires onto her finger. She had wrapped her arms around his neck and kissed him with all her love and dreams of their future. Now, a gold mourning ring with a single black stone adorned her finger. Perhaps riding with William would create fresh memories of horses that would wipe away her tears.

"Please prepare the gray mare for Miss Lizzie, while I tend to Chestnut," William said.

"Yes, sir." Ryan led out a small horse and her tack

Lizzie ran her hands down the mare's neck while Ryan placed on the saddle. "She's so sweet. I wish I had an apple."

"And she's gentle, Miss Lizzie," Ryan said. "You'll be friends in no time."

"Yes. What's her name?"

"Lottie, miss."

"For Charlotte?" Lizzie bit her lower lip. She and George had chosen that name for one of their future children.

"Yes, miss."

William assisted Lizzie onto the mare, and then he mounted Chestnut. "Which road?"

"Out the main road, then we'll turn left and head over towards the Sunny Mill." Lizzie picked up the reins and a trickle of fear ran down her back. With William at her side, plus Edith and her flock of children watching, Nate couldn't pester her. But he still could call her nasty names that hinted at her past mistakes.

They wound their way next to the small creek, ducking hemlock branches, skirting wide chestnut trees, and laurel thickets. The air was thick with the scent of green leaves and wet earth. A partridge drummed, and a red-headed woodpecker zipped across their path. Sitting on a horse and feeling the animal's muscles moving brought a sensation Lizzie had missed. When Nate's dogs smelled them, the hounds bayed; they ran up, making the horses dance.

"Call off your dogs!" Lizzie glimpsed Edith's sunbonnet out in her corn patch. "Edith, it's Lizzie!"

"Lay off!" Edith waved her hoe. "Git."

The hounds backed up, glaring at the couple. Edith's patched dress covered her raw-boned frame, and brown streaks smeared the front of her apron where she had dried her hands or wiped a child's face. Betsy stood in the cabin door holding a baby.

"Your corn looks good," Lizzie said.

"Thank you." Edith squinted at William.

"We're looking for your husband," William said. "I need to discuss his lack of progress on Miss Elizabeth's cottage."

"Nate left with his daddy. Be back in a day or two." Edith motioned to Betsy, and she gave her mother the fussing infant.

Lizzie shifted in the saddle. Nate probably rode off to peddle his daddy's moonshine, and to soak his anger in the liquor. At least he wouldn't strike his wife and children.

"What about the other carpenter?" William asked. "Why isn't Lucas working?"

"Lucas is busy hoeing corn. It's growing fast this time of the year." Edith jiggled the whimpering baby.

"Well, tell Nate that if they don't work harder, I will replace them." Red brushed William's neck.

Lizzie cringed, wishing that William would not be so direct, but it was too late to instruct him in mountain etiquette. Feuds could erupt from such blunt speech. Parents might decide to remove their children from the school, or worse, vandalize the building so others couldn't attend it.

Edith unbuttoned her bodice, and Lizzie noticed bruises on her shoulder. "Guess this one needs to fill his belly."

"Tell Nate howdy for us. We best be going." Lizzie turned her horse toward the path.

"I will, Miss Lizzie." Edith hefted the child to her breast, and the little one nursed. From the curve of Edith's belly, she was already carrying another baby. She counted each of her eight children as a blessing, while Nate bragged about keeping her in the family way. He should spend his days earning enough money to buy his children shoes.

A short way from the cabin, William reined in his horse. "Are most women here so open about…feeding their infants? I've never seen a woman do that." His face flushed.

"Yes, though most would cover themselves with a small quilt or blanket. Edith probably chose to expose herself, so you'd leave."

"I see." William wiped his forehead with this sleeve. "And those bruises…."

"Wives are the property of their husbands. Men think they have the right to strike their women if they get uppity, and no one interferes with the matter."

"No preachers speak out about it?"

"I've never heard a sermon about the subject. Mostly they preach how wives and children must obey their husbands, because they are the head of the home."

"But Mr. Hughes teaches men should respect women. Men and women are equals in Rugby."

"The local men think he's a fool. Because I worked at the Tabard, I heard his lectures, and saw how Mr. Hughes lived by his principals. I came to understand that his way of treating women reflected his idea about equality for everyone. But a foreigner will never convince Nate to change the way he thinks about his wife. Let's turn here."

They trotted down a different path leading to the main road. Lizzie glanced at William's troubled expression. If he completed the term, living on the ridge would continue to challenge and change him. William might find it difficult to reenter Cincinnati's society, and especially into the company of a certain young lady. From his comments, William did not want to blend into that world and would prefer to stay at Rugby.

"Do your ribs feel up for a race?" Lizzie smiled at William. "To the bridge?"

She dug in her heels, and Lottie galloped off. Lizzie leaned over the mare's neck and allowed the horse to choose the speed. She reveled in the beat of the mare's pounding hooves. So many months had passed since such happiness had quickened her heart and blown away the gloom. Hearing William in pursuit, Lizzie pressed her knees against Lottie and urged her on.

"We can do this. You're faster and lighter."

But as Lottie panted harder, Lizzie let up with her heels. Winning would be gratifying, but not if it injured the mare or William's ribs. His horse's hooves drummed across the wooden bridge while Lottie's pace dwindled to a walk. On the other side, Lizzie ducked her head to avoid an overhanging branch, but it still caught her hair.

"Whoa." Lizzie pulled on the reins. Beside the river, the tall spikes of red cardinal flowers bloomed. The water gurgled around rocks, and a thrush's silver voice floated from the woods.

"Allow me." William leaned over. His breath warmed her neck as he unsnarled her hair. "You have the loveliest curls."

For a second more than necessary, he slipped his fingers through the wayward locks. Lizzie turned away from his intense blue eyes, recognizing his desire to kiss her. She could taste the pleasure he would give, but fear of what the kiss would mean crippled her.

William exhaled and released her curls. "We should ride on."

They flicked their reins, and the pair trotted toward Rugby.

•   •   •

Silas and a few other older boys stood by a cluster of oak trees as William walked around the new swings. He pulled on the ropes, scanning the knots on the branches, and ran a hand over the board seats, checking for splinters.

"You lads did a great job. Thank you. The younger students will be thrilled," William said.

Most of the boys smiled and nodded their heads, accepting his praises. Silas muttered something and squinted at him. William determined to discover more about the boy's family. Even though they sent Silas to school, William mustn't assume that they were interested in the other educational opportunities that Rugby offered. None of the mountain folk attended the lectures that speakers presented every other Friday.

Mr. Hill rolled in and surveyed the construction. "Excellent work. When you graduate, come, and see me about jobs," he said.

William helped the lads pick up scraps of lumber, and they tossed them into Mr. Hill's wagon. The two men uttered more thanks, and the young men scattered.

"What can you tell me about Silas?" William leaned against the wagon. His sides throbbed, but he didn't regret the ride with Lizzie.

"He's the eldest son of five children, and his father died two years ago. His mother wants him to drop out of school and work on the farm."

"So why does he come? Most of the time, he refuses to cooperate in class." William could kick himself for sounding so callous. The youth was grieving; something he should understand.

"When you were in your teen years, did you fulfill your parent's expectations?" Mr. Hill picked up a hammer and set it down.

"Not really." William's mother could recite a list of criticisms resulting from his bad choices.

"Coming here is an act of rebellion against his mother. His life has spun out of control. Who can he manipulate? You. His mother ignores his bad attitudes because she fears that if she criticizes him, then he will leave the ridge. She could not manage the farm without Silas. When the school day is over, Silas tackles many chores, and has little time for homework."

"He's bright." William brushed sawdust from his waistcoat. He would try harder to show compassion, especially about the death of his father. If the lad would listen, William would share about Rose and how he still grieved for his sister.

"I have a hunch more knowledge has entered his head than Silas will let you know. Don't give up. That he came today shows he cares what you think of him." Mr. Hill climbed onto the wagon seat.

"Thank you." William untied the reins from the hitching post. If he could improve his relationship with Silas and the other lads, then he could concentrate on teaching and spending more time with Lizzie.

CHAPTER NINE

As fair art thou, my bonny lass,
So deep in love am I.
–Robert Burns

Fireflies sparkled inside Lizzie as she lifted the lid of a round top trunk. William stood in her doorway; his eyes filled with mirth. Mrs. Carroll also peeked in.

"I suppose you know something about this?" Lizzie leaned back the lid, and a lavender silk gown shimmered in the sunshine. The perfume of Damask roses floated from the trunk. Lizzie lifted out the silk gown with a skirt edged by a deep ruffle. Delicate tatted lace embellished the round neckline and the narrow cuffs.

"Sweet Joseph, look at that lace!" Mrs. Carroll gasped. "What treasures. I wish I could stay, but dinner won't cook itself." She stepped down the hall toward the kitchen.

Lizzie shouldn't accept this gift, yet in a few weeks, folks would expect a change in her attire. Like a box of chocolates, the frocks drew her hands, and she ran them over a dotted Swiss shirtwaist and a deep maroon woolen skirt. She hadn't realized how much she had yearned for color, for ruffles and bits of lace. For a man's loving gaze admiring her, when she glided into the dining room and settled at a table adorned with linens and glowing candles.

William pulled out the chair by her desk and sat down. "I need to rest."

"Yes, you do." She glanced at him. "How are your ribs feeling?"

"They hurt a little, but mostly I'm tired from teaching."

"Everything is so beautiful. Thank you." Lizzie found a fine lawn sprigged with pink rosebuds and a rich gray velvet riding habit. Soon, she would suggest another ride now that she had the proper attire. She marveled at the yards and yards of crocheted Irish lace trimming the petticoats. If she were alone, she would slide into the lavender dress and twirl, hearing the whisper of the fabric and feeling the silk tickle her ankles.

"Again, thank you. How did you know?" Lizzie stroked the riding habit, wondering if it was proper for her to accept clothing from a gentleman. While she understood what Lucas had wanted after giving her gifts, what sort of notions lingered in William's mind?

"When we were at the commissary, I saw you fingering the lavender silk, so I asked Mother to send some of Rose's things. They were hanging in her wardrobe, reminding my parents of her death and you're about my sister's size. I encouraged my parents to keep a couple of things as mementos and part with the rest."

"She agreed to this?" Lizzie stared at William. Had his mother had second thoughts about her and Rugby? From the woman's demeanor, Lizzie couldn't envision Mrs. MacLeod changing her opinion.

"No." William shifted in his chair. "When I went home, I talked to my father about the clothing. He also sent another trunk with some of my clothes to donate. Father was impressed by how you cared for me when I injured my ribs and wanted to thank you."

Lizzie's cheeks flushed, wondering if William had described how she had bathed his chest and had sat by his bedside. No single woman should enter a man's bed chamber. She couldn't imagine his wealthy father approving of her compared to the young woman William's mother had mentioned.

"My father is not like my mother. Remember, he believes in Rugby, has invested in rebuilding the Tabard, and even sided with me about teaching. Usually, he goes along with Mother about social engagements, but he has his quirks. She doesn't know he keeps a set of bagpipes at the mill. I think you and the Cumberland Mountains remind him of his humble home in Scotland."

"He sounds quite nice, but I don't want to make trouble." After dallying with different boys and causing dissention between their mothers and herself, Lizzie didn't want to cause a family strife.

"He sent you a note. It should be in the trunk." William stretched out his legs.

Lizzie found an envelope tucked between a dozen linen hankies edged with tatted lace. Rose may have wanted to teach the less fortunate, but she shared the same love of lace as Lizzie.

Dear Miss Walker,

Thank you for assisting my son and for encouraging him in his new position. From his descriptions, you sound like a resilient and gracious woman, and I hope to meet you some day. Please accept these frocks as a symbol of my gratitude for helping my son discover more about the world and himself.

Sincerely, Alasdair MacLeod.

"I will have to write him." Lizzie folded his note and slipped it into the envelope. "My father left when I was little, so I never had a daddy."

"I had wondered, and I'm sorry. While I don't agree with some of my father's business practices, he's special. Because he immigrated as a poor crofter and created his wealth, he has a different view of Cincinnati's privileged families. Please accept his gift and remember that wearing dark colors binds you to your grief. I'm sure George would want you to set aside the black dresses."

"I suppose so." But was Lizzie ready to release her grief? The mourning widow had become her identity. If she let it go, then she would have to find another way to define herself. She had no talents like her sister, Viney, who wove stunning coverlets. She enjoyed teaching the little ones and instructing the girls in sewing, but those jobs would soon end. Then she would have to find something else to give her life meaning and purpose.

"In two weeks, you will enter half mourning like me." William spoke the words with gentleness, as if he brushed leaves away from emerging spring flowers. "Tying on a blue cravat didn't diminish my love for Rose. Nor will wearing a lavender dress banish your love for George."

Lizzie nodded. Perhaps this clothing would lighten her heart and usher in brighter days.

.   .   .

William climbed the stairs to the second level of the Tabard and found Mr. Hill inspecting a row of rooms. The chambers still needed wallpaper and trim for the windows, door, and baseboards.

"Are you pleased with them, sir?" William stood next to Mr. Hill, who wrote notes into a small journal.

"I am. Mrs. Hill has ordered the wallpaper, and it should arrive this week. Thank you for giving me the information about the furniture and I agree with your selections. But I still want to feature pieces crafted by local men. If you are available, would you ride out and visit a certain fellow?"

"Certainly, sir. I'll wait for you at the livery."

The horses splashed through a creek that served as the road leading to the Buckley farm. William appreciated the mountaineer's resourcefulness in utilizing a stream as their road. A few trails threaded off towards hollows where some of his students lived. They had a far piece to walk to Rugby.

"Come in," Mr. Buckley said as he stood in the doorway to a shed. "Pay no never mind to the clutter. I'm almost done making a rocking chair for my wife's granny."

"We'd love to see it," Mr. Hill said. "Have you met our schoolmaster? Your daughters attend the school, right?"

"Yes, they do, and they speak kind words about Mr. William." Mr. Buckley stuck out his hand and William shook it. "They also enjoy those sewing lessons with Miss Lizzie."

They entered the shed, and William blinked as his eyes adjusted to the dim light coming through an opening in the log wall. He couldn't imagine how Buckley could see when he needed to drill holes or cut lumber. Yet a graceful rocking chair sat near the opening. He ran his hands over the smooth finish and inspected how the spindles fit into the seat.

"That's white walnut or some folks call them butternut trees."

"It's beautiful. Do you have any regular chairs, the kind to fit around a table?" William asked.

"I'm making one." Mr. Buckley lifted several pieces cut into the different shapes of the seat, the back and four thin posts. "I'll whittle them posts into the legs. Someday, I need to build one of those lathes that a fellow can pump with his foot."

"That would be handy," Mr. Hill said. "I'm sure you can construct one. Then you could turn the spindles and build more furniture faster."

"I figured it would save me nicking my hands. Almost took off a finger last week." Mr. Buckley raised a bandaged finger. "But it's healing."

"Take good care of it. How many chairs do you think you can build before October?" Mr. Hill took out his small notebook.

"Maybe one a week, sir. Pretty busy keeping the weeds out of the corn."

"Do you have friends who would want to build a few chairs and bedsteads for us?" William asked. One chair a week would leave him scrambling for more furniture.

"I can ask around. How many do you need?" Mr. Buckley brushed sawdust from his beard.

"A dozen coordinating chairs, beds, tables and a small chifforobe would be grand, but I will buy whatever you can make." William stuck out his hand. "And thank you."

"Thanks for showing us your work," Mr. Hill said as he and William slipped back into the sunshine and mounted their horses.

"Do you think he can find enough helpers to assist him, sir?" William ducked a low hemlock branch.

"I don't know. When we furnished the first Tabard with local furniture, Buckley was the most reliable of the mountain men. Some delivered their orders after the opening."

"Perhaps we should purchase mostly pieces from my contact in Cincinnati."

"Probably so, but I hope at least a few of the rooms will feature local craftsmen."

"I agree, sir. A combination would be best."

. . .

When Lizzie stepped into the dining room wearing a gray calico dress sprinkled with forget-me-nots, a shadow crossed William's face. His sister had often worn the frock to breakfast. The pale gray had contrasted with Rose's flushed cheeks and hazel eyes. Mother would demand Rose to change into a more suitable outfit for when they made their morning social calls, and then the daily arguments began.

"The gown reminds you of your sister," Lizzie said. "Would you like me to change?"

"No, you are beautiful in it. Perhaps you can give the dress some fresh memories."

When he pushed in Lizzie's chair, his hands brushed her shoulders, and he recalled the feel of her arms around him as she helped him into the buggy seat. Soft, inviting, and comforting, in a way that warmed his blood. While he didn't want to crack anymore ribs, William longed for a reason to hold Lizzie and inhale her lily-of-the-valley perfume. He settled in his chair as Mrs. Carroll brought a tray laden with a platter of fried chicken, biscuits, a bowl of gravy, mashed potatoes, and green beans.

"Sweet Virgin Mary, look at you, Lizzie." Mrs. Carroll set the platter on the table. "Makes my heart glad to see you in something other than black."

Lizzie laughed. "I had better hide my black dresses or you'll pinch them when I'm at school."

"Now, that's a good idea. 'Tis time for you to pack those widow's weeds away." Mrs. Carroll straightened up. "You ladle a second helping of potatoes on your plate and put more flesh on those lovely bones."

William reveled in Lizzie's blush. He adored Mrs. Carroll's wit and her fiddle playing. After the woman completed her work, she sat on the small back porch practicing jigs and reels, her feet slapping the wooden floor, keeping time with the music. A few had sounded like the tunes his father played on his pipes. His father had once told him how folks from Donegal, Ireland sailed to Scotland to dig potatoes. Probably they had shared a few tunes along with a drop of whiskey.

"Please tell me about Viney, you mention her often. And do you have any brothers?" William spooned gravy onto a heap of mashed potatoes.

"Yes, one, Jacob. He lives on the family farm with his wife and child and has another one on the way. Viney's the talented one, spinning yarn, drafting new weaving patterns, and turning them into coverlets. She sells them at the commissary and to individuals. She has sold several of her weavings to folks living in Cincinnati." Lizzie lifted a forkful of beans.

"But she left for the summer? Or for longer?" William buttered a biscuit, inhaling the rich scent of shortening and sweet strawberry jam.

"A couple of weeks ago, our father showed up. He abandoned us almost twenty years ago."

"Great heavens. Why? Where did he go?" William set down his knife. "How hard that must have been."

"It was. After Mama died, Daddy ran away. He left no note and never wrote a letter to us. I've struggled for years with my questions."

"Such as?" William gazed at Lizzie. Sorrow filled her face as she nibbled her biscuit.

"Why did he leave when we needed him the most? Why couldn't he write to us and let us know he was alive? Was it because we didn't deserve his love?" Lizzie glanced at the two gentlemen dining at the end of the table.

"Surely, you don't believe that." William's stomach flinched; what he had done was worse than her father's misdeeds.

"But why would a father abandon his children? We had lost our mother and desperately needed our daddy." Lizzie shook her head. "Parents should love and protect their children. We didn't mind having little money, but it hurt knowing our father didn't want us."

"Yes, it would hurt. But you forgave him?" William scrunched his napkin in his hands.

"Yes, because over time our aunts heaped love on us. They raised us until we could live on our own. Especially Aunt Alta kept telling us to let go of our bitterness and forgive him. Turned out, Daddy was roaming the west, hiding from his memories of fighting in the War Between the States. When he returned, he asked for one of us to move to his new home in the Great Smoky Mountains. Daddy has the palsy, so Viney went with him."

"I see." William stared out the window. Like Lizzie's father, he needed forgiveness from several people, but to seek it would demand more courage than he could muster.

"I stayed because of my cottage, but I offered to come at the end of summer."

Four more weeks to persuade Lizzie to allow him to court her. A month to sow affections and nurture them. His mother had written that in the fall, William needed to resume his responsibilities at the mills, so his father mustn't have explained that William would manage the Inn a little longer. If he moved back to Cincinnati, he and Lizzie could write letters, but did he want to reenter that frantic life? While Lizzie might enjoy visiting the city, he couldn't imagine her living in one, especially after completing her new cottage.

Following dinner, the other boarders retired to their rooms, but William and Lizzie drifted into the parlor. Mrs. Carroll lit several kerosene lamps, including the one hanging from the ceiling, and the prisms dangling from the shade sparkled. The glow from the lamps cast their shadows across the cream-colored wallpaper scattered with deep red roses and green leaves. Maroon velvet covered the settee and wing-backed chairs, and a large woven carpet protected the wooden floor.

"Mrs. Carroll mentioned that you have a lovely voice." William sat down on the piano stool. He had spent hours at his sister's piano, playing her favorite etudes and Bach fugues, along with Scottish songs for his father. Playing each piece had brought memories of when Rose had learned a certain sonata and the joy she had found in music. He raised the lid protecting the piano keys, and a waltz floated through the room.

.   .   .

"I haven't sung since George died." Lizzie sat on the settee and lifted her knitting basket off an end table.

She doubted her voice could sing. No melodies or words bubbled up from inside her, as the ever-present pain had consumed each note and syllable. Lizzie stared at the forget-me-not flowers sprinkled across the gray calico dress. Some nights, she dreamed of rocking and singing to George's baby, but the morning showed an empty pillow next to her head. Perhaps her voice would return to her if love renewed her heart. But love required time to flourish and to build new dreams.

As William played a familiar melody, Lizzie picked up a pair of steel needles from which dangled several inches of a lace edging and slipped the thin cotton thread through her fingers. Knitting lace was magical. She knitted five stitches and then looped the white thread over a needle and knitted the next two stitches together. Repeating this process created holes in a gossamer netting. At the end of the row, Lizzie knitted back to the top of the edging and started the pattern over. She liked the regularity of the pattern and yearned to feel the same stability in her life. No surprises. No threats from Nate or Lucas. Just peaceful days in her cottage, sipping tea and tending to her flower garden, with the company of an orange cat or two. And perhaps in time, William.

"Do you know any of Robert Burns' songs?" William played a few chords. "Rose loved them, as does my father."

"A few, and not very well."

Which of Burn's love songs would William choose? *Coming Through the Rye* or *My Love is Like a Red, Red Rose?* Lizzie counted the stitches on the needles. Perhaps she should suggest they sing hymns or less romantic songs. Or maybe she should ask William to play something by Bach or Beethoven.

One evening, she and George had attended a concert at the Tabard where a traveling pianist from England had performed. Sitting side-by-side, George had linked his fingers with hers as the musician plunged into one of Bach's fugues. The man had played the dominate theme with one hand while his other hand repeated the melody in different variations. The two voices wove in and out, creating an intricate tapestry of music; just like her love and George's had blended as they had hoped to knit together a joyous life. Tears blurred Lizzie's vision; her heart might never feel such hope and love again.

After a few opening notes, William sang,

"It came upon a Lammas night,
When corn rigs are bonnie,
Beneath the moon's unclouded light,
I held awa to Annie....
I'll no forget that happy night,
Among the rigs with Annie."

Lizzie froze. The words could have described her time with Lucas beneath the laurel bush. Despite Lucas' reminders, she had stuffed the memory of that warm August night far back into her mind and willed it to stay there. She hoped William had not chosen this song because he had discovered her past foolishness. No, he played the song to honor his father's heritage and his deceased sister. She mustn't think William's every action was about her.

.   .   .

At the end of the song, William closed his eyes. The words drew him back to a maid's room, the pewter light from the moon, and her hands on his bare chest as he pulled her to him. A month later, shame, terror, and grief had struck. Rose's death had fogged his mind and had brought his numb consent and more sorrows. If Lizzie knew of his foolish choices, she would slam the door to her heart and refuse further contact with him. Because of his growing affections for her, his secret must remain hidden. William's bruised heart matched his favorite Burn's song. Softly, he sang.

"Had we never love'd sae kindly,
Had we never lov'd sae blindly,
Never met---or never parted—
We had ne'er been broken hearted."

.   .   .

Lizzie set down her knitting. Something troubled William; even when speaking of Rose, his expression didn't show this torment. What battled with his soul? Her feet propelled her to the piano. She longed to console him and soothe the tremor in his voice. So many times, she had sat at George's grave singing these same words. Her lips opened.

"Ae fond kiss, and then we sever,
Ae farewell, and then forever..."

Their voices twined like honeysuckle vines. The music flowed out of the room, and from the back porch, Mrs. Carroll's fiddle carried the tune. Instead of the rush of despair Lizzie had expected, a calmness settled around her like a warm shawl, and the words melted something hard and icy. Closing her eyes, her voice soared as her joy of loving George cascaded from her lips. She yearned for the same ecstasy that would restore wonder and meaning to her life. As the final notes faded, a similar peace flooded William's face.

"Thank you, sweet Elizabeth." William took her hand, turned it over and kissed her palm. "Thank you for sharing music with me."

A thousand stars shone inside her as Lizzie remembered William's arms around her when he had carried her out of the flooded mud hole. Solid. Strong. Comforting. She yearned for a gentle man who could offer her solace. William closed the lid over the piano keys and stood up.

"Sweet dreams. I'll see you at breakfast."

"Yes, sweet dreams."

Back in her own room, Lizzie pulled the curtains over the opened windows, as the night was too warm to close them. The windows were so tall that when the sashes were raised, she could walk out onto the porch and gaze at the moon. Lizzie donned her nightgown and lounged on her bed, running a finger over where William had kissed her. Finally, she read from *Jane Eyre*, savoring the scene where Mr. Rochester played the fortune teller and told Jane how fate would give her "a measure of happiness". Lizzie prayed she would find the same measure of happiness as Jane. Blowing out her lamp, she rolled onto her back, as William's kiss lingered in her mind. Outside her window, something tapped against a porch board, and she froze. Her ears searched for the patter of a possum's feet, hoping to find crumbs left by a boarder.

Instead, boots descended the porch steps and crunched on the gravel path. A chill rippled through her. Who had that been, and how long had that person lingered in the shadows? If the person was a boarder, why hadn't he unlocked and entered by the main door? Lizzie struggled to breathe and shook so hard that she couldn't sit up. No one stirred along the hall, and Mrs. Carroll did not keep a dog.

Lizzie had neither a fire poker nor even a frying pan to defend herself. William's derringer. She would ask him to teach her how to shoot it and then buy a pistol. She would not tell him or Mrs. Carroll about the stranger on the porch. If William should stand guard and injured one of the mountain men, trouble would follow.

But could she trust herself with a gun? Not many months ago, she had pondered ending her life with Jacob's rifle and fleeing to heaven. But teaching beside William and singing with him had lit an ember of hope. Now Lizzie needed a gun to defend her life.

CHAPTER TEN

I dream'd I lay where flowers were springing,
Gaily in the sunny beam,
–Robert Burns

"Teacher, push me, please," one of the youngest girls said.

William ambled over to the swings and stood beside Silas, who pushed his youngest brother. William shoved, and the girl squealed, begging to go higher. If only he had understood how rewarding it was to share fun with children. His mother had relegated his care to a nanny, and on Sundays at church, she had paraded him in front of her friends. William glanced at Silas. Maybe now was the moment to talk with the lad.

"Thank you again for helping to build these swings. Have you thought about becoming a carpenter?"

"No, sir. I'll probably farm." Silas pressed his lips together as an emptiness filled his eyes.

"I think it was Thomas Jefferson who said that farming is a noble pursuit, but if you enjoy building things, you should try carpentry. Or seek further education and become an engineer."

"Like the men driving the locomotives, sir?" Silas asked.

"That's one type of engineer. But I mean the men who figure out how to build tall buildings or the bridges for the trains."

"You think I could do that, sir?"

"With the proper education and training, yes."

William stopped the little girl's swing as Lizzie rang a small bell from the front steps and its sound rippled over the clearing. The students dashed for the door and their feet stomped into the schoolroom.

"Time for learning." William headed inside, and Silas and his brother followed. He hoped his words would encourage Silas to dream about his talents. May the youth realize how Rugby was more than a settlement, but also showed how to pursue different paths in life. William picked up the third-grade reader and called the class forward.

. . .

After spending an hour correcting essays and arithmetic papers, William ambled into the room across the hall. Betsy swept the floor, gathering up tiny fabric scraps as the girls stowed their sewing projects into drawstring bags. Lizzie packed supplies into a bushel basket and stored it in a corner.

"How are the sewing lessons?" William glanced around. "When will we see you young ladies in your new frocks?"

"I was thinking they should wear them on the day of the school program."

"Hmm, a time of recitations and singing?"

"And reading essays and answering mathematical problems," Lizzie added.

"We've less than a month to prepare for it. After dinner, why don't we spend the evening planning for the event?" They would need several evenings to decide the details, and even a few Saturday afternoons.

"Yes, I'll see you ladies tomorrow." Lizzie watched the girls as they scampered out the schoolhouse door, then turned to William. "Now it's time for my lesson."

William delighted in her smile, offered his arm, and she linked her elbow with his. He wished they could end every day sharing a stroll, chatting about the students' work. They ambled down the path leading to the Big South Fork. The feathery branches of hemlock trees brushed against William's shoulders and silvery beech trees spread out wide arms. A partridge burst from the undergrowth and flew away.

"No pranks today," Lizzie said. "Most of them worked hard on their assignments, too."

"Thank God, but I'm sure more will come when we aren't expecting them."

"Probably, but I have a feeling the boys will tease the girls more than you."

"Silas completed all of his assignments," William said. "That's a miracle."

"I think your words inspired him." Lizzie paused and freed a blackberry cane that clutched her sleeve.

"I hope so." William had noticed the same dull expression lingered on the male students' countenances as on his mill workers. The lads lacked a sense of vision of the opportunities they could cultivate in the greater world. Their community needed them to study medicine and teaching, plus carpentry and blacksmithing, and then return to assist their mountain friends.

"What prompted this urge to learn how to shoot a gun?" William held back a branch for Lizzie. "Wouldn't you rather be knitting lace?"

How she moved those thin wire needles baffled him. Such magic flowed from her fingers as they turned the thread into delicate stars and flowers. Lizzie's lace was as fine as the yards and yards of edging his mother bought from the Irish women, crocheted by those poor immigrants living a dozen to a room. Or by the Germans sliding their tatting shuttles, another mysterious process of knotting together cobwebs. Rose had preferred their narrow lace for her hankies.

"When I live in my cottage, I need to know how to shoot some varmint. Jacob's too busy with his farm and family to teach me. Plus, I like the idea of hiding a pistol in my reticule. I suppose my mountain blood wants to prepare for any unknown attacks. Why do you carry a firearm?" Lizzie picked up her skirt and shook off a twig clinging to the hem.

"For protection. To shoot snakes." William kicked a stick out of the path.

"Literally or figuratively?" Lizzie gazed up at him.

"Both." William gave Lizzie a hand and helped her over a log.

"I need one for the same reasons."

. . .

The gurgling of water flowing around rocks reached them before Lizzie spied the river. On scorching afternoons, settlers would race to the Gentlemen's Swimming Hole and jump into the pool. Floating on their backs, they would gaze at the layers of limestone forming low cliffs or at the tree limbs overhanging the river. They would breathe in air thick with the fragrances of sun-warmed earth and green leaves. While cicadas droned from the woods, the men would lounge on the stone slabs thrust along the riverbank and rest from the hours spent hoeing crops.

Lizzie's boots slipped on the pebbles littering the sloping path, and William grabbed her waist. She welcomed his firm grip and his instinct to protect her. Unlike Lucas, George had assisted her when descending stairs. When strolling on the gravel paths, George would pick up sticks that might catch on her skirt.

"Steady. Last night's shower made it slick." William guided them around a muddy spot and released his hold when the path ended by the river.

"Thank you." Lizzie gazed at the rushing water and exhaled. How could a river instill peace into her soul while also urging her spirit to float away on its current? To leave behind the darkness of the past year. One day, she wanted to ride on a paddlewheel steamboat down the Ohio River, onto the Mississippi and travel to New Orleans.

"First lesson, here is how you load my derringer." William released a small lever, and the pistol opened. He pushed a cartridge into each of the two barrels, tucked the gun back together, and gave it to her.

"It's beautiful." Engraved leaves wandered across the metal shaft that gleamed in the sunlight, and she rubbed her thumb over the smooth ivory handle. "Is it meant for ladies?"

"No, the maker, Remington probably thinks the art makes it more appealing to gentlemen. I like the size, as it's handy to slip into a small pocket. Now let's practice shooting it. Plant your feet like so. We'll use that oak on the far left as a target."

Lizzie matched his stance and lifted the derringer. How peculiar it felt to squint at a tree branch with her finger on the gun's trigger. She may need several practice sessions, but she would master this skill and feel safer at night.

"In case you stumble, I'll be here to catch you." William moved behind her. "Ready?"

Lizzy held her breath, aimed and fired. A small cloud of smoke billowed around her, and she winced at the acrid smell. Her shot missed the tree and flew into the underbrush. While William positioned a chunk of wood on a stump, she reloaded the derringer. She aimed and nicked the corner of the wood.

"Good, try again." William handed her more cartridges.

Before they left, she would hit the center of the target. Lizzie reloaded and raised the pistol. But when she aimed, William grabbed her wrist..

"Lizzie don't move. Give me the pistol."

He snatched the gun and fired at a diamond-backed rattler resting four feet away by a boulder. The snake leaped from the shadows with its mouth wide open ready to strike. Lizzie screamed and jumped back as the bullet blasted the serpent. It writhed. William shot again, and the snake lay motionless.

"Thank God, you spied it. I should have checked around the big rocks. Snakes like to sleep in the shade and near the water." Lizzie slumped against William.

"I should have searched, too. Mr. Hill warned me about snakes. When I made my quip, it was supposed to be a joke."

"My brother says, if you see a snake, kill it and then check to see what kind it is."

"That seems a little extreme. Do you want to end our lesson?" William rested a hand on her arm.

"No." Although Lizzie longed to press herself against William and feel his breath on her neck, warm and delicious, she straightened up. "I want to hit the target." She must practice until she felt comfortable using a gun.

"Good. Now, relax your shoulders, and try again."

When a bullet struck near to the center of the chunk of wood, Lizzie grinned. So, what if she had to shoot over a dozen times? Success with a gun was almost as satisfying as knitting lace. As each shot inched closer to the center, confidence trickled into Lizzie, and she no longer noticed the smell of the gun smoke. She shifted her feet, digging her boot heels into the damp soil, and fired again. The bullet struck the center of the target, and Lizzie almost tossed the derringer into the air.

"Excellent. You're a fast learner." William pointed at an oak tree. "See if you can hit that lump where a branch fell off."

Lizzie stared at the spot and aimed. Bark splattered as the bullet slammed beneath the target and into the tree. "Blast it all." Viney's favorite curse flew from Lizzie's lips. If her sister could witness this new skill, she would cheer her on.

"Are you interested in learning to shoot a rifle? In Scotland some women hunt." William stuck his hands in his pockets. The shadows were deepening, and a thrush lilted from a beech tree. From far off, someone rang a bell to alert her family of supper time.

"Maybe someday." Lizzie offered William his derringer, but he shook his head.

"You keep it. I figure you want to know how to shoot because something has scared you. I'll order a replacement."

"Thank you." Lizzie stared at the gun. Should she accept another gift? If William were like Lucas, he would expect something in return. But William looked concerned and not lustful.

"Perhaps you could tell me why you need it?" William handed her a soft rag to clean the weapon.

"I can't, at least not now."

. . .

William wished Lizzie would trust him with her secret, but why should she when he kept quiet about his situation. As she cleaned the derringer, he gave her a few more tips about how to care for it. When they were back at the boardinghouse, he would give her a box of cartridges. What an odd gift for a lady! His mother would never understand it, but his father would approve. Teaching Lizzie to handle a gun was another way to fulfill Mr. Hughes' dream to create equality between men and women. William would suggest to Mr. Hill that they organize a shooting club with some sort of contest. Yet how odd the derringer looked poking out of Lizzie's pocket, its ivory handle gleaming in the twilight.

"We best be off, or Mrs. Carroll will scold us for delaying supper." William offered his elbow, and they climbed up the path. Never would he compromise Lizzie's character by giving the ridge folk a reason to gossip about his assistant. But he might leak the news about how Lizzie owned a pistol to keep away whomever had frightened her.

"Now, I need to discover what other skills you wish to learn so our times together can continue." The sound of rushing water faded as they arrived at the main road.

"Chess. I'd like to learn it."

"We shall start soon. We need to correct papers tonight and discuss the school program."

William wished Lizzie would choose an activity where they could be alone, but sitting in the parlor would be safer for them.

"I never thought shooting a gun would make me hungry." Lizzie touched the derringer in her pocket.

"Shooting always gives me an appetite." William opened the boardinghouse door. "And Mrs. Carroll's roast smells wonderful."

"I'll be there in a minute." Lizzie's boots tapped down the hallway.

William's eyes followed her ankles, so slim yet sturdy. He best wash-up, too, and make himself presentable.

. . .

While Mrs. Carroll played her fiddle on the porch, William corrected arithmetic papers, and Lizzie commented on the handwriting exercises in the student's copybooks. She had enjoyed practicing penmanship, feeling the flow of her arm as her pen moved across the paper and shaded the capital letters. Now and then, she showed William a student's outstanding work, or he spoke about a perfect algebra paper.

"What shall we include in the school program?" William asked.

"Why don't the youngest students read a few sentences to show what they have learned? You could quiz older students about geography as you point to places on the map." Lizzie stared at Mrs. Carroll's silhouette as she played a sweet slow air.

"Good ideas. And you could teach the students a few songs or hymns."

"Their parents would prefer the hymns. The older boys could solve a couple of math problems."

"Yes. And recite pieces like the Gettysburg Address." William leaned back in his chair. As the clock struck ten, Mrs. Carroll entered the room and placed her fiddle on a shelf.

"Time to say goodnight. Mornings come early these days."

"Thank you for the music." William stacked the papers and slipped them into his satchel.

"It was lovely, especially the slow tune." Lizzie rose.

"It's a favorite slow air of mine, *Lament for Limerick*. I'll see you at breakfast." Mrs. Carroll opened the door to her room off the parlor.

"Good night," William and Lizzie called after Mrs. Carroll.

"Good night to you, too." William squeezed Lizzie's hand and departed.

"Sleep well," she said.

After he rounded the corner, Lizzie leaned against the wall, listening to his boots and the click of his door before she entered her room. She would always love George, but William's tender ways had swept away many of the cobwebs of grief. Helping him at school and learning how to fire a pistol had built a desire to be more than a pretty woman. She wanted to engage in the culture Rugby offered and become a person with thoughtful opinions. Then if she married, she could pass those qualities onto her children.

Like every night since hearing those footsteps, Lizzie walked the length of the porch, searching the shadows for any forms. Nothing moved in the warm night air, and not even the whip-poor-wills called. Stepping over the low windowsill, she slipped back into her darkened room and drew the curtains over the open windows. She placed the derringer on a chair and slid into her bed. Lizzie yawned. Target practice wore a person out.

CHAPTER ELEVEN

Now's the day and now's the hour.
–Robert Burns

A horse's snort awoke Lizzie, and she listened to its clip-clop. Who would ride through town in the wee hours of the night? Moonshiners would not travel the main road. The horse stopped. Footsteps crunched on the gravel path to the boardinghouse. Men muttered.

Lizzie crept to her chair, found the derringer, and slid in two cartridges. Boots clomped on the first porch step. She kneeled at the open window, aimed at the legs, and fired twice. A man shrieked. Nate's voice shouted, "The bitch!" Another man cursed.

Lucas! Her heart pounded and her legs quivered. Lizzie slumped to the floor. What had she done? What would those two do to her? Doors banged, and voices ran down the hall. The horses galloped away, as Mrs. Carroll burst into the room.

"Are you hurt?" She helped Lizzie onto the bed as William joined them.

"What happened?" William dropped next to Lizzie.

"Two men. Outside my window." Lizzie shuddered. "I heard them a few nights ago."

"Sweet Joseph and Mary! I'll alert the others." Mrs. Carroll dashed off.

"Thank God, you had the pistol." William wrapped his arms around Lizzie, and she pressed her cheek against his chest. "Why didn't you tell me?"

Sobs rolled out of her; great waves filled with fear. Her body shook and her voice refused to cooperate. Nate and Lucas would torment her. They would pursue revenge until she groveled at their feet, begging for mercy. Lizzie clutched William's linen nightshirt as he stroked her hair. How foolish she was to think a gun would make her brave. Nothing inside her could conquer the fear roiling through her veins.

"To think I might have lost you." William kissed the top of Lizzie's head. "I must go help."

Lizzie nodded and hid her shaking hands in the folds of her nightgown. The ridge folk would learn how William had given her the pistol. If she had injured either Lucas or Nate, they would attack William. For the next few weeks, the gossips would retell the story until it expanded into high drama that could ruin her future and William's, too.

• • •

"Somebody fetch Mr. Hill!" William said, as he carried a lantern and joined the other men. Lights flickered across the lawn as they searched the grounds. Every window in the boardinghouse glowed, throwing faint rays across the porch. William examined the hoof prints to discern in what direction the intruders had gone. He would follow them until he apprehended the culprits and locked them up.

Who were these fellows? Why had they come for Lizzie? Lucas must be one of the men, which meant Nate was the other. William clenched his jaw, longing to bash their heads together, but justice must first prove their guilt. If Lizzie had recognized either of the men, she was too afraid to tell him.

He glanced at the silhouette of Lizzie and Mrs. Carroll etched in the light of her window. While he longed to console her, she needed another woman's comfort and wise advice. He wished his mother could be that sort of woman, but she wasn't. Perhaps after Mrs.

Carroll calmed Lizzie's nerves, the lass might reveal what she knew about the intruders.

"Over here! I found blood on the gravel," Tom said.

William dashed to Tom and squatted down. The other men also encircled them with their lanterns, and a ring of light illuminated the earth. Splotches of blood spattered the gray gravel and dribbled across the grass towards the road. Lizzie had injured someone; that fact should help them as they searched the area.

"What should we do next?" William eyed Tom.

"By morning, the teamsters and their wagons will have smothered their trail."

"If we leave now, we will need the lanterns to show us the tracks," William said. "We'll never catch up to them on foot."

"Guess we should wait and see what Mr. Hill has to say."

Waiting. William hated waiting. Wasting time when he wanted to gallop. But if he had waited, he wouldn't have become a father. If he had waited to make certain choices, he would have met his son. Rushing ahead blindly had made him vulnerable to making mistakes.

How many times had Rose gazed at him and quoted, "They that wait upon the Lord shall renew their strength; they shall mount up with wings as eagles." He should have heeded Rose. William vowed not to act in any reckless manner that might harm Lizzie.

• • •

"Allow me." The mattress dipped as Mrs. Carroll sat by Lizzie and tucked a shawl around her. "Here, I'll hold the cup, and you take a sip of tea."

The steam warmed Lizzie's cheeks. The hot liquid eased her outward trembling, but her innards screamed. What should she do? How could she protect William and herself from the revenge lurking inside Nate and Lucas? Lizzie looked into Mrs. Carroll's eyes.

"One man is Lucas; I heard his voice. The other is probably Nate. I must get away from them."

"Aye. No telling what they'll do, but what about your gentleman? He'll not let you ride off alone."

Her gentleman, William, who didn't want to lose her, whose gun had protected her. Lizzie could still feel William's nightshirt in her fingers and his arms around her. But she couldn't risk Nate injuring William because of her, nor did she want him to confront the two men. Fury would fuel whomever she had wounded.

"You must help me slip away. The gossip will fade faster if I'm not here."

"Yes, but it's too risky to leave immediately. But I have an idea," Mrs. Carroll said.

The parlor clock struck one as William knocked on Lizzie's door and opened it. "We found the tracks of two horses and blood. We will start searching at daylight."

"Thank you, but nobody will tell you where the men are hiding."

"We must arrest them before they harm some other woman." William leaned against the door frame.

"That might make matters worse. When it comes to handing out justice, the ridge folk have their ways," Mrs. Carroll said.

"But Rugby's laws mean those ways will have to change." William yawned.

"Come, lassie, and finish the night in my room. We'll be needing our rest," Mrs. Carroll said.

"Please sleep as long as you wish. Mr. Hill canceled school for tomorrow." William touched Lizzie's hand and departed.

"Gather what you will need, dearie." Mrs. Carroll glanced at Lizzie.

Along the hall, doors clicked as the men returned to their rooms. A breeze ruffled the curtain and a chorus of crickets chirped. How could everything sound so normal? Lizzie's heartbeat still raced, and thoughts tumbled around in her head. Even if she fled, Lucas would seek her. William would think that she didn't trust him to protect her, because he did not understand the ways of the ridge.

Lizzie stuffed a few shirtwaists, skirts, and undergarments into a small carpetbag, and added the copy of Jane Eyre, her knitting needles, and cotton thread. At the bottom of Rose's trunk, she located a short cape with a hood. No mountain woman would wear such a frivolous thing. If anyone spied her, they would think she was one of the English girls.

The fragrance of beeswax candles floated from Mrs. Carroll's room as she shut her door behind Lizzie. "I packed you a basket of food. Where do you plan to go? Knoxville?"

"I don't know anyone there, so I'll ride to my cousin's. My Aunt Ida is staying with his family over by Jamestown. That's closer. I'll leave a bit before dawn."

"What should I tell William?" Settling onto her bed, Mrs. Carroll tucked her braid under her nightcap.

"Please tell him I'm visiting a relative." Lizzie thanked God that she wasn't lying to cover her actions.

"When will you return?" Mrs. Carroll held back a yawn.

"I don't know. I guess when I feel it is safe. You had better sleep, so you can wake up and make breakfast."

"Aye." Mrs. Carroll blew out the candles and soon slumbered.

Lizzie stretched out on a settee and covered herself with a quilt as she listened to the clock. From down the hall, some man snored. Outside the boardinghouse, tree branches rustled, a dog barked, and bats swooped and circled as they feasted on insects. When the parlor clock struck three, she picked up the basket and carpetbag, crept out of the house, and saddled her horse. She loaded everything into the saddlebags and mounted Bessie.

"North." Lizzie pressed her heels against the mare, praying that no one else traveled the pike at this early hour.

Clouds of mist threaded through the hollows as the trace dipped and curved around the hills. The dark hid Lizzie as she rode through Allardt. But outside the village, she spied a wagon parked by the river with a man sleeping beneath it. He had to be a teamster hauling goods from Jamestown or perhaps from Kentucky, because no moonshiner would expose himself. Lizzie leaned low over Bessie, and the horse clip-clopped over the wooden bridge and trotted on.

As the heavens turned to peach and rose, a cardinal sang, wood smoked floated from cabins, and lanterns glowed in barn windows. The shapes of cows and horses blossomed in pastures and the sunlight glistened on the dewy cornstalks. Lizzie's stomach growled. Last night, she had reckoned she wouldn't eat for a week, but now Lizzie couldn't find a hiding spot quick enough. Around the next bend, sunlight shone on a grassy patch near a shallow branch trickling across the pike. While Bessie drank and grazed, Lizzie munched on boiled eggs, buttered biscuits filled with slices of cheese, and a peach so juicy that she had to wash its stickiness from her face. Finally, she stuffed the fancy cloak in a saddlebag and inhaled the morning freshness.

Lizzie's nerve strings eased as if invisible fingers had rubbed the stiffness from her neck. No longer was she a fugitive, but merely a woman traveling to visit kin, and soon she would hug her beloved Aunt Ida. Sitting straight on her horse, Lizzie rode through Jamestown, passing the courthouse and storefronts, before heading east toward her cousin Hank's home.

CHAPTER TWELVE

Amid this mighty fuss just let me mention,
The Rights of Women merit some attention.
–Robert Burns

The path to her cousin's cabin slithered around laurel thickets, followed a creek bed for a short lick, and ended at a clearing surrounded by tall oak trees. A baby's wail greeted Lizzie, and two tow-headed young children stood on a scrap of a porch with blue morning glories climbing up the posts. A rooster crowed as Aunt Ida rose from a rocker, patting an infant's back.

"Lizzie! You're the answer to my prayers." Aunt Ida closed her eyes. "Thank you for coming. Meet Hank's newest son, Joseph." A tuft of blond hair sprang from the boy's head; tears seeped out from his closed eyes. His face grew redder as he howled, thrashing his thin legs, and waving his fists.

"I'm sorry that I didn't write first." Lizzie embraced her aunt. "Where's Cousin Mary?"

"We buried her a week ago. After the funeral, Hank returned to Kentucky where he's cutting timber, and he's hoping to coax a young gal into marrying him. She had a baby two weeks ago by a lumberjack who dallied with her. Reckon she needs a husband as much as Hank needs a woman, and this little one needs a wet nurse."

The way of the hills, bury a wife and find another. But at least Hank hadn't run off like Lizzie's father and would provide a mama for his children and be a daddy to the girl's babe. After unsaddling Bessie and putting her in the paddock, Lizzie surveyed the small log cabin. Aunt Ida had kept up with the dishes, but a funky odor rose from a basket of dirty clothing and linens. Dust bunnies huddled in the corners, and cobwebs dangled from the loft joists. Bare feet pattered against the floorboards.

"Are you our new mama?" the little boy asked. "I'm Thomas and four years old, and she's Ginny. She's two."

Lizzie kneeled and hugged them. "No, sweethearts, I'm your granny's niece, Cousin Lizzie. I've come to help for a bit." She needed to heat water for a hot bath as dirt ringed the children's necks and their hair needed combing.

But worse was the despair filling their blue eyes. Lizzie had been the same age as Ginny when her mother departed for heaven. A similar darkness had smothered her childhood until the aunties embraced her. Like a sliver sunk deep in Lizzie's flesh, the longing for her mama still haunted her. Even if Hank remarried, life would be different for these two children who would not remember their mother.

On the porch, the rocker creaked as Aunt Ida attempted to shush the crying infant. "Hank borrowed a goat from a neighbor, but this little one keeps spitting out the sucking cloth." Aunt Ida held up a limp square of muslin tied to a cow's horn.

"Let me try." As Lizzie lifted the boy into her arms, a memory of Jacob's wife suckling her son washed over her. First, Hazel would brush her cheek against her infant, while cooing and calling him sweet names, and then the baby would nuzzle her chest and nurse. In a quiet corner of the cabin, Lizzie rubbed the baby's face against her cheek, and kissed the top of his head. He hiccupped and stared at her.

"I don't have what you need, nor do I smell like your mama, but try this." Lizzie stuck the tip of her finger in his mouth, and he began to suck. With her other hand grasping the cow's horn, she slipped the cloth nipple between his lips and withdrew her finger. Lizzie leaned back in the rocker, and she listened to him sucking milk. When his little hands patted her face, pleasure warmed her bones. But instead of dreaming that the child belonged to George, an image of William rippled through Lizzie's mind. Her memories showed her those moments when he had lifted her from the mud hole, had kissed her hands, and guided her away from George's grave toward a new life as a teacher, all acts of love. Other than clinging to William last night, she hadn't given him any signs of her budding affections. Fear of another loss had built a moat around her heart, but she hoped William would paddle a boat across it. Lizzie winced. Would he feel rejected when he discovered she had fled? She should have considered that his heart still ached from the loss of Rose.

By the time Joseph had finished the goat's milk, his little belly was round, and he blew a small bubble. Lizzie patted his back, burping him, and then he stretched out with his cheek on her shoulder. They rocked until his breathing slowed, and then they both fell asleep.

The tap of Aunt Ida's cane woke Lizzie. "That's the most peaceful I've seen him. After your heart has healed from George, and you find the right man, you'll make a good mama."

"I best start on the washing." Lizzie needed to busy her hands and avoid Aunt Ida inquiring if she had affections for any new man. She would not burden her aunt by explaining last night's frightening events and fill her with concern that Lucas might come riding into their yard. Picking up two buckets, Lizzie headed to the stream to fill the wash kettle.

"Want to help?" she asked Thomas and Ginny, who trailed after her. "Why don't you collect kindling for the fire?"

•   •   •

In the faint morning light, William scanned the small group of settlers who clustered around Mr. Hill. A few of the young men had spent a year at the colony, but others had just arrived. Probably none of them knew the local folks well. At least he had had contact with his students' parents, but he could not claim a working relationship with any of them. Would the mountain people think the settlers should mind their own business? Or would they sympathize with Lizzie's plight? From her comments, the mountaineers considered her a wanton flirt and would think she had prompted last night's attack.

"You lads will follow the bloody trail as far as you can," Mr. Hill said. "Then break into pairs and knock on doors. Tell folks that Mr. Hill sent you because most of them respect my name. But if they refuse to talk, thank them for their time and move on." Mr. Hill adjusted his hat. "William, you'll come with me."

"Yes, sir." William held the reins to Chestnut.

"We will check a certain place. Follow me." Mr. Hill mounted his horse and trotted off.

They rode out of town for several miles and turned onto a game trail. A turkey exploded from the underbrush and flew away. William hoped no snakes would cross the path or fall out of a tree. Low branches swept across his face, and the path swerved around a broad laurel thicket.

"The mountain folk call them laurel hells," Mr. Hill said.

A gurgling stream accompanied them for half-a-mile until the men reached a clearing with a tiny log cabin with one window, but no smoke rose from the chimney. Did one of his students live here? No one had planted a garden or a patch of corn.

"Hello!" Mr. Hill looked around. "I don't think anyone is here, but let's look for footprints."

"Where are we, sir?" William scanned the rocks jutting out of the hill behind the cabin. A foreboding feeling trickled down his spine as if a tick had crawled onto his back.

"This is Nate's father's moonshine cabin. I was hunting one day and stumbled upon it, but I told no one of my discovery. The still is farther upstream."

"So, you believe Nate was one of the men, sir?" Nate and his father would be furious if they found them here.

"After your strong words with Nate, who else would want to harm Lizzie? And Lucas doesn't like the growing relationship between you and her."

"So, I endangered her, sir?" William dismounted. He would hate himself if his actions had provoked these men to attack Lizzie.

"Probably, and now that she's injured one of them, their anger will kindle further revenge. After we return to the settlement, we'll devise a plan for her safety."

He and Mr. Hill scanned the ground. Turkey tracks etched the creek bank along with bear prints. William shivered, hoping the bear had visited during the night and now slept. But no horse's hooves or boots had left an imprint.

"I don't think they came here." Mr. Hill ran his fingers through his hair. "Next stops are the granny women."

They cantered back towards Rugby and turned onto a two-track, winding through a small hollow. The horses splashed through a stream flowing over the road, and they stopped at a log cabin. A split-rail fence surrounded a tidy garden of pole beans, squash, and potato plants. A row of purple, blue, white, and pink larkspurs bloomed by a small porch.

"Granny Coleman's place. When someone needs nursing, they seek her help. Hello!" Mr. Hill called.

A short, thin, gray-haired woman walked out, wiping her hands on her apron. "Good to see you, Amos. But they ain't here."

"Perhaps I've dropped by to be neighborly," Mr. Hill said.

"That would be kind, but I heard about the ruckus." Granny Coleman shook her head. "I don't know anything about those fellers."

"If an injured man comes here, please tell me."

Granny stared at Mr. Hill. "I'm heading over to Sally's soon. Doubt if I'll see anyone back in that holler."

"Probably not. Good day, Granny." Mr. Hill clucked to his horse.

"Living way back here, how did she know so much, sir?" William brought Chestnut closer to Mr. Hill's horse.

"Gossip travels faster across this ridge than storm clouds. Her son is helping build the Tabard and stays in one of those tents pitched in the woods. He told some woman who raced over and told her. If Granny Coleman knows, the other midwife has heard the story."

"What about our doctor?" William adjusted his seating.

"No. The mountaineers don't go to him because they wouldn't want him to know anything."

Their horses stepped through the creek rippling over the road and when they rounded a corner, Mr. Hill held up a hand and stopped. William reined in Chestnut and froze.

A few yards away, two bear cubs played, while their mother watched from the side of the trail. William's heart hammered against his ribs; Lizzie had his pistol. Yet what a fool he was to think such a small weapon could kill a bear. More likely, an injured beast would maul him. The bear stood on her hind legs, sniffing, and rotating her head. He hoped she smelled the odor from the horses and not his terror. Sensing the danger, Chestnut fidgeted, and William stroked her neck.

"Shh," he said, although, like Chestnut, he yearned to turn around and bolt for cover. But running from a bear would provoke her to attack.

"Steady," Mr. Hill said. "Try to calm yourself so she doesn't sense your fear."

William forced himself not to look at the bear's eyes as he inhaled and exhaled, praying the bear would depart. She dropped to all fours, nudged her cubs, and they ambled into the underbrush.

"We'll give her a minute to distance herself. Bears are common around Rugby, so you must learn how to react."

"Do they come into the settlement, sir?" William vowed to buy both a pistol and a gun and carry them whenever he rode. He could shoot into the air and scare away a bear.

"Now and then, last week, someone spied them at Beacon Hill."

"Near Lizzie's cottage?" Perhaps Lizzie *should* practice with a rifle. He admired how she walked through the woods, unarmed, and seemly unconcerned about bears.

"Yes. We should return and see what the others have discovered." Mr. Hill urged on his horse.

William dug in his heels, longing to speak with Lizzie and make plans for her safety, even if he had to guard her throughout the night.

. . .

After several hours of scrubbing laundry, sheets decorated the rail fences, britches hung from tree limbs, and a flock of diapers dripped from the porch railing. Usually, Lizzie dreaded washing clothes, wringing out endless pairs of socks, and hanging everything up, because most often, a dog's wagging tail would knock something on the ground, and the pillowslip or shirtwaist had to be rinsed again. But today, happiness bubbled inside Lizzie at the cheerful sight of clean linens. How good the sheets would smell when everyone retired for the night.

Sitting in a tin tub, Thomas splashed at the soap suds as Lizzie rubbed away the dirt rings and washed his hair. He squealed when she dried him off and tapped his little bare bottom. Thomas would have to wear his nightshirt until his clothes dried.

"Where's my next pumpkin?" Lizzie lifted Ginny into the tub. "Close your eyes, honey." She poured water over the girl's head, relishing the sweetness of seeing Ginny's skin turn pink as soap removed the grime. Lizzie reckoned Cousin Mary had been so weary from carrying a baby in her belly that she had forgotten about baths. She had only met Mary on her wedding day, a puny, flat-chested girl who now lay in her grave. Ginny looked more like Aunt Ida, with her oval face and delicate bones.

While Aunt Ida and the children napped, Lizzie swept and scoured the floor, wiped sticky fingerprints off the chairs and table, and washed the one window. A pot of soup beans and smoked hocks simmered over the fire, filling the room with the scent of ham and summer savory. Lizzie didn't miss living in a log cabin or fetching water, but there was a peacefulness in a humble home. If she had married Lucas, they would have lived in such a place. She shuddered at the remembrance of his marriage proposal, offering her a pair of shoes and ten yards of calico. She didn't need wallpaper and fancy wooden window trim to find contentment. But Lizzie wanted a man who would cherish her and see her worth as more than a pair of shoes.

What had the morning brought to Rugby? Lizzie prayed Nate hadn't died, leaving Edith to support her brood, then she might charge Lizzie with murder. Should she have stayed and told her side of the situation? But then she would have had to face Lucas and Nate's hateful accusations. She was better off allowing some time to flow by before that confrontation. Soon enough, Cousin Hank would return, and she would need a plan for her future. Lizzie's innards felt as tangled as a kitten with a ball of yarn.

She set William's derringer on the fireplace mantel, and each time Lizzie spied it, his arms seemed to encircle her, like when he had demonstrated how to fire it. Lizzie hoped William missed her presence as much as she craved his company. One bullet had ripped apart their daily pattern of sharing the wonder of teaching children; the quick smiles they had given each other, and his elbow linking with hers when they had walked home. Although Lizzie yearned to hear his boot clattering up the porch steps. William needed to stay in Rugby and teach school.

· · ·

The screen door thumped behind William as he walked into the kitchen, where Mrs. Carroll was cutting out biscuits. He backed away from the hot stove, but his stomach growled at the fragrance of baked ham.

"Have you seen Lizzie?" William picked up a warm biscuit and took a bite.

"No." Mrs. Carroll turned her back as she slipped a baking tray into the oven.

"Do you know where she is?"

Mrs. Carroll's blue eyes stared into his. "She went to see a relative. That'd taste better with butter and honey."

"Her brother?" William plucked a knife from a bin and scanned the worktable for butter. Perhaps Lizzie went to help Hazel with the new baby or maybe pull weeds in their garden. With two young children, Jacob and Hazel would appreciate Lizzie's support.

"No." Mrs. Carroll dusted the flour off her hands.

William swallowed. Was Mrs. Carroll keeping some secret or weary from the lack of sleep? "Could you please explain where Miss Walker has gone?"

"She told me to tell you she was going to visit a relative."

"And when will she return?"

"She didn't say."

Blast it all. He was too tired for such games. William grabbed a couple of sugar cookies and stomped to the carriage house. Lizzie's horse had disappeared, so she hadn't walked to a relative's home. As far as he knew, Jacob and Hazel were her only family on the ridge. William leaned against the door frame and chomped on a cookie. She could have at least provided some information about where she had gone.

Lizzie was supposed to lead the sewing lessons and help plan the end of the semester program. Miss Emily might complete the dressmaking, but she had no obligation to assume Lizzie's teaching responsibilities. William took another bite of a cookie. If he hadn't given his word about completing the summer term, he would hop on a train and begin his investigation for his son. Lizzie's comments about fathers abandoning their children had picked at a scab that had refused to heal.

·   ·   ·

William glanced around the room as a first grader read a passage. He wished he could see Lizzie sitting with the older female students, keeping them focused on their studies. It looked as if Silas was doodling or writing a note instead of working on his algebra. With his nerves taunt and his whirling thoughts of Lizzie, William didn't want a confrontation with Silas, but the lad must learn accountability. After praising and dismissing the wee ones, William strolled around the room. The students bowed their heads and tended to their assignments. He paused at Silas' desk. Although the arithmetic book was open, Silas drew two sets of train tracks.

"Silas, aren't you supposed to be working on the algebra problems?" William laid a hand on the boy's shoulder. Silas must understand his responsibility to complete his work.

"But I am, sir. If I can visualize the problem, it's easier for me to figure it out." Silas drew a locomotive on one track. "This is one of those problems with one train being faster than the other, and they both leave the station at the same time."

William had and still hated those kinds of equations, as he had no patience with them. Frankly, who cared about speeding trains? Probably the managers at his mills who needed their shipments to arrive on time, so actually, William should care, too. Maybe Silas had discovered a way to help other struggling students solve algebra problems.

"Here's the other train rushing along." Silas added another locomotive. "I'm supposed to use the formula: rate equals distance/time."

"That's correct." Perhaps this was why teachers called these story problems. A few illustrations might help a student understand the situation. William bent lower, trying to remember how the teacher's manual explained the solution.

Silas' pencil scratched out numbers as he worked the equation. His ink-stained fingers paused for a moment, and then he wrote the answer. "Is that right, sir?"

"I believe so." William picked up the manual and flipped pages until he found the assignment, sensing how the other boys watched him. Like the mother bear crossing the trail, they recognized his insecurities with math. "Yes, it is. Good job."

•   •   •

After dinner, William read the older students' essays about their favorite activities. The boys cited fishing and hunting along with exploring a local cave while the girls wrote about singing and baking. Lizzie had suggested the assignment to help him discover more about everyone. While she would have known many of the details, he wished she was reading them with him so they could discuss each person.

William opened the arithmetic manual and checked the older students' papers. How had those boys perceived his limited knowledge of higher mathematics? Because his tutor had refused to dismiss William for his afternoon ride unless he finished his work, William had cheated. Not on every problem, but for the ones he couldn't solve, he had acquired the correct answers. When the tutor had left the room, William had searched the teacher's manual and copied the solutions on a small piece of paper. He had solved most of the problems, so why worry about a little fudging?

William rubbed his forehead. If he had known how his lack of self-control would haunt him, would rob him of his child and would dissolve his confidence as a teacher, he would have reformed his behavior. While he couldn't erase the consequences of the passions shared in the secluded spots in the garden, he could discipline his mind. William picked up a pencil and worked the next day's algebra assignment.

CHAPTER THIRTEEN

Be blest with health, and peace, and sweet content.
–Robert Burns

A week after Lizzie had arrived, Joseph's body had gained flesh and Aunt Ida no longer looked so pale and weary. Thomas and Ginny had tidy hair and wore clean, patched clothes. In the evenings, they sat on the porch, and her aunt told tall tales about a mountain lad named Jack who outwitted kings and giants. The creaking of Aunt Ida's rocker accompanied her voice as Joseph slept on her boney shoulder. Lizzie knitted socks with a child on either side of her. Layers of fog would settle over the creek bottom as the air cooled, and clouds of fireflies hovered around the yard. If only Lizzie could transport this peace back to Rugby and share it with William. This joy matched Jane Eyre's delight in the company of her cousins, as they created a refuge from Jane's sorrow of losing Mr. Rochester. But any day soon, Cousin Hank would return, and she would have to leave.

One afternoon, while everyone was napping, she tackled the garden Cousin Mary had planted. Lizzie pulled out chickweed and quack grass, freeing rows of string beans, potatoes, collard greens, and winter squash. Sweat slicked the space between her shoulder blades, but she didn't care, because bringing order to the chaos brought an inner satisfaction. Lizzie longed to hoe away the fears and sorrows troubling her life and plant seeds of hope. What was William doing now? Perhaps he listened to the little ones read or handed out copy slips so the students could practice their handwriting. Lizzie missed the smell of chalk dust and seeing his elegant penmanship lettering out the day's Bible verse. She hoped anger didn't blaze inside William because she had left without telling him her plans.

Lizzie plopped down in the shade and chewed a mint leaf as her ears caught the snort of a horse. A woman's sunbonnet flickered through the tree branches that draped over the winding path leading to the cabin. Lizzie squinted at the mule and rider; the woman ducked, and they trotted into the clearing. Where had Lizzie seen that sunbonnet? On Nate's wife, Edith.

Had Mrs. Carroll broken her promise? Lizzie grabbed the mule's bridle as Edith alighted. "Welcome. How did you find me? Would you like some water?"

"That'd be right nice. And my mule would relish a drink." Edith dusted off her skirt and apron.

While Edith cared for her animal, Lizzie fetched a pitcher of water from the creek and poured two mugs for them. They settled under the shade of a large oak, far enough away from the cabin, so that no one would hear their conversation. The faded yellow of a black-eye tinted Edith's left cheek.

"I know what you're thinking, but nobody told me where to find you," Edith said. "Folks like you might think all I do is make babies, but a body has time to ponder while nursing or rocking the least one to sleep."

Red crept over Lizzie's neck, and she picked at a cocklebur attached to the hem of her skirt. Edith's plain words reflected how she viewed most of the women on the ridge. "You're right. I am sorry."

"I forgive you." Edith rested one hand on her rounded belly. "One day, you'll understand. So, I asked myself, seeing how Miss Lizzie probably shot Nate, where would she go? And I remembered your aunts. Alta's gone to her reward, so Ida's the only one left. I asked around about her."

"But why do you think I shot Nate?" Lizzie's shoulders slumped. She hated how everyone on the ridge assumed her guilty. It appeared more time must pass before she could return to Rugby and William.

"I minded how Lucas ranted to Nate about you jilting him again for Mr. William. Nate's still irked about that rich foreigner telling him how to build your cottage." Edith patted Lizzie's hand. "Your bullet punched a hole through Nate's thigh. Granny Slone cleaned him up, but the wound's not closing properly. It's festering. I reckon the meanness in Nate is a poison that fights the healing. Pain's real bad."

"I'm sorry. I just wanted to scare the intruders away, not hurt anyone." Even as mean as Nate was, Lizzie wanted his leg to heal otherwise, he and his friend would hate her until eternity. The man needed to work and feed his family.

"Granny Slone told only me that the bullet come from a pistol. Your brother owns rifles, so I know that he didn't give you a gun. Betsy told me how she spied a pistol in Mr. MacLeod's waistcoat pocket, so I reckon you used his. You and Mr. MacLeod seem pretty close these days."

Lizzie's cheeks flamed. "William and I are merely friends."

Edith glanced at her. "Time will tell about that. Nate hasn't named you because he's ashamed of being bested by a woman, but he will never forgive you."

"Is William in danger?" Lizzie closed her eyes. If he was, she was to blame. Edith's black-eye revealed Nate's frustrations and how his temper continued to rule his household.

"There are tongues flapping about the teacher; folks saying that he shot my husband. But being close to the end of the term, the women are begging the men to let things slide. Nate's kin blame you for causing the ruckus, and I can't say what they might do when school closes." Edith pushed back her sunbonnet. Threads of gray streaked her bun, and crinkles wove their way around her thin neck, but the strength of the mountains rested in her brown eyes.

"Hit be better if you stayed here for a spell. Even when your cousin returns, his new wife might need some help. Best come back at the end of the term."

Meek and humble Edith was right, again. But what made her husband so ornery?

"Why do you stay married to Nate?" Lizzie focused on an ant carrying a snippet of a leaf toward his home. Edith shifted her weight and stretched her back, and the scent of crushed grass drifted around them.

"Honey, when we wed, Nate had a temper, but the meanness hadn't entered him. When we were hoeing corn, he'd take the hoe out of my hand and carry me to a soft spot beneath a tree. Love and joy filled those tender moments. Even after the first couple of young ones arrived, he'd sneak me into the hay mow while they napped. He never picked me flowers, but when he went trading in Sedgemore, he'd bring me a few lemon drops. I miss that part of him." Edith plucked a handful of chickweed and let the greenery fall from her fingers.

"Having so many bellies to fill, too many dry summers with puny corn crops, and after those uppity English folks took over our ridge, anger gnawed a hole in his heart, and bitterness trickled in." Edith turned her head, looking up at a noisy flock of crows. "If I left, where would I go? My kin, especially my daddy, would tell me to go back to my man and accept my lot."

"It doesn't seem fair." Lizzie knew Aunt Ida would never insist upon her staying with a man as mean as a copperhead snake. She and Aunt Alta had taught her how a husband should protect and cherish his wife.

"When's life ever fair? We make do the best we can." Edith's hand, with ragged nails and thick knuckles patted Lizzie's arm. "Promise me you'll heed my warning."

"Thank you. I will. How is Mr. William?" Lizzie understood how much this trip would cost Edith if Nate heard about it, yet she needed to warn William of the dangers that lurked for them.

"Oh my, that man is like a dog with too many fleas." Edith laughed. "His name brings pink to your cheeks. Good to see you flustered and in love, after grieving so hard for Mr. George. When things change for the better and it's safe, I'll tell Mrs. Carroll."

"Thank you. I'm beholden to you. I wish I could repay your kindness." Like any highlander, Edith wouldn't take charity.

"Well, it pains me that I can't help my children with their schoolwork. My folks didn't believe in giving girls book learning. I'd like to know how to write my name, but Betsy's scared to teach me my letters." Edith picked at the frayed strings of her sunbonnet.

"I could spell out your name, and when Nate's asleep, you could practice writing it. Let me fetch some paper." Lizzie brushed dirt off the back of her skirt and headed to the cabin.

She dug into her saddle bags dangling from a peg in the wall and pulled out a few sheets of stationery and a pencil. After printing Edith's name on one sheet, Lizzie wrote on the second piece of paper, "I am safe and will return soon. L." She folded it in half and wrote William's name on it.

"Here, this is your name E d i t h. Perhaps somewhere, like near the creek, you can draw the letters in the dirt, and then dust them away so the children don't see them. And please slip this note under Mrs. Carroll's door so she can give it to Mr. William."

"Thank you. I best be off." Edith slipped both papers into her apron pocket. "I'll stop by the boardinghouse." She heaved herself onto the mule, clicked her tongue, and rode off.

The patter of feet sounded on the porch. Lizzie sat down on a step and drew the children to her. Thomas rested his head on her shoulder while Ginny snuggled against Lizzie's chest with her thumb in her mouth. She inhaled the scent of the little girl's sweet skin. If only Lizzie could wake up from a nap and find herself back in Rugby, listening to William play the piano. How long would it take for tempers to cool, and for the gossip to turn toward something else?

"I'm hungry," Thomas said as Joseph's cry rippled to the porch. Ginny nodded.

"Guess Joseph is, too. He needs his diaper changed." Lizzie kissed the tops of their heads. "How about cornbread and milk?"

While she fetched a pitcher of milk, Thomas crumbled cornbread in their bowls, and then they ate. She changed Joseph, and he curled against her shoulder, sucking on the muslin nipple while they rocked. Lizzie dreaded the day when Joseph's new mother would hold him;

she wanted to slip him into her apron pocket and take him home as her child. Her mama must have experienced the same love when she had suckled Lizzie. But why hadn't her father felt this way about his children? As if Lizzie had stepped on a yellow jacket's nest, resentment toward her father buzzed inside her brain. Aunt Ida and Aunt Alta had heaped love onto the three of them, always telling them to forgive their father. But staring into Joseph's tiny face, Lizzie understood the resentment that plagued Viney.

.   .   .

William sank onto a boulder and reread Lizzie's note. Was she safe, or had she written those words to placate him? Every afternoon, he hoped to see her ride up to the carriage shed and return to teaching with him. Because he had studied along with his students, no longer did he stand at the chalkboard with the teacher's manual open to the algebra solutions. The lads recognized his growing command of the subject, and school wasn't as troublesome. William still didn't enjoy challenging story problems, but he appreciated the boys' respect. Thank goodness, he understood geometry, but probably some other teacher would instruct that subject during the fall term.

William gazed at Lizzie's cottage. After the lies Lucas had spread about her, William had banished him from her land. With the Tabard nearing completion, he could send over a couple of carpenters to finish the job. But he wanted to act like the settlers, who not only believed in equality but worked for a new type of society. He set a board on two sawhorses, marked it with a pencil and picked up a saw.

The slanted sun illuminated a jumble of rejected lumber and the blisters on William's hands. Sweat soaked his shirt, and he craved a drink of water. William had learned to measure three times before cutting. Then if he tapped in a few nails at the top of a board, he could hold it in place with one hand while nailing it to the wall. The pine siding gleamed and scented the air. William should be proud of the small accomplishment, but how could he finish this project by the end of the term? He put away the tools and walked to the Tabard.

A few men lingered as they pitched scraps of lumber into a wagon or locked up tools inside the inn. William gazed at the towering white structure which would open in the fall. He hoped his father and mother would want to come to the celebration and witness what their investment had created. And his father could meet Lizzie. He walked toward Jimmy Keane.

"Tomorrow we've a half day of school, and I wondered if you could help me in the afternoon." William ran his fingers through his hair as he described Lizzie's cottage.

"Certainly, sir. I'll be there." Jimmy nodded.

"Thank you." William extended his hand, wincing when Jimmy squeezed it.

• • •

"These are the drawings for the cottage." William spread the papers out in front of Jimmy. "We need to finish the walls and then plaster them."

"Do you know if the young lady wants plaster?"

"I don't know. She enjoys the parlor at Mrs. Carroll's and its walls are plastered and covered with wallpaper." Not that William had any idea how to perform either task.

"Then she probably will want wallpaper." Jimmy placed a board on the sawhorses and measured it.

As they worked, Jimmy explained how to trim a board so it would fit the corner space. William tucked away each bit of information and asked many questions. By twilight, they had completed the interior walls, leaving spaces for the doors.

"Thank you." William looked about. "I can't believe we accomplished so much."

"The job always goes faster when two work together." Jimmy brushed sawdust off his trousers. "Let me show you how to nail up the lath that will hold the plaster. I'll stop by after work on Monday."

"Have a good evening." William nodded as they walked their separate ways.

William had missed so much of life by being raised a gentleman. The satisfaction of watching walls take shape. The bonding with another fellow as they worked together. Of feeling useful and having a goal other than making money and marrying a rich young lady. William hummed the melody to *Ae Fond Kiss*. Although Lizzie wasn't as wealthy as the girls in Cincinnati, her bank account might convince his father to approve of their match.

William whistled as he walked into the entryway of the boardinghouse and cringed at the sound of Violet's voice floating from the parlor. Blast it all! His mother had conspired again and brought the girl to his sanctuary. As the days had slipped by, he had hoped Violet would forget about Rugby, but she was like the buzzards circling the wooded hills. Violet had her eye on him and would not fly away. William longed to hide in his room, but his mother would drag him out to face these guests.

"Rugby is so quaint, isn't it, Papa?" Violet said. "I wonder when William will return?"

"Any minute now," Mrs. Carroll said. "Would you like some more cookies? William is quite fond of shortbread."

"Please. I'll have to remember that detail for when he visits again."

Now or never. William straightened his shoulders and marched into the parlor. Mrs. Carroll cocked her head and raised an eyebrow before heading to the kitchen. She had listened to him complain about Violet and had offered suggestions on how to discourage the lass. But it appeared her ideas had not worked.

"What a surprise!" William squeezed Violet's hand and then shook Mr. Underhill's. "Are you here for a brief holiday, sir?"

"Yes. Violet wanted to escape the heat of the city for the cool mountain air. I am sorry that your mother could not accompany us.

This is also a bit of a business trip. We brought several pieces of furniture, so you can see how they look in a room. Violet can arrange them to display their beauty. A woman's touch can make a difference in creating a cozy feeling for the guests."

"Yes, how true. Thank you for bringing the furniture." William accepted a cup of tea and sat in a winged-backed chair, avoiding the space Violet had left on the settee.

"I would love to tour the village and see the Inn." Violet passed him the plate of shortbread. "I am sure with your attention to details that the new hotel will be grand."

"There's not enough time before dinner for a tour." William bit into his cookie. "And I need to correct school papers after we eat."

"But it's Friday! Surely, you can take the evening off and correct them on Sunday." Violet sipped her tea. "Please, William?"

Blast it all. Today was Friday, which was why Mr. Underhill had slipped away. The gossips would observe him strolling through Rugby with Violet, and they would scatter the news like pollen falling from a pine tree.

• • •

The morning sunlight slanted through the canopy of oak leaves and illuminated the gravel path to the Tabard. A few summer visitors strolled through the village and glanced at William and his guests; at least those folks didn't know that usually he and Lizzie walked together. A wagon loaded with lumber rumbled past, heading towards Beacon Hill where new settlers built more homes.

The Tabard's white clapboard gleamed, and the stained shingles surrounding the dormers radiated a humble warmth. Scalloped gingerbread adorned the porch that wrapped around the two-and-a-half story building. In places, small balconies would allow future patrons to sit outside their rooms and gaze across the village.

"How lovely! Papa, we will have to attend the grand opening and see how the guests like the furnishings." Violet pressed her hand on

William's arm. "You've done a splendid job of overseeing the construction, but I'm sure you will be glad when it is finished so you can come home."

"This is my home now. My father suggested that I manage the Inn, so I will stay on for a while." William pulled away as they climbed the steps to the porch, and he unlocked the door.

Violet frowned. "Aren't you overseeing it just until the opening?"

"That was our original plan. But if I like inn keeping and do well, then I can choose to stay on."

"I see." Violet gazed at the dusty dirt road running through the village. "I assume that over time, other merchants will establish shops in the village?"

"I do not think so." Good. Perhaps William had found one way to discourage Violet's pursuit of him. Although Rugby's society offered a roster of lectures, plays, and brass band concerts, the commissary was the only place where women could shop. Violet would wither without brick streets lined with stores displaying the artistic skills of milliners, dressmakers, cobblers, and whatever else women wanted.

"It appears both the Inn, and the village need women of good breeding to encourage more refined commerce," Mr. Underhill said.

"Yes, sir. This way, please." William guided them inside.

Mr. Underhill gazed about the entryway. "Stunning. Let's look around, shall we? I ordered the wagon driver to drop off a crate of furniture. He asked several fellows to help carry it to a bedroom."

"I'll fetch a crowbar from where we store the tools so we can pry it open." William walked into a small room and searched through a bin.

"Splendid, then Violet can arrange the furniture."

One-by-one, William showed them the dining room, kitchen, parlors, and then they climbed the stairs to the rows of bedrooms. Wallpaper printed with vining ivy covered the hallway and wainscoting protected the lower half of the walls.

"We still have a great deal of inside work," William said. "But we're pretty much on schedule. Here's the crate."

He stuck the crowbar underneath the lid and the nails screeched as he pried off the boards. Violet stuck her fingers in her ears, and Mr. Underhill laughed.

"I'm impressed with your new carpentry skills, William. Let me give you a hand." Mr. Underhill pulled a small table from the crate.

"Thank you, sir." William carried out the head and footboards for a bed.

After they unloaded everything, Violet gave orders. "Place the bed near that window so the person can feel the breeze. The small table and chair would look nice next to this window."

"Excellent." Mr. Underhill turned to William. "Violet has a talent for decorating, doesn't she? With a rug and a few paintings, this room will appeal to all visitors."

"Yes, sir." William refused to look at Violet. Fighting off his mother's prodding to court this young lady sapped his energy, and Mr. Underhill had joined the fight to banish his bachelorhood.

•   •   •

On a fine morning with sunshine crowning the mountains, Cousin Hank arrived with his bride and her babe. A pile of quilts filled a large splint basket stuffed in the back of his wagon, along with a few cast-iron pots and frying pans heaped in a crate. With Joseph sleeping on her shoulder, Lizzie, Thomas, Ginny, and Aunt Ida surrounded the newlywed couple. Lizzie tightened her grip on the baby.

"Meet Mandy," Hank said. "Here's your new mama." Hank lifted her from the wagon seat.

Mandy pushed back her blue-check sunbonnet and smiled. She had pinned her brown hair into a thick bun and her plump bosom stretched the bodice of her blue calico dress covered with a flour sack apron. In the crook of her elbow, she held a sleeping infant wrapped in a colorful nine-patch quilt.

"Can you swap howdies with me?" She shook Aunt Ida's hand first and then Lizzie's, before bending over the children. Hank slipped an arm around her waist, smiling down at his bride.

"And this here is Jeanie," Mandy said. "I can't wait to hold her brother; reckon they'll grow up as twins." Mandy handed Jeanie to Aunt Ida and looked at Lizzie.

Pain sliced through Lizzie as she inched her arms forward. Mandy didn't need another baby. Lizzie had considered asking Hank if she could adopt Joseph, but seeing how he gazed at his son, her cousin would never agree to such an idea. As Joseph left the security of Lizzie's shoulder, he fussed.

"He's a mite touchy this morning," Lizzie said.

"Oh, after he knows that his new mama can fill his belly, he'll come to me." Mandy rocked Joseph in her arms. "We're going to fatten you up, little man." He whimpered, waving about his fists, before scrunching up his face and howling. "Reckon I'd best find a quiet place to feed him."

"Go on in," Hank said. "I'll bring in your plunder. Lizzie, could you grab the other handle on that big basket?"

After helping Hank, Lizzie ran down to the creek and tossed in pebbles. How could a child latch onto her heart in only a few weeks? Although she relished teaching, she longed for the simple pleasures of marrying, birthing a child, and kissing his cheeks. When the ache subsided, she pulled the derringer from her pocket and studied the pearl coating the barrel. With his festering wound, it would be a while before Nate could confront her. Aunt Ida didn't need her, nor would the newlyweds want Lizzie sleeping in the loft, listening to them rustling their corn-shuck mattress. It was time to root hog or die! Lizzie must warn William and face the gossips.

Following the noon meal, Lizzie said her farewells, strapped her saddle bags onto Bessie, and mounted her horse. "Come on, girl, let's go home."

CHAPTER FOURTEEN

Ye powers wha mak mankind your care,
And dish them out their bill o'fare.
–Robert Burns

Lizzie left Bessie with Tom at the carriage house and slipped through the back door into the kitchen, where Mrs. Carroll was baking oatmeal raisin cookies. The aroma of cinnamon and vanilla welcomed her, and she stole one off a cooling rack.

"Would you like a cup of tea with it?" Mrs. Carroll hugged Lizzie with one arm. Concern darkened her blue eyes. "Weren't you supposed to wait until Edith sent word that William should fetch you?"

"My cousin brought home his new wife, and they didn't need my help. And I'm tired of living in fear of some stupid man. I want to finish my cottage."

"Well, then. I moved your belongings upstairs to the last room on the hall. You should be safer there." Mrs. Carroll glanced at the parlor and laid a hand on Lizzie's arm. "There is something you should know."

William's voice chatted with someone in the parlor, and Lizzie cracked the door to peek at him. A lovely young woman dressed in a navy-blue traveling suit stood next to a gray-haired gentleman who must be her father. Several carpet bags and a hat box rested at their feet. She took William's hands, rose onto her tiptoes, and kissed his cheek. Lizzie's face blanched.

While she had been away, William had invited his intended to visit him! What a fool she was to think that this man might love her. He was like those lads from England who used mountain girls and tossed them aside when they sailed home to their privileged brides. Lizzie wanted to slap William for toying with her affections. As she released the door, William looked her way and gasped. Blast it all. He was the last person she wanted to speak to. Lizzie fled out the back door.

"Wait!" Mrs. Carroll called.

Lizzie dashed up the stairs of the carriage house that led to the hayloft. William would not search for her in this place. She folded her knees to her chin and wept, wishing she had stayed with her cousin. Yet Lizzie knew his new bride would not want another woman cooking at her hearth. If not for the construction of her cottage, she would board the train heading east and visit Viney and her father. But she would not allow William and his wealthy fiancé to destroy her dream of a small, tidy home surrounded by rose and lilac bushes.

She dried her eyes and trudged along the path to Madam Hughes' home. She wanted to hear what Emily thought about William's actions and how she should respond. Lizzie found Emily sitting beneath the grape arbor with her knitting.

"Lizzie! I missed you. When did you come back?" Emily hugged Lizzie.

"This afternoon. My cousin brought home his new wife." Lizzie sank onto a bench and inhaled the fragrance of ripening grapes. In another month, they could make jelly together.

"William was delighted to see you?" Emily picked up her knitting.

Lizzie explained what she had observed. "I didn't think he was that type of man."

"And he may not be. You said that Mrs. Carroll tried to talk to you." Emily patted Lizzie's hand.

"Yes. But I was in too much pain to listen." Lizzie dabbed at her eyes.

"Did you feel pain or anger?"

"Both. Wouldn't you be outraged?" Lizzie exhaled. Any woman would feel hurt if she saw the man she loved, dallying with the girl chosen by his mother.

"I think you should listen to what Mrs. Carroll has to say before you judge William. And he needs to explain his side of the story, too."

"I guess so." Lizzie rose and smoothed the wrinkles from her skirt. "Thank you."

"Please let me know what happens." Emily embraced Lizzie. "Before you leave, we need to determine a date for the tea party. While you were away, the girls finished their new frocks, and they are eager to wear them."

"I'll ask Mrs. Carroll if we can use the parlor next Saturday in the early afternoon, then we could finish before she prepares dinner."

"Splendid. If that day doesn't work, then we'll find another date." Emily hugged Lizzie.

When Lizzie reached the boardinghouse, she climbed to the second story room, where she found a stack of letters on her new bed. She spied a Boston postmark, opened the long envelope, and sank down onto a chair.

Dear Miss Walker,

We regret to inform you that because of economic circumstances in England, your investments have depreciated by fifty percent. Your diminished income will reflect these losses, so please budget accordingly. We do not foresee any increases in your wealth in the future. If the downturn continues, you may lose more of your capital.

Respectfully, Mr. Park

Tears trickled down her cheeks, and her heart thumped against her ribs. Lizzie longed to scream out her frustrations, or curl into a tiny ball and fit into a cocoon until this new trouble resolved itself. Why had *this* happened? Did she have sufficient funds to finish her cottage and still have money to live on? Perhaps she should sell the cottage to a new family settling in Rugby? But to lose her new home would rip away another piece of George, who had selected the building site. She pulled out her hanky and wiped away her tears. Screaming or pounding her pillow would not solve her problems; she must find employment as soon as possible. Slipping the letter into her pocket, she took it to Mrs. Carroll.

"Oh, my. I am so sorry." Mrs. Carroll set down the missive. "I had heard that times were hard in England."

"And then to see William and that girl together! It's all too much." Lizzie grabbed a molasses cookie and stuffed half of it in her mouth.

"You misjudge the lad."

"I saw her kiss his cheek."

Mrs. Carroll grimaced. "But did he kiss hers?"

"No." Lizzie munched the rest of the cookie.

"If you had been here, you would have observed how the lassie is chasing after William, but he did his best to refuse her advances. He even retired to his room at 8:30 last night."

Lizzie poured boiling water into a small teapot and tossed in a teaspoon of black tea leaves. "He shouldn't have let her kiss him. Is she the girl that his mother talked about?"

"Yes. Her name is Violet, but she should have been named Foxglove because of her poisonous behavior. It appears that her father is also part of the scheme to have her marry William."

"Well, he can have her. I don't think I can ever trust him again."

"You will have to determine that, but at least allow William the chance to defend himself. For now, please peel those potatoes and slice them into thin sections."

Lizzie scraped the brown skins into a bucket so she could feed the scraps to the chickens. Mrs. Carroll had protected her from Nate and Lucas and had provided advice like a mother, surely, she spoke the truth about William. But if he loved her, he should have told Violet how another woman had claimed his affections. Lizzie sliced the potatoes and tossed a handful in a pot, wishing that she could cut out the pain ruling her heart. She longed to shred the letter in her apron pocket, so she would never have to worry about earning an income.

. . .

"Lizzie, please, could we talk for a few minutes before dinner?" William caught her elbow. She glared at him, walked to a corner of the porch, and sat in a rocking chair while he took a seat.

"I realize that what you saw seems suspicious...."

"If you prefer Violet to me, then so be it." Lizzie stared at the orange daylilies blooming in the flower garden.

"But I don't! My mother keeps foisting her on me, and now her father is part of the plot. I have no interest in Violet, or in any other girl. I only want to be with you."

"Allowing a young lady to kiss you shows other intentions."

"Please forgive me. I can't irritate her father, as his factory is building the furniture for the Inn. I didn't know that she would kiss me, and I certainly didn't want it."

The glint in Lizzie's eyes told William how he had only assuaged a few of her feelings of rejection. Fear and anger still lingered in her expression, and only rebuilding her trust would remove those emotions.

"I'm so thankful that you are home. Please give me a chance to prove myself. Are you still afraid of what Nate and Lucas could do?"

"No, not really." Lizzie's voice shook. "But a letter arrived with bad news."

"About your father?" William longed to take her hand but hid his in his pockets.

"No, about my investments. Oh, here." Lizzie pulled the envelope from her pocket and tossed it at him.

William scanned the letter, and his stomach sank to his toes. His father had mentioned the continuing recession in England and how the situation would affect America's economy. The lack of jobs in England would mean more immigrants looking for work at his family's factories, and more settlers coming to Rugby, seeking a new way of life.

If she would allow it, he needed to review her bank statements to discover how much wealth Lizzie had lost and what remained of her nest egg. He doubted if she would accept a loan from him. Considering the ruckus about Violet, this was not the moment to ask to court her, to invite her to marry, and benefit from his wealth.

"Do you think I can afford to finish my cottage?" Lizzie recited the last figures she could remember from her bank account in Boston.

"Maybe." William hoped Lizzie would appreciate the work he and Jimmy had accomplished over the past few weeks and how much money they had saved her. Hearing the dinner bell, William escorted Lizzie to the dining room and pulled out her chair.

"After the troubles with Nate and Lucas, the students' parents will not approve of me teaching. When the Tabard is completed, will you give me a job, please?" Lizzie bit her lower lip.

"Of course. After dinner, why don't we look at your cottage? We can discuss other options, too."

Mrs. Carroll placed a bowl of green beans on the table. "You could work here, lassie. With so many visitors escaping the heat of Cincinnati, I can't keep up in the kitchen. I hired a couple of the new settlement girls to help with the laundry."

"Thank you so much! You're an angel." Lizzie jumped from her chair and hugged Mrs. Carroll. "I would love to work here."

"And you're like a daughter to me. You enjoy your dinner and don't fret anymore."

· · ·

The slanted sunlight glowed on the fresh pine flooring and danced on the whitewashed walls as William escorted Lizzie around her cottage, taking pleasure in how the sparkle had returned to her eyes.

"I can't believe you accomplished so much. You're remarkable."

"Thank you, but remember that Jimmy Keane helped me and taught me how to do everything."

"Perhaps you should work as a carpenter?" Lizzie placed her hand on his arm.

"I think I prefer teaching." William wanted to add, especially with you, but such words might remind Lizzie of how she would not return to the classroom.

Lizzie's touch sparked a warmth in his veins and William yearned to kiss her. But with what had happened in the last month, Lizzie might misinterpret his advances. While his youthful affair had grown from lust, his affections for Lizzie blossomed from his love for the remarkable and courageous woman. Lizzie would understand his past misguided passions, but she would not approve if he disclosed the complete truth about his behavior.

Back at the parlor, William raised the lid over the piano keys while Lizzie reclined on a settee with her knitting.

"A little music before we retire?" He slid onto the piano seat and his fingers found the melody for *My Love is Like a Red, Red Rose*, then *Bonnie Wee Thing*, and finally, *Ae Fond Kiss*. A sweet peace settled over the room, and Lizzie's expression relaxed. William allowed the last chord to linger until the notes faded. Lizzie was home, and he would do everything he could to ensure they never parted again.

CHAPTER FIFTEEN

God knows I'm no the thing I should be,
Nor am I even the thing I could be.
–Robert Burns

A large sunbonnet hid Edith's face as she knocked on the kitchen door and glanced around. "Miss Lizzie? Do you have time for a lesson?"

Lizzie eyed Mrs. Carroll, hoping that she would allow this break. Her hands were tired from gripping the knife and tears streaked her cheeks.

"You go ahead. I can finish the onions." Mrs. Carroll nodded her head.

Lizzie placed a large chopping knife by a cluster of green onions. "Let's sit on the back porch."

After Lizzie gathered up paper, a pencil, and a primer, she sat down with Edith on the chairs where Mrs. Carroll and she often snapped beans. A wren trilled from a nearby lilac bush, and Bessie gazed at them from the paddock. Edith pulled a scrap of paper from her apron pocket.

"I wrote my name on this bill, but I need to learn the rest of the alphabet."

"Can't Betsy help you?" Lizzie wiped her sweaty palms on her apron. Having her daughter teach Edith would reduce the risk of further angering Nate.

"Didn't you hear? The day after I visited you, Nate gave his blessing, and Betsy wed Lucas. She's bragging about being the first of her friends to have a husband. I reckon Lucas married her to spite you, but my Betsy could do worse."

"She'll make him a good wife." Never again would she have to fret about his advances. Knowing how Betsy had longed for a husband, Lizzie prayed she would find happiness with Lucas. Yet remorse trickled through Lizzie. Despite her encouragement for the girl to work in Rugby and wait a few years, Betsy had succumbed to the ways of the ridge. Soon, she would birth numerous children. At least the girl had a basic education and a new dress.

"Please teach me the other letters so I can read my Daddy's Bible." Edith removed her sunbonnet.

As Edith learned the sounds of the alphabet, she placed a finger beneath each letter and repeated them a dozen times. By the end of the hour, Edith could read a few simple words like cat and rat. While teaching the little students had been pleasing, watching Edith's mind absorb learning filled Lizzie with joy. She had lectured the older girls about how they would need reading to decipher signs and notices, and they would use arithmetic when tallying up prices while shopping. If the other adult women on the ridge learned to read well, then they could peruse *The Rugbian*, which would expose them to new ideas.

Edith sighed, closed the primer, and leaned back in her chair. She pointed at Lizzie's dress.

"You might think it queer, but I've yearned to make pretty things like that there lace collar. I'm weary of knitting socks and mittens. Reckon it's like planting a few hollyhocks beside my beans. Nate names it all foolishness, but I love my flowers. Could you teach me to knit lace?"

"Certainly. Let me go fetch some needles and cotton." Lizzie chided herself for her selfish ways. Why hadn't she thought about how the women of the ridge eyed her lace-edged handkerchiefs with envy? She vowed to right the situation.

Lizzie casted on sixteen stitches for a simple edging. Edith fumbled with the cotton thread until she mastered keeping the correct tension on the tiny needles. After she repeated the process several times, the rows of delicate holes formed in a web with a zig-zag edge.

"Looks like the frost on a windowpane." Edith held up the lace. "Hard to understand how the same stitches that make a sock can turn into something so fine. Reckon I could stitch some to the pillow slips I just sewed and sell them at the Commissary? I always envied your sister earning cash money."

"Would Nate mind?" Lizzie studied Edith's determined look; perhaps seeing Nate laid low by a bullet had emboldened her. Lizzie had never met a mountain man who would allow his woman to earn money. Yet, what better way for his wife to bring in cash that she could spend on her family and perhaps even herself?

Edith resumed knitting. "I reckon he'd be like your brother Jacob, bellowing complaints, but once Nate gets a few tools for the farm, he'll come around. After I shoe my children, I plan to buy me fine kid boots, with rows of buttons that need a buttonhook."

Lizzie stared at her black boots. She should have known that Edith might want something like them. Growing up barefoot, Lizzie had yearned for shoes like the ones worn by her English neighbor, Mrs. Hill. Even if Lizzie had to knit yards of lace, she would help Edith gain those boots both for herself and her children.

"Do you think any of your friends would like to make fancy goods to sell? And would any be interested in learning to read?"

Edith rubbed the small of her back. "Tongues are wagging about you losing your money and how you can no longer put on airs like those English folk. Now you're just a mountain woman like the rest of us. Give 'em time. Let them watch how I like making lace, then they might want to learn fancy knitting. I'll ask a few others if they hanker to learn to read. I best be heading home. What do I owe you for these needles and the cotton?"

"Think of them as a way I can repay your kindness for being my friend." Lizzie folded her knitting.

Edith's back stiffened. "No, I don't take charity."

"When you sell those pillow slips, give a little extra to the church." Perhaps the donation would atone for Lizzie's past.

"I could do that." Edith stuck her knitting in her apron pocket and tied on her sunbonnet. Suddenly, she squeezed Lizzie's hand. "I pray that one day the good Lord will give you and Mr. William much happiness. He's a fine man."

"Thank you." Lizzie picked at a hangnail as she watched Edith trudge homeward. When Nate spied Edith's coins glinting in a jar, would he grin or slap his wife? But with his injury, he could not seek revenge soon. And Lucas was busy enjoying the delights of his bride.

.   .   .

William nodded his head, and young Saul straightened his shoulders. His patched overalls had worn spots and his faded blue shirt from his older brother billowed around his thin frame.

"To be or not to be, that is the question." Saul continued his recitation while the other students either doodled, swung their legs, or stared out the window.

William ran his fingers through his hair. The children needed to listen and encourage each other and help make the program outstanding. But when had William ever modeled a scholarly attitude? Saul returned to his seat, and William called out, "Samantha."

"What is man that Thou art mindful of him?" Samantha quoted Psalm 8. Her dark brown dress showed her calves, as the hem needed to be let down. With her blonde braids tied together with a blue ribbon and her freckled face, Samantha looked like a character from *Little Women*.

William scowled at the back row. Two older boys slugged each other in the shoulder, each punch growing more intense. He wished Lizzie would reconsider and assist him in preparing for the end of the school program. The children needed her voice to lead them in the few songs they were practicing. William glanced at the wall clock and divided the time by the three remaining students who needed to speak. The door clicked open. Every head turned as Edith slipped in and stood in the back of the room.

"Go on, children." She nodded and stared at a couple of boys who smirked at each other, but her look erased their grins.

"Next." William prayed his students would remember their lines. He should separate the boys in the back row, but in ten minutes school would be over for the day. Then he could rest his weary brain.

"'What should I bring Him as poor as I am?'" Edith's little son, Danny, recited a poem by Christina Rossetti. "If I were a shepherd, I would bring him a lamb."

The irony of the poem's words slapped William, because most of the ridge folk displayed the same poverty as the boy in the verses. Yet Edith's face glowed with pride when Danny finished, and her twin girls skipped forward. Back and forth, they recited the love passage from I Corinthians 13, while the two older boys made faces for each adjective.

"Love is patient."

"Love is kind."

As the girls returned to their seats, Edith cleared her throat. "Mister MacLeod, may I say something to your students?"

"Certainly, we have a few minutes left." William hoped her little something would guide him as he attempted to manage this hoard.

"You'uns are lucky to have such a fine teacher, one who cares about you and has so much book learning. I wish I could have gone to this school with its fancy maps and shelves of books and desks! Now, you boys back there, stop acting like knuckleheads, making more work for your teacher. If Mr. MacLeod tells me that you all are still shoving and making faces, I'll have a talk with your mamas. They won't put up with such foolishness." Edith glanced at William. "Thank you for letting me speak my piece."

"Thank you! School is dismissed." William shook Edith's hand as the children streamed from the room. She smiled, gripped her twin's hands, and walked away.

William slumped in his chair, grateful for whatever had prompted Edith to come today and scold those boys. Perhaps a parent had complained about his lack of control over the older students, or perhaps Edith had felt some inner premonition that he needed assistance. Lizzie could elucidate on what might have motivated this humble mother to observe the practice.

. . .

After settling in his place at the dinner table, William admired how his sister's lavender shirtwaist and dark brown skirt emphasized Lizzie's trim waist. A tenderness stirred in him as Lizzie gazed up from beneath her eyelashes. How he had missed sharing meals and concerns with her. None of the other boarders knew much about him, or for that matter, cared about his teaching woes. Lizzie and Rugby had claimed his heart, and he wanted a home with the beautiful woman sitting across from him.

"You look stunning tonight." William blessed Mrs. Carroll for the bouquet of red, pink, and yellow zinnias mixed with blue delphiniums. Did the silverware shine brighter because Lizzie had polished it?

"Thank you. It feels so good to dine with you. How was school?" Lizzie cocked one eyebrow.

Why hadn't he noticed that endearing little action before tonight? Every inch of him wanted to lift her chin and kiss Lizzie until she swooned in his arms. But first she must agree to a courtship before he could claim her kisses.

"Well, the students are working hard at their subjects, but several of them have not learned their lines for the school program. When we were almost finished, Edith came to watch the practice."

"Edith!" Lizzie set down her fork.

"Yes, and she told those older boys to mind themselves or she'd tell their mothers."

"Good for her. I hope they behave now."

"I do, too. But could you please coach the singing?" William spooned creamed corn onto his plate.

"Let me speak with Mrs. Carroll about it. Perhaps I could slip over after washing the lunch dishes and before we prepare supper. But you understand how tongues will criticize you for bringing me back to school."

"Don't worry about the gossips," Mrs. Carroll said as she set down a platter of golden pork chops. "Your lovely voice will inspire the little ones."

"I will come but only for that hour." Lizzie took a roll from a breadbasket.

"Then it's settled." William's shoulders relaxed. With Lizzie's help, the children would learn their parts. When their parents watched the performances, they would forget about Lizzie's recent misfortunes and understand her talent for teaching.

• • •

As they sat correcting papers, Lizzie sniffed. Where had she smelled that acrid odor? She poked her head out of a raised window and sniffed again. "Smoke! Something's burning!"

Lizzie and William rushed to the porch as a group of men and boys ran toward Beacon Hill.

"Fire!" one of them yelled.

A team of horses hauling a water wagon raced by, followed by more men. Lizzie and William dashed after them. The smoke thickened, swirling around Lizzie, as did her dark memories of escaping the Tabard. Not again, not again. Her brain repeated the words as her feet ran down the familiar trail to her cottage. Up ahead, fingers of fire shot over the tops of trees and raced along the peak of the cottage's roof. Flames crackled and rose along the outside walls.

While three firemen pumped, the others aimed their hose at the conflagration.

William grabbed her arm. "Stay away!" He ran to the water wagon.

"Step back," Mr. Hill yelled. "Everyone, back!"

The blaze leapt higher, tossing embers against the darkening sky. The cottage walls caved inward, and the roof slammed to the earth. Ashes flew from the chaos along with her dreams. Lizzie doubled over, coughing. Tears blurred her vision as the fire consumed her future home that she could not afford to rebuild. Why must she lose everything?

The men tossed buckets of water in a circle around the burning rubble to contain the fire, and William worked with them, stomping out patches of burning grass.

"I'm sorry." Mrs. Carroll slid an arm around her. "Someone must have kindled this. How else could a fire start?"

"Nate." Lizzie wiped tears from her sooty cheeks. "And there will be no justice, no punishment."

Her ridge would never change. Ignorance turned men into bullies who had to rule over other folks, especially women. Aunt Alta had taught Lizzie how compassion flowed from the Almighty, and she must show the same kindness. William had said that education would teach the children better ways to control their anger, but few of his students had accepted his ideas. Lizzie sided with her aunt, that each person must choose to transform their thinking or plod along in the familiar ways.

"Come, lass," Mrs. Carroll pulled her to the path. "You've seen enough."

Lizzie trudged home and carried warm water to her room, where she washed the soot and tears from her face. At last, she settled on the porch swing. The sun slid behind the wooded hills, and ribbons of rose and violet flowed across the sky. Whip-poor-wills called, and nighthawks dipped and dived, searching for insects. She yearned to flop down on her bed next to her sister and pour out her woes to Viney. Her sister would know what Lizzie should do about the troubles that tormented her. William's form appeared in the twilight, his boots clattered up the steps, and he sank down beside her on the porch swing.

"I'm so sorry, Lizzie." Soot smeared his face and arms, and ash dusted his clothes.

"No one could have saved it," Lizzie said. "I'm sure Nate's cronies flooded it with kerosene before they lit the match and ran off."

"Most of the men believe Nate ordered someone to torch it." William's sooty fingers interlaced with hers, and a wistful look crept across his face. "If you would allow me to court you, then one day, I will build whatever house you desire."

Lizzie swallowed back a lump in her throat, thinking how her feelings for George were like an old quilt, too tattered to keep her warm, but too full of memories to cut up. But her loss of George had shown her how swiftly a spouse's death transformed a woman from protected to bewildered. Her heart cherished William, but she could not survive losing another beloved. She gazed at William's tender blue eyes until he looked away.

She needed to unfold something about William's past that still tormented him; something that if they wed, would become part of her life, and could control their future. He must trust her with his secret. Lizzie slid her fingers from his hand.

"I am sorry, but not at this time. I just lost my cottage and my fortune and need to sort out everything."

William flinched. Lizzie hated herself as pain and dismay flooded his expression. He had shown her so much love, how could she disappoint him? William stood up.

"I see. How foolish of me to speak too soon. Good night, Miss Elizabeth." William strode into the boardinghouse.

Lizzie returned to her room and wept as she unhooked the buttons on her boots, slid out of her clothes, and pulled on a nightgown. Already, she regretted her response to William's offer. Yet she knew her decision to wait to court would prepare them for a more peaceful future, if at last they wedded. Lizzie sank down on her bed and opened *Jane Eyre*; she read the passage where Jane learned of Mr. Rochester's first wife.

•   •   •

On Saturday, Lizzie and Emily spread a linen cloth on a small table that they had carried into the parlor and arranged gleaming silverware on it.

"I thought we would use a basic place setting because the girls don't need to know the difference between a salad fork and a dinner fork." Lizzie straightened a knife.

"Good idea. And we don't need multiple layers of plates. Just a small luncheon plate will suffice." Emily placed one at each setting.

"Water goblets would be lovely, but they might intimidate the girls."

"I think using a teacup and saucer will thrill them."

"Here they come." Lizzie opened the door to excited voices and escorted the girls into the parlor. "Your new dresses are beautiful, and you did a splendid job in sewing them. You look lovely." Lizzie walked around, complimenting each lass as she inspected the frocks.

"And now to celebrate your creations." Emily wrapped an arm around Victoria's waist and ushered her to the table. "We made name cards for where you should sit. Many hostesses use them."

"Never seen such pretty dishes," one girl said as they scanned the cards and sat in their selected chairs.

"These are Mrs. Carroll's personal dishes, so we must be extra careful with them. I love the garland of pink flowers." Lizzie picked up her napkin and placed it in her lap, and each girl followed her lead. Before working at the Tabard, Lizzie had only experienced napkins in Mrs. Hill's home. While the girls needed to learn the good manners used off the ridge, she did not want to belittle their mountain heritage.

"Let us pray first." Emily bowed her head. As she finished speaking, the door opened, and Betsy entered the parlor wearing her new frock.

Lizzie scanned the table, determining where they could add another seat. She should have thought that Betsy would want to take part in the party. The girl might be a married woman, but she had just turned sixteen. The other teens hugged Betsy and complimented her on the dress.

"I wore it on my wedding day." Betsy twirled around. "Lucas thought it right pretty."

"Here, you can have my seat, and I will pull up a chair." Lizzie rose.

"I didn't want to miss this. And soon, this dress ain't going to fit me." Betsy beamed as understanding settled over her friends' faces. "Lucas is crowing about how he planted his seed on our wedding night."

As Lizzie slid another place setting on the table, she froze. Thank God she was not the woman bearing Lucas' child and the subject of his bragging. The settlement lasses blushed, but the mountain girls giggled and hugged Betsy. Such explicit talk about making babies was part of their world. How odd that at a tea party organized to teach refined manners, they had encountered the highlanders' casual speech about marital intimacy.

"Congratulations, Betsy," Lizzie said. "Why don't I pour tea and Emily will pass the refreshments."

An hour later, Emily arranged the girls in two rows, ducked behind her dark cloth and focused her camera. With a puff of smoke, she captured their youthful innocence and Lizzie laughed as the girls squealed. While the new dresses would be saved for going to church, each family would show off their photograph to visitors.

Lizzie and Emily hugged each girl goodbye and encouraged them to wear their frocks to the end of the school program. As Lizzie wrapped her arms around Betsy, she prayed that Lucas would provide a decent life for the young woman and her child.

"Don't be shy. You come visit me, hear? Let me know how you are feeling as time goes by."

"I will, ma'am. My mama has already given me some raspberry tea to help, and I talked to Granny Coleman."

Lizzie watched Betsy's braid swing as the lass rounded the curve and headed home. "I feel as if I failed her. I tried so hard to convince her to wait a few years before marrying."

Emily placed a hand on Lizzie's shoulder. "You have embraced my uncle's philosophies. But most mountain folk will need many years before they accept the idea that women are equal to men."

"I suppose not having a father controlling us made Viney and I different." Lizzie picked up a tray of dirty dishes. Because William believed in Mr. Hughes' ideas, he was an uncommon sort of man. But was he the man for her?

CHAPTER SIXTEEN

Fain, would I hide, what I fear to discover.
–Robert Burns

William pried open a large crate and stared at the dark mahogany headboard of another bed. He had expected more chairs and tables for the dining room because most of the bedrooms were furnished. They only needed rugs and a few paintings to set a cozy tone. His guests would have to balance their dinner plates on their knees if the other furniture didn't arrive in time. Perhaps Violet and his mother had planned this stunt so that he would travel home and investigate the matter. But between preparing for the school program and the Inn's grand opening, William had more tasks than he could handle. Maybe Violet hoped he would beg her to come to Rugby and take over the decorating.

"Please take these pieces to the second story and find an empty bedroom. I need to ride to Sedgemore." William strode to the livery, saddled Chestnut, and cantered down the pike. He wished Lizzie could accompany him, but she was meeting with Edith.

At Sedgemore, William watered Chestnut at the train depot's trough before entering the telegraph office. He wanted to send the missive to his father, but that would reflect badly upon his ability to manage the Inn.

"Please send this to Mr. Underhill's factory in Cincinnati. *Need dining room chairs, tables.*"

"Is that all, sir?" The clerk looked at William.

"Yes, that should suffice." William counted out some coins. "The rest are for your troubles."

"Thank you, sir!" The clerk sat down at his telegraph station and clicked out the message.

William allowed Chestnut to trot for a while before stopping on the wooden bridge. He gazed at the current as the river twisted around a bend. His summer had flowed away as swiftly as the water rushing beneath him. In a month, the Tabard would open, and he would have to decide if managing the Inn was the correct future for him. Mr. Hill had offered him a permanent teaching job, but without Lizzie's help, William did not want to continue as a schoolmaster. Yet, he longed to remain at Rugby with the woman he loved, and if they married, he would need to support Lizzie and their family. William closed his eyes, envisioning Lizzie cuddling their daughter, but instead of a wee girl, the image of a blond boy filled his mind and he winced.

*   *   *

Lizzie watched the parlor clock pendulum swing back and forth, sweeping away her hopes that Edith would visit today. During the other times they had met for lessons, Edith had completed enough lace to edge a pair of pillow slips. Lizzie carried her empty teacup to the kitchen, where Mrs. Carroll peeled potatoes.

"Would you like some help?" Lizzie picked up a knife and a potato.

"They're not here yet?" Mrs. Carroll toss the potato slices into a kettle.

"I don't think Edith is coming. And Emily had to stay with Madam Hughes today because she caught a cold."

The peel from the potato spiraled down in a long curl, and Lizzie's emotions slid with it. She hadn't realized how much she looked forward to Edith's female companionship. Except for attending church on Sundays, the rumors and housework kept her in the boardinghouse.

Someone knocked on the front door. Wiping her hands on her apron, Mrs. Carroll walked to the front hall. Voices murmured, and footsteps tapped into the parlor. Were these visitors who had come for the mountain air?

"Lizzie, you have guests." Mrs. Carroll nodded at the open doorway.

A dozen women from the ridge stood in the parlor, untying their calico sunbonnets. They gazed at the lace curtains, the velvet settee, and the two lamps with frosted globes painted with red roses. Most had looked in the window when they passed by the boardinghouse, but none of them had stepped into the settler's world.

"Miss Lizzie," Eliza Jane said. "We've come to learn how to make fancy goods." The other women nodded. They wore their hair pulled into buns. Worry lines gathered at the edges of their eyes, and their lips formed thin lines.

Lizzie swallowed. "How wonderful. Please come in. You can hang your sunbonnets on the hall tree." She nodded toward the oak pole. "Would you like tea?"

"No, miss," another woman said. "Just learning."

"You wonder why we came, but Edith didn't." Eliza Jane rested her hands on her swollen belly.

"Well, yes, in ways. Mainly, I'm glad you're here." Lizzie pulled open a drawer in a small chest and removed sets of knitting pins and cotton thread she had purchased. If these women could set aside the gossip about her, then she resolved to forgive them and teach what they wanted to learn.

"It's on account of Edith losing her baby. When Nate found out about the reading lessons and lace making, he punched Edith with his crutch, sending her to the floor. She started bleeding and weren't nothing the granny woman could do. His meanness killed the baby, and that ain't right." The other women looked at their hands, lined with bulging veins, and knuckles thick from scrubbing clothes.

"Nothing as sweet as a baby." One woman wiped tears from her eyes. "Nate allowed Edith a single day in bed, then set her to hoeing, said to use her hands to weed corn."

Dizziness swept over Lizzie, and she clutched the back of a chair. Edith had suffered because of her. That baby had died because of her, and she could do nothing to restore the child, or banish Edith's grief. Lizzie should have listened to her inner voice, that expressed concerns about Nate's anger. A gray-haired woman slipped an arm around Lizzie's waist, steadying her.

"She's taking it bad. Never met a woman so plumb crazy about babies," the gray-haired woman said. "I'm Deborah, honey."

"Edith bragged about how she was going to make enough fancy goods to buy shoes for her children, and boots for herself," Eliza Jane said. "Now, we aim to do that for her. If we like the work, might earn a bit for our families."

"What about your husbands?" Lizzie gazed about the group as she set out balls of pearl cotton. "I want no more trouble." The determined looks on their faces amazed her. These women deeply loved Edith and would risk their husband's ire to help their friend. For the first time, Lizzie wished for such devoted female friends.

"Oh, they'll fuss and fart, but our men don't hit us," Eliza Jane said. "A few of us are kin to Nate, and I already told him off!"

"Edith's my sister," said the woman who had cried. "Even my man, Bobby, says what Nate did was wicked."

"The men folk knows we's mad, and that there's too many of us to stop," another woman said. "For once, they'd better listen."

"How is Betsy?" Lizzie couldn't imagine Lucas hitting Betsy, but Nate would encourage such behavior. Two women chuckled.

"Don't fret about her. Lucas is fanning his tail like a Tom turkey and boasting that his baby will be a boy because of how much Betsy's puking. He told her she didn't need no lace making lessons but should start knitting booties. Laws, that gal can get him to do anything. He even carries buckets of water to the house," Eliza Jane said.

"That's wonderful. Let's begin our lesson. Here's how you need to hold the thread when you cast on the correct number of stitches for the pattern."

The pearl cotton snagged on their chapped fingers, yet they persevered. These women had knitted endless pairs of socks, mittens, and even long underwear for their families, but their hands needed to learn how to work with the thin thread. Lizzie remembered how most of them had frowned at her when she had flirted with their brothers or sons. She had assumed they were jealous of the way boys hovered around her. But now, she wished when they were younger that she had become friends with these women.

"Is this right, Miz Lizzie?" Eliza Jane held up about three inches of an edging. "The other rows don't look like the first."

"Sometimes, the first one looks a little slimmer, and the rest are fuller. Your tension is even, and the edging is beautiful." Lizzie enjoyed seeing how praises tugged a smile from Eliza Jane as she concentrated on the pattern. Lizzie had missed assisting William, but an even greater satisfaction blossomed from teaching the women. Perhaps, as she encouraged these mothers to develop various handcrafts, their new skills would inspire their daughters to knit lace or learn to weave baskets.

"Queer, ain't it," Eliza Jane said. "Same stitches knit thick socks that keep a body's feet warm, but with this here pearly thread, they loop together like netting, sort of stretchy, too." She spread the edging between her fingers. "Looks like it should break, but it doesn't."

Deborah looked up. "Reckon this knitting is like women folk. We need to be sturdy to birth children. Yet each time I set a new babe to my breast, I feel as light and gauzy as this here lace." She glanced at Lizzie. "You're feeling it, ain't you? Seen it in your eyes. You're wanting to wake up next to your man, but you're still ashamed of how you twisted men's desires to suit your needs."

The women paused and stared at Lizzie. The clock's pendulum swished. Red crept over her neck, and she licked her lips as tears dripped down her cheeks. Lizzie yearned to be free from her shame and to prove to these women that she had become a new person.

Deborah wrapped one arm around Lizzie's shoulders. "It's good to grieve when we've made bad choices. We've all made mistakes. After today, no more tears about the past." Deborah glanced around the room, and the others nodded their heads.

"Thank you." For a moment, Lizzie was a child with her head in Aunt Ida's lap, feeling her aunt's hands smoothing her hair, and rubbing her back while speaking encouraging words. She hoped William would forgive her for not accepting his proposal and would understand how she needed more time to grow into a compassionate woman like Deborah.

They resumed knitting. Outside the open window, a horse whinnied, and a breeze lifted the edges of the curtains. The afternoon sunlight filled the room, sparkling on the prisms hanging from the chandelier.

"How many repeats of this pattern until I have enough to edge a pillow slip?" Eliza Jane asked.

"About forty-eight," Lizzie answered. "If you keep an even tension."

"Law, that's what we all need," Deborah said. "Enough tension to keep things hoppin', but not too tight, because then we'd pop."

Everyone laughed. The front door clicked. William stepped in and looked around.

"Good afternoon, ladies. I don't think I've had the pleasure of making everyone's acquaintance." He bowed a little, and walked about the circle of chairs, shaking hands, asking their names. The women murmured their appreciation for teaching their children and pleaded with William to continue as a schoolmaster. After the last pleasantry, William fled to the kitchen in pursuit of a cup of tea, and whatever treats that he could beg from Mrs. Carroll.

Deborah nudged her. "You best be knitting yards of lace for your wedding dress."

Lizzie's experiences as a maid at the Tabard had taught her how society could be cruel toward those from a lower class. No matter how fine she dressed or refined her speech patterns, William's mother and that Violet would view her as a backwoods mountain girl. Lizzie lifted her chin. She *was* mountain born like these feisty women and refused to refute her heritage.

"There's plenty of time before I'll need a wedding dress." Lizzie counted her stitches. Like Jane Eyre, she must discover what haunted William before she could say yes.

The women hooted and began chattering about how each of their husbands had proposed to them. Lizzie concentrated on the intricate lace pattern. One day, she hoped for a story to share.

•   •   •

In the twilight, William escorted Lizzie to her cottage site. At least she had welcomed his offer to take a walk. He had ordered his workmen to clear the rubble and trim the singed branches on the nearby trees. Already tufts of grass and a few dandelion leaves poked through patches of ashes. Small birds flitted around the hemlocks, searching for a place to roost while a rabbit loped along the trail. William leaned against a tree.

"Have you decided if you want to rebuild here or perhaps somewhere else in the settlement?"

"I really don't know what I want to do. This is a pretty spot. But it's as if a slug has smeared a sticky trail across this place."

William pulled off a thin sassafras branch and snapped it into fragments. Perhaps Lizzie had refused to court him because she sensed something about his former life. He had to explain about his mistakes so she would know everything. But how could he open his heart and face further rejection? Considering how she had described her father's actions; his tale would distress her.

"My cousin wrote to me, asking for advice, and I thought perhaps you could give me your opinion." William forced himself to speak evenly. He did not want to alarm Lizzie.

"I can try." A puzzled expression spread across her face as she sat down on a stump and smoothed her skirts.

"A year ago, my cousin became involved with one of his family's servants. When they learned that the young maid was with child, his parents hid the girl, paid for her care, and arranged for the baby to enter an orphanage. After she gave birth, my cousin's parents had planned to provide the girl with a good reference and send her to a distant city to work for an acquaintance."

"It sounds as if your cousin's parents were more generous than some employers. Many would have turned her out. But why didn't the young man offer to marry her and keep his child?"

"He wanted to, but his parents threatened to take away his inheritance. Then the woman died, so it seemed best to place the baby in an orphanage." William snapped another stick. "Now, my cousin would like to marry, but doesn't know if he should explain the situation to the lady or keep his past a secret."

"He needs to tell her. A few of the local girls birthed woods colts without a husband, yet they kept their babies." Lizzie twisted the edge of her apron. "Your cousin was thinking about money and that's selfish."

William stared at the moon rising in the east. "What do you think the young lady will say if he tells her?" He held his breath, praying for mercy.

"That he should bring his child home and accept his responsibilities as a father. A child is priceless. If only my daddy had understood how much we had needed him. Look at how angry Viney is, and even though I've forgiven him, sometimes I still hurt from being abandoned."

He should have known better than to lie. Once again, he had stumbled and fallen. His head pounded as tension tightened a leather strap around his skull. William saw only one way to regain Lizzie's trust and approval.

. . .

Lizzie knew there was no cousin. Frost seeped through her veins, burning her fingertips, chilling her toes. How could William have chosen an inheritance instead of his child? She recalled the softness of little Joseph in her arms, and how Hank had sought a new mother for his children. It wasn't right that William's child was an orphan when he had a wealthy father who could provide an abundance of food, toys, and clothing, and most of all, his love.

"Didn't your cousin want to hold his son, even one time?" Lizzie could play along with this charade. "Did he search the local orphanages?"

"My cousin found a receipt for a large donation to the institution in his father's office, and a letter from the director of an orphanage."

"Well, I'm sure the orphanage appreciated the generous donation, but I hope your cousin looks for his son. That child needs him, and probably your cousin needs him, too." Lizzie stood up and dusted off her skirts. "We'd better walk home while there is still light."

Back in her room, Lizzie pulled on a nightgown and curled up in bed. How could a few sentences instantly change her life? Her heart had plummeted as she realized that William wasn't half the man that George had been. Like Mr. Rochester's insane and shackled wife, William had hidden a secret that revealed the selfishness lingering in his soul. Lizzie shouldn't have behaved like Jane Eyre and allowed her heart to gallop ahead of common sense. How little she knew about this man who said he loved her.

Lizzie sobbed into her pillow, as William's betrayal raked open the scabs covering the wounds of her father's rejection. A three-year-old Lizzie had wondered if she and her siblings had made their daddy so mad that he did not want them. After growing older, Lizzie had noticed how when a friend's mother died, the father had hurried and soon married another woman, often a widow needing a daddy for her brood. One winter, a couple of men had gone to work in Knoxville, but they had sent home money, and in the spring, they had returned to their families.

What would William's boy think as he grew older, and people called him a bastard? Folks along the ridge urged their unwed daughters to keep their babies. Kin took in their orphaned relatives, even though sometimes the children had to be divided between several families. Wealthy folks didn't adopt a child from an orphanage because they feared it would have "bad blood". William's child might live in an institution until he turned eighteen. Then he might end up working in his blood family's factory or some other miserable place when he should assist his father and learn to manage the mill. How could the man Lizzie love treat his baby in a despicable way?

CHAPTER SEVENTEEN

A woman can make an average man great, and a great man average.
–Robert Burns

Lizzie wanted to contribute to earning Edith's new boots, so she knitted an hour each morning, but her mind scrambled the pattern. Instead of knitting two stitches together, she would add an extra one, or she would forget to bind off the correct number of stitches at the end of a round and would have to rip out the work. Finally, Mrs. Carroll heard her muttering and plopped in a chair beside her.

"Have the wee folk been playing tricks with your needles? You've been glum for several days." She dumped a mound of green beans in her lap and began snapping them into a kettle.

"Here, I'll help." Lizzie stuck her needles into the ball of cotton thread and took a handful of beans. She longed to confide but didn't want Mrs. Carroll to think ill of William. "There's a great deal on my mind."

Mrs. Carroll lifted one eyebrow as her hands moved. "And?"

"Will you keep this a secret?" William might be angry if she told Mrs. Carroll, but so be it. He had not been honest with her.

"You and I have other secrets." The older woman leaned over and hugged Lizzie.

"William made up a story that revealed something from his past. Now I question if I can trust him, and if I love him enough to marry him."

"From what I've observed, you're in love with William and he adores you. Whatever has he done?" Mrs. Carroll frowned and reached for another handful of beans.

Like a flock of crows rising from a tree, William's story flew from Lizzie's lips, along with her misgivings. Mrs. Carroll ran her fingers along the arm of the rocking chair, while the beans sat in her lap.

"If you could write an end to this story, what would you say?" Mrs. Carroll leaned back in her chair and closed her eyes.

"William would claim his son and bring him to Rugby, where folks would accept the child, and then I would marry him." Lizzie wiped away tears with her hanky. "And William's parents would come to know their grandson and learn to love him."

"Then tell William that. Many a young man has dallied with a maid and created a child. But most times, the girl's father insists the lad care for his wee family. Now, it is William's turn to accept his responsibility." Mrs. Carroll brushed a ladybug from her skirt.

"I don't give two figs about William losing his inheritance. He could continue teaching to support his child."

"Over my lifetime, I've learned those who work with their hands find a deeper happiness than inherited riches. As the Irish say, contentment is wealth." Mrs. Carroll patted Lizzie's knee.

After finishing the beans, Lizzie dusted the parlor and gazed at the piano, remembering William's fingers moving across the keys and coaxing her to sing.

Once, in anticipation of biting into warm shortbread, he had lingered in the kitchen as she blended butter and sugar and flour. He had sniffed the fragrance as the cookies baked and a delighted expression filled his countenance. Drat the man! Everywhere she turned, from the boardinghouse to the schoolhouse to the path to her burned cottage, memories plagued her. Lizzie forced her thoughts to plan the songs the children should sing for the school program, but images of William working with the students flickered in her head.

At dinnertime, Lizzie slid her chair in at the table and greeted several new male settlers, along with a family of six from Knoxville who had fled the heat of summer. But William never appeared. She avoided the men's flirtations and instead answered the family's questions about Rugby and Mr. Hughes. While clearing away the dirty dishes, Lizzie asked Mrs. Carroll about William's absence.

"'Tis Friday evening. In Ireland, this is the night when lads go out together. Perhaps William is with his friends." Holding a tray stacked with dishes, Mrs. Carroll turned away and nudged the kitchen door with her shoulder.

But William seldom hobnobbed with other men. She was his closest friend. Sometimes he had tea with Mr. Hill, so they could discuss the Tabard's progress and other matters, but then he told her where he was going. Lizzie pulled her bonnet from the hall tree and stepped out toward the Hill's farm.

A split-rail fence enclosed several pastures sprinkled with sheep, plus a small orchard filled with peach and apple trees. Chickens roamed outside a modest barn, and pink, yellow, and red hollyhocks grew around the Hill's cabin. As Lizzie knocked on their door, guilt nibbled at her for neglecting this English couple who had treated her like a niece. She and Emily should visit them more often.

"Lizzie! Let me fetch another teacup." Mrs. Hill wrapped her arms around Lizzie and led her to the parlor. Except for the company of an orange and white cat, Mrs. Hill had been knitting alone beside a west window. Lizzie sank into a brown winged-back chair next to a table holding a tray with a blue and white teapot, and Mrs. Hill added another teacup and saucer.

"I'm sorry that I haven't visited recently. Thank you, ma'am." Lizzie accepted a cup of tea. Her ears didn't detect the sound of Mr. Hill's voice talking to William elsewhere in the house.

"Ah, you've been occupied. We're so glad that you and William have become close friends." Mrs. Hill chattered about the new settlers, the peach crop, and other tidbits about Rugby.

Lizzie sipped her tea and answered questions, wondering if the men were in the barn. She should have searched the Tabard, but visiting that place still gave her chills, plus she hated how Violet had toured the inside before she had.

"Mrs. Hill, do you know where William is? We are supposed to be discussing the last details of the school program." Lizzie set down her teacup.

"No, I am sorry, but I don't know. Amos didn't say anything about meeting William at the Tabard. Perhaps he went with Amos to pick up the chairs from Mr. Buckley."

"If you see him, ma'am, please remind William that we need to talk." Lizzie rose from her chair.

"I will. I'm sure William is somewhere nearby." Mrs. Hill handed Lizzie her bonnet.

"Thank you, ma'am." Lizzie tied on her bonnet.

Through the twilight, Lizzie walked the path back to the boardinghouse as a cardinal chipped his evening song and she sank into a rocker. What had become of William? Perhaps her harsh words about his cousin propelled him to seek out Violet to assuage his feelings. If so, Lizzie would have destroyed her chances of repairing their relationship. His mother would do all she could to snare her son into marrying Violet. Lizzie slumped in the chair as a whip-poor-will called from behind the carriage shed.

If William didn't return before Monday, she would have to return to the classroom and finish preparing for the program. She shuddered. The gossips would love whispering about how her pride had caused William to abandon her.

.   .   .

William picked up his small carpet bag, strode out of the Cincinnati train station, and hailed a carriage. He must act while courage and determination flowed through him. Pulling out a scrap of paper, he handed it to the driver. So many times, he had considered entering this institution and asking about his child, but doubts had enveloped him. Lizzie's pluck had taught him to plow through his fears and to focus on hope.

He stared at the four-story brick building with the words *General Protestant Orphanage Asylum* chiseled into the limestone arching the main porch. On the opposite sides of the archway rose two rectangular dormitories. His boots sounded on the thick stone steps as he passed through the archway and pushed open a pair of wooden doors. William glanced around and spied a door with the gold letters spelling *Administrator.* He knocked and turned the knob. This spiraling in his gut resembled the way his factory workers felt when called to his office.

"Do you have an appointment, sir?" The dark-haired young man wore round spectacles, a white cotton shirt, black cravat, and a dark gray waistcoat.

"No, I am sorry. I've been out of town for the summer, but I have a pressing need." William removed his hat and forced himself not to fiddle with the rim. He hated mentioning his last name, but he must find his son. "I am William MacLeod of MacLeod Manufacturing; my family often donates to this institution." William extended his hand.

"Yes, Mr. MacLeod, how may I help you, sir?" The young man rose and shook his hand.

"I wish to speak to the Administrator, please." William hoped adding the word please would help him to not appear as if he considered himself better than the clerk.

"Certainly, sir. Right this way." The young man escorted him down a short hallway, knocked, and opened a heavy oak door. "Mr. Mueller, William MacLeod would like to see you, sir."

The gray-haired man rose and shook William's hand. "I know your father well but have only noticed you dancing at the benefits. Good to meet you. How are your parents?"

"Well, sir. They still grieve the passing of Rose, but father has taken an interest in the Rugby Settlement down in Tennessee. I've been there watching over his investments."

"Very good. How may I help you?" Mr. Mueller motioned to a large wing-backed chair for William before sitting down at his desk.

"I am looking for a child, sir." How much should he explain? William wiped sweat from his forehead.

Mr. Mueller looked over his spectacles, studying William. "I assume you are seeking your infant son. Your father told me the details, but I never shared the information with another person."

"Thank you, sir." William swallowed. "Is the lad here? May I see him, please?"

"About five months ago, a family took him home."

He was too late. Pain roared through William, ripping, and tearing at his heart. He should have fought for his child and the adoption would never have happened. His fingernails bit into his thighs. He was too late to make up for his mistakes. Now what would he tell Lizzie?

"But there have been complications..." Mr. Mueller rose and looked out his large window. "When the family adopted your son, they had no children, but a couple of months ago, the wife learned she was in the family way. The doctor ordered bed rest for the next five months, or she will lose the baby. They are not wealthy enough to hire help, so they came to me, seeking to relinquish the boy."

William released his grip on his thighs. "So, he *is* here?" Hope filled his lungs with air. He could prove to Lizzie that he wanted to correct his mistakes.

"No, we agreed it would be cruel to bring him back here. George, that's what they named him, remains with the family until we can find a new set of parents."

William ran his hands down his trousers. Would his son's name give Lizzie sorrow or a bittersweetness from the memories she cherished? Perhaps they could give the lad a middle name and call him by it.

"Because George is one year old, no one wants him. Those willing to adopt an orphan prefer babies. Bad blood and all that nonsense. With each passing day, we are running out of time, because soon the wife can't care for the lad. Are you still interested in meeting him?"

"Yes, sir. Can we go now?" With all my heart, William wanted to shout. To hold him, to carry him to bed, to sing him to sleep. Over the summer, his students had brought wonder and gladness back into his life. His own son would provide even more joy.

"I have a meeting in a few minutes. Why don't you return about five? By then, the husband will be home. I will send them a note, so they will know we are coming."

"Thank you, sir." William's shoulders relaxed. One hour more to wait. To pace the streets like a nervous father while the midwives attended to his son's birth. He had missed that event, but William would mark today as the birthday of his family.

He strolled by shop windows, gazing at little blue sweaters and small trousers. His son would need clothes. So, what if he didn't know his size? William pushed open a door and strode to a counter where a female clerk wrapped a parcel in brown paper for a well-dressed matron. After the woman and her large black hat covered with silk flowers swept by William, the clerk turned to him.

"How may I help you, sir?" Her white shirtwaist and dark brown skirt resembled Lizzie's outfits, and William's heart skipped a beat.

"I need clothes for a one-year-old boy." William rolled his hat in his hand. "I am sorry, but I don't know his size."

The clerk cocked her head. "Is he tall or short for his age? Thin or still chubby? I assume he still wears diapers?"

"Yes, I assume so, too." William nodded. He had been short as a child, and then grew three inches when he turned sixteen. From the clerk's expression, she questioned his sanity. "I'm his uncle and haven't met him, but of course have heard wonderful things about the lad. I want to surprise his mother with a complete wardrobe for the rest of the year." God forgive him for stretching the truth.

"Perhaps I could buy two sizes of everything and then return what doesn't fit." Such a plan sounded good. He would give away any extra clothing to families on the ridge.

"I suppose that would work. Two of everything?"

"Yes, boots, stockings, coats, mittens, everything." William took out a couple of gold coins. "This should cover the costs."

"Yes, sir." The clerk's heels clicked across the wooden floor.

· · ·

"What is all this?" Mr. Mueller asked as he entered the carriage.

"I went shopping, sir. Since I didn't know George's size, I bought clothing in several sizes." William pushed the wrapped parcels aside so Mr. Mueller could settle on a seat. Perhaps he should have first seen how big George was before raiding the clothing shop.

"He shouldn't lack for anything," Mr. Mueller said. "There are other children in our institution who could benefit from your largess."

"Yes, sir. I won't forget." William gazed at the four small faces peering from the second story of the orphanage. The image seared his mind, compelling him to remember to assist these little ones in the memory of his sister and the mother of his child. After twenty minutes, the driver called to the horses and parked. A row of two-story brick houses sharing a common wall with each other lined the street. Two windows graced each floor, and a couple of stone steps led to each front door. Mr. Mueller knocked. A tall man with brown hair, wearing a white cotton shirt and black trousers with suspenders, opened the door.

"Please come in, sirs." He ushered them into the narrow front room. "Marie is feeding George his supper. I'm Fredrick Beyer. Mr. Mueller, I am sorry about this." A strong German accent filtered through his words.

"Yes, this situation is awkward, but we understand how your wife needs extra care. Please meet a man who wants to adopt George. I will refrain from speaking his name."

William shook Beyer's hand, watching how the man's eyes widened as he recognized his employer. William had noticed this man scurrying about the factory but couldn't recollect what Beyer's job was. The fellow would realize something was amiss when he recalled how William was not married. Depending upon how much Beyer told people, soon the entire workforce would learn that a MacLeod had sired a bastard. No, he would never allow that word to be spoken in front of George.

Mrs. Beyer held George as she walked into the parlor and paused. Tears trickled over her cheeks and her lips trembled. She said something in German to her husband, who patted her shoulder and whispered a response.

George's curls resembled Rose's and his eyes were the same cornflower blue as his, while his chin echoed his grandfather's. The lad reached out a hand and his long fingers matched William's. Only the lad's mouth resembled the woman who had birthed him.

"May I?" William held out his arms, and Mrs. Beyer gave him George.

Tears filled William's eyes as he inhaled his son's sweetness. He wanted that scent to percolate through every inch of his body. He kissed the top of George's head and stroked his little hands. One year lost because of his pride and society's prejudices. He swallowed.

"George looks healthy. Thank you for raising him."

Mrs. Beyer looked at her husband, and he translated for her. Nodding her head, she wiped away her tears with a handkerchief. A few threads dragged the floor from the frayed hem of her dark gray dress. William doubted if they would accept any coins from him, but he would tell the accountants to increase Beyer's wages.

"Here." Beyer handed William a brown paper bag as his wife slipped from the room. "His clothes, sir."

"Thank you, but you should save them for the new baby." William turned towards the front door as George played with the ends of his black cravat.

"Thank you, but please take these, sir." Mr. Beyer handed William a small stuffed cat sewn from faded calico, and a baby quilt composed of dozens of blue stars. "My wife makes for him."

"Thank you and thank you for all you have done for this child." William gazed into Mr. Beyer's eyes. "I'm forever indebted to you."

The man nodded and ushered them to the front door. As William and Mr. Mueller hastened to the carriage, he slipped the cat into his pocket and tossed the quilt with the packages. George flailed his fists and feet and howled. William whispered soft words, but George arched his back and screamed.

"Try jiggling him a bit," Mr. Mueller said. "When you reach your home, walk the halls until he quiets. He will need time to adjust to you. Some children require weeks before they feel safe and trust their new parents."

"Thank you, sir." Why had he thought his son would welcome him, a stranger? William bounced George on his knee and prayed. He would need heavenly help to remedy this situation.

CHAPTER EIGHTEEN

Fear not clouds will always lower,
–Robert Burns

The butler held open the door and stared at George as the carriage driver carried in numerous packages. "Welcome home, Master William."

"Thank you. Is my father here?" William rubbed George's back, whose face had turned red from his howling.

"No, sir, but your mother is in the parlor with a friend. Shall I fetch her?"

"Goodness, what is that racket? What's all this?" William's mother asked as she and Violet strode into the foyer. "Why did you bring home a baby!"

William twisted his body to turn the boy towards his mother. "Please meet your grandson, George."

His mother's eyes widened, and she leaned against the wall, breathing in short bursts. The butler raced to bring her a chair. Violet blanched.

"Your son? How can you say that?" The young woman's eyes glinted.

"Because it's true." William tightened his embrace of George, who continued to wail.

No matter what his mother said, he would not abandon his son a second time. Violet's expression proved that she was not the woman to care for George. He knew that just as Lizzie had chosen to love their students, she would open her arms to his child.

"Lord, have mercy! How dare you bring him here! You know what will happen if our friends learn about him. Think about your poor parents' reputation and return him this instant." Mrs. MacLeod glanced at Violet." Please, my dear, say nothing to anyone until I speak with your parents."

"I will honor your wishes, ma'am. I will leave, so you can continue your conversation without me." Violet straightened her shoulders. "I am disappointed in you, William. That awful settlement has changed you, and not for the better."

"Please see to Miss Violet," his mother said to the butler as she closed her eyes.

"Yes, madam. This way, please, miss." The butler marched to the entryway and Violet followed him.

"Take him back," his mother's voice shook, and she clenched her fists. "This instant, before your father arrives. This surprise will harm his heart."

In the recesses of his conscience, William cared about how his actions might affect his parents' health and happiness, but the fate of his son concerned him more. Hopefully, because of their families' long friendship, Violet would remain silent about his child. His parents had wealth and privilege to insulate them, while his son had no one other than himself. Lizzie had convinced him of that truth, and he would provide George with the security and love he deserved. Mr. Mueller had assured him that over the next few months, George would learn to trust William as his father. Just like with teaching the older boys, William would need patience.

"No, mother. I am his father, and he will return with me to Rugby."

His mother's mouth hardened into a thin line. "I should never have left you in that ridiculous place. Did that girl make you do this? And look at all these parcels!"

William shook his head, jiggling George. "My son needs more outfits. And no, Lizzie is not involved in this matter." The less his mother knew about their relationship, the better.

"Lizzie is it! Your father can deal with you. I must lie down before I faint." His mother stumbled away, and a maid trailed her up the stairs.

Now what? William rubbed George's back the way he had seen Lizzie comfort a small child after the girl had skinned her knee. His mother wouldn't allow George to live in the family's nursery, so he would have to move the crib to his room.

"Dan, could you please help me?" William explained his plan to the servant, and the fellow headed toward the nursery.

From around the corner, stepped a young maid with black hair and blue eyes. "Please, sir, I might be able to quiet the lad. I've five brothers and four sisters and one of them always needs comforting." She held out her arms. "Please let me try with the wee lamb."

"What's your name?" William watched the girl rock from side to side as she made soothing sounds.

"Kate, sir. It's a pity he has no favorite blanket to cuddle. Just its scent might calm him."

William pulled the stuffed cat from his pocket. He would look for the quilt among the packages. "His adoptive mother made this."

"Ah, good sir." Kate rubbed George's cheek with the toy. "Your kitty's come with you, sweetheart."

George hiccupped and grabbed for the cat, clutching it to his chest. A few more tears rolled down his rosy cheeks. William's heart ached. If he hadn't fled from his responsibilities, George would not be suffering now. William would never forgive himself for hurting his child and creating this trauma.

The front door opened. "Welcome home, my lad!" His father wrapped an arm around William. "Whom do we have here?"

William prayed his father would understand his motives and have mercy on his child. "This is George, your grandson. I fetched him from the orphanage and plan to keep him."

Tears glistened in his father's eyes, and they trickled down his cheeks, wetting his salt and pepper beard. "I've regretted our decision every day. I thought about finding a foster family for the baby and paying them to care for him, but your mother said that would give her heart apoplexy. You're a better man than I am, son." His father reached out and stroked George's cheek. "May I?"

George gazed up at his grandfather. William cherished the look of wonder sweeping across his father's face and the joy erasing his tears as he brushed his lips against his grandson's forehead. At least one other person living in the house wanted to love George.

"Unfortunately, Violet was here when I arrived, so unless you can convince her parents to not spread the gossip, she knows the news. Mother stormed to her room. I hope you can change her mind. This is Kate, and she has a way with him."

His father nodded at Kate. "You're now his nanny, no matter what the missus says."

"I was going to move the crib into my room." William rubbed his chin.

"Nonsense." His father tickled George's chin. "Kate can sleep in the nursery and see to his needs. You decided to give up your position at Rugby?"

"No, I must return to Rugby for the end of the school performance. I had planned to take George with me, but now I'm unsure how many more changes he can tolerate. Perhaps I should stay a few days."

"If you decide to manage the Inn, then Kate and George should come reside in Rugby. But how will a certain young lady feel if you don't return on Monday?" His father handed George to Kate.

Rejected. Outraged. She would think another man had toyed with her and abandoned her. In that state of mind, Lizzie would harden her heart towards him and would not listen when he explained about George. And if he didn't bring his son with him to Rugby, she might not believe that he had reclaimed him. What a muddle he had created in trying to redeem his past choices.

After dinner with only his father present, William sat down at the piano and opened the lid that protected the keys. Perhaps music would soothe his son and help him fall asleep. "Anything you would like me to play?"

"Something by Robbie Burns. How about *Bonnie Wee Thing*." Mr. MacLeod settled George's head on his shoulder and circled the parlor. The lad stopped whimpered when his grandfather cooed to him in Gaelic.

If William didn't hasten to bring George to Rugby, his father would have him speaking in his Scottish tongue and playing the bagpipes. William's fingers found the notes of the song, and music rippled around the room. His father hummed along as he strolled. George stared at William, mesmerized by the music. William continued to play different selections until he finished with *My Love is Like a Red, Red Rose.* His father handed a sleeping George to Kate, who bundled him off to bed.

"I'll be up in a minute to kiss him goodnight," William said.

"And is Lizzie like a red rose?" Mr. MacLeod sank onto the settee.

"Yes, like a rose bush smothered in blossoms. I've never met a more beautiful woman with a heart as wide as the Ohio River." William closed his eyes, missing her scent and her voice mingling with his. Then he explained their parting conversation. "I am afraid that I ruined my chances with her."

"You must woo her until her heart melts. Bring her a bouquet of red roses, a box of fine tea, and add a lovely tea set. When she comprehends your contriteness, then she will marry you." His father's eyes sparkled. "But remember, this time, a wedding must come before the wedding night."

"Yes, sir. I understand now how much pain a mistake can create for a family." William nodded. "I pray Lizzie will accept my son. His foster family gave him her late fiancé's name and she will find that unsettling."

"Her breath might falter when she first hears his name, but from how you have described Lizzie, compassion fills this lass. I look forward to when I can meet her."

"Yes." William rose. "Time to put my child to bed."

William climbed the stairs and tip-toed into the nursery as Kate placed a drowsy George wearing a tiny nightshirt into his crib. While unpacking the many parcels, she had found George's baby quilt.

"Allow me." William tucked the blue star quilt around George and kissed his cheek. Like a rose unfurling its petals in the morning sunshine, his heart opened. Never had he experienced such love sweeping through him, melting his bones, claiming every part of him. May Lizzie feel the same tenderness when she spied him holding his son.

CHAPTER NINETEEN

What is life, when wanting love?
Night without a morning.
–Robert Burns

Lizzie plunked a stack of dishes onto the worktable in the kitchen. "Do you know what is going on? Can't you tell me anything about William?"

Mrs. Carroll sighed. "On Friday, he said he'd be gone for a few days. For all I know, he went with some lads to that cave the settlers like to explore."

Caving? William? Lizzie turned back her sleeves and washed the dishes. William should have explained why he had to leave Rugby, instead of making her second guess his reason for fleeing. The image of Violet kissing his cheek haunted her. Lizzie set aside a couple of tin cans.

As soon as she stacked the last dish in its place, she walked to her cabin site, set the cans on a stump, and practiced shooting. She hoped the pop of the derringer would alert the local men that she had a gun and knew how to fire it. Lizzie riddled the cans, and then aimed at chunks of charred wood until sweat trickled down her neck and soaked her bodice. She cleaned the pistol and stuck it in her apron pocket.

That afternoon, Lizzie and the ridge women met, and they each unrolled several yards of starched lace edging. Lizzie marveled how the women had found the time to knit with their gardens bursting with produce, meals to cook, and tending children. While nibbling cookies and sipping tea, the women sewed the edgings onto pillow slips.

"I memorized the pattern so I could knit in the dark," Deborah said. "Reckoned that if I can turn a heel of a sock in the twilight, I could keep on making lace. Can't wait to see what these slips will look like." She threaded her needle and stitched away.

They chatted about how Deborah's granddaughter had taken her first steps, and the ripening apple crop. Missy's eyes sparkled as she revealed she was expecting another one, and several women hugged her. Spending time together over the past weeks had taught Lizzie to appreciate these women in small ways. No longer did she see them as someone's wife or mother or sister, but as individuals, as friends with the courage to dream for their children and for themselves. Courage, the same word that William had used when he asked her to accompany him in the classroom. What her new friends didn't comprehend was how their boldness inspired Lizzie to embrace the ideas behind Rugby that encouraged unity in a fresh way. Finally, Eliza Jane tucked her needle and pins into a small calico poke.

"Before we go home," she said and straightened her shoulders, "Can we deliver these here pillow slips to the commissary? The sooner they sell, the faster we can help Edith."

"Yes, let's do that. How is Edith? Should I visit her?" Lizzie asked.

"Oh, no," Deborah said. "Best stay clear of Nate. He blames you for the infection. His leg looks mighty ugly. Some days, his mind wanders something fierce."

"Edith's gaining back her strength, and I'll tell her you asked about her," Eliza Jane said, as she tied on her sunbonnet. "Come on, you sluggard." She poked Missy.

They loaded two baskets and walked to the commissary. Men stared when the gaggle of women paraded through the door and swooped up to the two clerks. From the corner of her eye, Lizzie noticed how the mountain women raised their chins and straightened their backs. Eliza Jane set down her basket.

"We know you sell fancy goods and brought these pillow slips." She unfolded one, snapping the muslin so it would flatten. "They should fetch a good price, even more than those with the fancy stitching." She pointed at a set of pillow shams embroidered with pink cabbage roses.

Lizzie nodded at the clerk as the lady unfolded more pillow slips. This moment belonged to these women, and she wanted them to revel in it. Already, their eyes held more fire and their hands rested on the counter instead of hiding beneath their aprons. She prayed their handiwork would sell quickly so her new friends could reap from their labors. The clerks examined the edgings, whispered to each other, and the fair-haired one spoke.

"We will take them on commission and sell them for the same price as the shams."

"What does that mean, on commission?" Deborah brushed back her sunbonnet.

"When you bring in eggs or butter to barter, you trade them for what they are worth or gain credit for future purchases. But with items left on commission, we will pay you when they are sold."

"How long will that be?" Eliza Jane asked.

"Perhaps someone might buy them this week, or next month, or who knows. But until we are paid for them, we cannot give you any money."

Lizzie touched Eliza Jane's arm. "Trust them. Sometimes Viney waited a month before someone bought her weavings. There are still summer visitors coming to Rugby, and somebody will buy your work."

"I just want Edith to have them boots as soon as she can," Eliza Jane said.

"I'll come by on Saturday and see if they've sold," Deborah said. "Harder for y'all to get away."

"I'll keep an eye on them, too," Lizzie said. "I'll send word when they sell." Like her friends, she needed to earn cash money to support herself. Before the investors opened the new Tabard, they would need fancy goods to decorate the bedrooms. Lizzie needed to figure out how to convince them to buy these linens. Then she and the other women could market dozens of items.

. . .

William swayed back and forth in the rocking chair while George drank from a bottle. He had never been so tired in his life; even returning home at dawn from a night of reveling hadn't worn him out like caring for his child. He had instructed Kate to sleep while he kept George quiet. Kate had shown him how to warm a bottle of milk and how to hold George while he drank, how to rub his back and burp him, and how to change his diapers. His mother had never suffered the same loss of sleep because William's nanny had tended to him. How did the women on the ridge endure this endless weariness and still cook, wash clothes, and take care of a host of children?

George released his bottle and gazed up at William. Wonder and fear flowed through his veins, followed by an intense warmth. This child was his son to cherish, to nurture, and protect. Not just until George grew into manhood, but even when William's hair turned silver, he would be his father and his son would need his guidance. William prayed George was young enough that he would not remember any pain he had suffered during those early months.

Somehow, he would manage this new position that required greater strength and wisdom than he had ever shown during his twenty-odd years. He would succeed, but the task would be simpler if he shared it with a wife. With Lizzie. William brushed his fingertips across George's cheek. He hoped she could forgive him and open her heart to George.

But Lizzie might not forgive him for leaving her to prepare for the school performance on her own. She would not believe that she had the fortitude to undertake the task. Yet after a year of neglecting George, how could William hop on a train and leave behind his child? William stared out at the faint pink spreading across the eastern sky and yawned as the clip-clop of horses' hooves sounded on the street below the window. The door opened, and his father entered.

"How's our wee laddie this morning? It's good to see him relaxed and quiet. I hope you managed a few hours of sleep." Mr. MacLeod settled in a chair next to William. George accepted his grandfather's arms and patted the man's short beard.

"Do you think mother will ever acknowledge George as her grandson?" William closed his eyes and sank down in the chair.

"I'll do my best with her. But she's had a difficult year."

"Haven't we all? I miss Rose every single day." William steadied his voice. Losing Rose had influenced his decisions from teaching to wanting to parent his child to managing the Inn.

"Yes, we still grieve. But while you thrive at Rugby in new freedoms and experiences, the old ways bind your mother to how society dictates certain standards. She prefers to remain in that safe role." Mr. MacLeod patted George's back, and he burped. "It's harder to change when you reach our age."

"But you are willing to dismiss society and claim George as part of our family."

"He is a wee innocent bairn who should not have to endure prejudices because of our decisions." Mr. MacLeod gazed at William. "Now we must give the love we denied him. Rugby will offer George greater opportunities than if he grew up in Cincinnati."

"Mr. Underhill wrote that he shipped more furniture." William ran his fingers through his hair. "I should return, but I don't want to leave George. I wish I could take him with me." William kissed George's nose, and the lad cocked his head.

"But you must return to your responsibilities and help a certain young lady with that program. Your work is to build up Rugby so that George will have a future in a place that will accept him."

· · ·

Lizzie gripped the edges of William's desk, seeing not the confused expressions of the students, but the faces of their mothers who had revealed additional details as they bragged about their children. Hadn't she blithely instructed William to view them not as a gang determined to undermine his authority, but as unique young people who needed nurturing. She must heed her advice as she coaxed them into performing.

"Where's Mister MacLeod?" Seth asked. The other students stared at her.

"Away on business." Lizzie didn't want to lie, but she could not offer a better excuse. Why had Mrs. Carroll convinced her to step into this role? She had considered canceling the few remaining days of the term, but the parents anticipated the program. At least she was familiar with how she and William had organized the up-coming lessons and performance.

"Upper grades, please open your readers and complete the assignment on the blackboard. First and second graders, please come to the front."

All morning, Lizzie listened to students read or recite historical facts or work on an algebra problem on the blackboard. As the temperature and humidity rose, the students languished, and one small boy fell asleep. After the noon break, she gave up on lessons and focused on the up-coming program. "Let's start with the recitations. Victoria, please stand and speak your piece."

"Four score and seven years ago our fathers brought forth," Victoria quoted.

Lizzie smiled at each student as they recited a poem or a part of the Constitution or Bible verses. She prayed that over the next two days, they would continue to gain confidence. Outside the schoolhouse, gusts of wind bent the treetops, and gray clouds swooped over the mountains. The students needed to practice their songs, and then she would urge them to hurry home.

"One more time," Lizzie said. "Oh, the sun shines bright on My Old Kentucky Home…"

But the children could not remember the words that they had practiced many times. Lizzie glanced out the window at the darkening sky. Thunder rumbled, and the windowpanes rattled.

"Now for *Onward Christian Soldiers*," Lizzie started singing the hymn.

The children fidgeted and looked outside. She should let them go, but they hadn't finished rehearsing. Lizzie plowed through the last two verses, as large drops of rain splattered against the windows.

Thunder roared, and sheets of rain battered the schoolhouse. The youngest students ran to Lizzie and clutched her skirt while older siblings comforted their brothers and sisters. The building creaked in the gale force wind. Lizzie shuddered and prayed that a tornado would not form and strike the ridge.

"Everyone put away your books and come sit in the southwest corner." Lizzie gathered the little ones around her. The children's frightened faces stared back at her. She raised her voice over the thunder. "We are safest here. Why don't I tell you a story?"

"Once upon a time a girl named Mutsmag lived in the Tennessee hills and she outwitted a witch and a giant…" Lizzie wished she had the courage of Mutsmag to defy the giant storm pounding the schoolhouse, breaking off tree limbs, and flashing lightning every few seconds. She waved her hands, and changed her voice to sound like the villains and gave Mutsmag a thick drawl. The older boys stared out the window, but the tall tale charmed the younger students. As the storm moved away from the ridge, the darkness faded, and the rain ended, but the wind still pummeled the trees.

"Y'all hasten home," Lizzie said. "Take care on the paths. They'll be slick with mud."

Lizzie walked around the schoolyard as the wind continued to tear off leaves and twigs. One oak had sacrificed a large limb. A man would need to saw it into sections before hauling them away. If the storm damaged her friends' corn and other crops, would they feel like celebrating the end of the term?

· · ·

"Take this letter to the train station and give it to the conductor. He must see that it is delivered to someone at Sedgemore who's going on to Rugby. Tell him it's from a MacLeod."

"Yes, sir," the footman answered and dashed away.

William hated mentioning his family's name. *Hypocrite.* He liked to boast about Rugby's new social order while claiming the privilege attached to wealth. And today he would spend money on something that his students could never afford and something their parents would yearn to possess. William joined Kate in the parlor.

"I changed his nappy, sir. He just finished his bottle, and young George had a strong hold on it. May I teach him how to use a two-handled cup, sir? He is ready to learn, and to eat a bit of oatmeal."

"Of course, if you think that is best, and thank you, Kate." William took George into his arms and kissed his forehead. Any day, his son would toddle about the house. William had to move him to Rugby, or he would miss those important moments.

He held George on his lap while the photographer ducked beneath the cloth draped over his camera. Hopefully, this tin type would prove to Lizzie that he had brought his son home and had committed to caring for him. Kate chattered at George.

"Look this way, sweetheart. That's our boy. Show the man your lovely eyes." Kate waved a hand.

George flinched when the flash of powder erupted and blazed. He howled and buried his head on William's shoulder, and he rubbed his son's back. "There, there. You're safe. It was only a bit of light."

William rose and walked around the room. "I guess we're done for today." While he continued to stroll, the photographer packed his equipment.

"I should have it done by late afternoon, sir." The man shook William's hand. "I'll drop by with it."

"Thank you, I'd appreciate it, because I leave in the morning." William hoped tomorrow would be soon enough.

·   ·   ·

On the walk home, Lizzie's stomach dropped lower and lower. Trees uprooted. Shingles blown off roofs. Rugby's field of tomato plants smashed, and the vines floated in large puddles. Surely her friends' crops looked the same. Unless her people could salvage something, hunger would stalk the mountain folk this winter. If the women could sell more linens, quilts, and fancy goods, then their families might squeak by. But they would need to unearth time to create them. Lizzie opened the door to the boardinghouse.

Mrs. Carroll hugged her. "I was worried about you and the children. We need a cup of tea."

Lizzie sank into a chair. "Do you know anything about my friends?"

"Mr. Hill stopped to check on me and said hail shredded the corn plants and pocked the apples. It was a brutal storm."

"Oh, dear, that's not good. Thank goodness the tall pine by the porch fell away from the house." Lizzie sipped her tea.

Mrs. Carroll stirred cream into her tea. "Rugby will need a brigade of men to clear away the fallen timbers."

"Do you think we should hold the presentation?" Lizzie nibbled on a molasses cookie. "With so much to do, only a few people will come."

Mrs. Carroll looked out over the yard, littered with leaves and small branches. "We've a day to clean up the worst of this mess. Most parents will want to watch their children perform because they are proud of their offspring and understand how hard everyone has worked."

"I suppose so. Still, it seems rather frivolous after so much loss."

"Sometimes we need a bit of lightheartedness after a storm." Mrs. Carroll drank the last of her tea and pulled an envelope from her apron pocket. "I forgot that this arrived on the early train before the storm. Good thing, who knows how many trees fell on the tracks."

William's handwriting. Lizzie tore open the letter and stared. Blast that man! This was all he had to say to her. *Will return soon.*

CHAPTER TWENTY

Thee, sweet maid, hae I offended?
My offence is loving thee.
–Robert Burns

William faced his father. "Do you think I'm doing the right thing? Will George recognize me when I return? A month is a long time for a baby." He kissed the top of George's head.

"It is, but Kate will take good care of him."

"But I want him to love me." William didn't want anyone else to be first in George's heart except Lizzie. After causing so much pain, William wanted his son to smile every time he spied his father. George rubbed his eyes and yawned.

"Aye, but what about a certain young lady? She deserves to know why you left and how your life has changed. And you promised to direct the program."

Would he ever reach a point in his life where William wouldn't regret his actions? He had not wanted to tell anyone his reason for leaving, as William had feared he might not find George, and his pride had fed his fears. Both had ruled his emotions and damaged his relationship with Lizzie.

Kate knocked on the parlor door and entered. "Look at him now, nodding off in his daddy's arms. Do you want to put him to sleep or should I, sir?"

"Please get him ready for his nap, and I'll be up in a few minutes." Despite a wave of sorrow, William relinquished George to the maid. After all, George would spend every day with her.

"I'll leave tomorrow on the earliest morning train, so I can arrive before the presentation."

"Good. Take her roses. Woo her heart back to yours." His father placed his hat on his head and headed out the door.

While Lizzie would enjoy roses, yards of silk and lace would impress her more. Perhaps Kate could recommend a shop that sold those goods. William climbed the stairs to the nursery.

Curled on his side, with his quilt tucked around him, George's eyelids fluttered. Pink brushed his cheeks, and one chubby hand clutched the stuffed cat. Toys, his son, lacked toys. How had William turned twenty-four years-old without knowing what children needed? Because he was a self-centered fool.

"Kate, can you recommend a shop where I can buy lace and yard goods?"

"Stewarts on Third Street sells trimmings and fine fabrics, sir." Kate folded George's clean clothing and placed it in a wardrobe.

"And toys. My toys are probably in a trunk somewhere in the attic, but I'd like to buy George a few playthings and books."

"On Fourth Street is Armstrong's, and he carries wonderful toys. My sisters and brothers love to stare at the displays."

But a family like Kate's couldn't afford anything in the window. William rubbed the back of his neck. His students would have the same yearnings, but their parents would view any gifts as charity. Perhaps he could buy a few toys for the school.

"What do you think George would enjoy?"

"Boys love balls. But purchase a large one, so he can't stick it in his mouth. Blocks are good, sir."

"Thank you, Kate." William leaned over and smoothed George's hair away from his eyes. "You will have the finest blocks I can find."

The driver parked outside Armstrong's and opened the carriage door for William. "Here you be, sir."

"Thank you. Please wait while I shop."

A bell rang when William pulled open the door. Shelves lined the walls of the shop, displaying dolls, puzzles, books, and other toys. William shook his head; he needed time to figure out which ones to purchase.

Several women strolled down the aisle where dolls with porcelain heads, hands, and boots sat on shelves. Tiny tea sets and doll-size chairs were placed near them. William spied a stack of wooden blocks on another shelf and hurried over. Carved with images of animals on one side, the blocks were painted in primary colors and packed in a small wooden box.

"Can I help you, sir?" A clerk with salt and pepper hair and a striped apron covering his clothes approached William. His Scottish accent lilted the words.

"I want to purchase a set of blocks for a toddler. And a large ball. And anything else you can think of." William surveyed the tin soldiers set up on a shelf and a couple of rocking horses near a window.

"Those rocking horses are the rage, but he might be too young for one, sir. Unless you held onto him as he rocked." Mr. Armstrong showed William the horses.

"That's what I'll do. I'll take the one with the red saddle and a real horsehair mane."

"A fine choice. Here we have rubber balls of all sizes, sir." Mr. Armstrong pointed to several baskets heaped with balls of many colors. "These fit a small child's hands, sir."

William picked up a blue ball. Should he take this one or the yellow ball? Along with a red and a green ball, he placed both into Mr. Armstrong's hands. "I need three boxes of blocks, please. And a dozen of those nursery rhyme books, and the fairy tale books."

"A dozen?" Mr. Armstrong raised his eyebrows.

"Yes." William nodded. The store owner didn't need to know William planned to send the extra toys and books to the orphanage and give some to Kate to take home to her siblings. The rest would grace his classroom, where they could play with them after they finished their lessons.

As the driver loaded the parcels into the carriage, William said, "I will walk to Stewarts. It's just around the corner, so please wait for me there."

"Right, sir." The man climbed onto his seat and flicked the reins.

William gazed into the shop windows featuring ladies' high topped button boots, and wide-brimmed velvet hats adorned with feathers and ribbons. Lizzie would look splendid in all these lovely hats, but grief had changed her perspective about such attire.

In the next shop, candy gleamed in glass jars beside boxes of fudge. Candy. His students would love it and could share some with their parents. William marched into the store. Sweets were the perfect family gift.

"Please fill thirty of those small striped bags with a selection of everything. Peppermint sticks, lemon drops, licorice. Please package them in a sturdy crate and give it to my driver waiting outside Stewarts." William handed the clerk several coins. "Keep the change."

"Thank you, sir!" The man opened a sack and scooped in lemon drops.

At Stewarts, William inhaled and pushed open the door. Only women fingered bolts of taffeta, silk, linen, lawn, and wool cloth. Hundreds of small drawers labeled *buttons, snaps,* and *hooks* filled a large wooden cabinet. A clerk with blonde hair in a chignon and dressed in a striped silk frock approached William.

"May I help you, Mr. MacLeod? Are you looking for the tailor's shop? That's in the next block."

"Thank you, but no, I don't need the tailor. I would like to buy some lace." How had the clerk known his name? Perhaps she had worked in his factory. Red crept up William's neck as the women stared at him. As a gentleman, he should show no interest in the lace edgings women stitched to their petticoats and drawers.

"Our lace trims and ribbons are over here, sir. What sort of lace do you need?"

The clerk guided William to a shelf where a rainbow of ribbons shimmered along with cards filled with lace edgings, some with narrow points while others flowed in gentle scallops.

What a foolish idea to shop here. William hadn't a clue what Lizzie would do with such trims. Besides unmentionables, where had his sister worn lace? He recalled the collars and cuffs that his mother's lady's maid stitched onto Rose's freshly laundered frocks.

"Do you have lace collars? And maybe a pair of matching cuffs?"

"Yes, we keep a selection in this drawer, sir. Which do you prefer, the ones made of bobbin lace or crocheted?"

"I'd like to see the bobbin lace ones." Whatever bobbin lace was. William had only watched Lizzie knit lace, but the wives of his Irish workers crocheted and sold the flimsy stuff to his mother's friends.

The clerk lifted several collars from a drawer and spread them on a counter. Each one was a delicate web featuring leaves and flowers woven from fine linen thread. William picked one up, marveling at the intricate twisting and knotting of the threads. One collar featured roses and hearts, and he set it aside along with the matching cuffs.

"We import them from Belgium, France, and Scotland. Have you ever watched lacemaking, sir?"

"Not this sort, but a friend knits lace." William blushed, and the clerk smiled.

"And the collar is for your lady friend, sir?"

"Yes." He needed to hurry and flee from this cage staffed by women. "I'll take this one. And I'd like a bolt of blue silk, with stripes like your dress."

"Certainly, sir. You wish to purchase the whole bolt?" The clerk's boots clicked across the wooden floor, and she pulled a bolt off a shelf. The silk glistened in a ray of sunshine. "Like this? It was woven in France."

"Yes, perfect. Thank you. Please make them into a parcel." If he had bought too many yards, Lizzie could sew a frock for Mrs. Carroll.

William longed to escape from the perfumes drifting through the shop and fill his lungs with fresh air.

"Yes, sir." The clerk wrapped everything in brown paper, tied the parcel with a red ribbon and cited a sum. "Or would you like to add it to your mother's account, sir?"

"No." William handed her several bills and headed for the door. His mother was the last person who should know about this purchase. He would leave the package in the carriage where it could wait for his morning departure.

.   .   .

A faint streak of pink brushed away the gray dawn as William settled into his seat in the train car. Before leaving, he had kissed his sleeping son, spoken a few words with Kate, and felt his heart split when he walked out of the nursery. He hoped this would be the last time he had to leave George. Even if Lizzie refused to reconcile, William would bring his son to Rugby, where George could thrive without society calling him illegitimate. William nodded off as the locomotive chugged south into Kentucky.

The hiss of brakes and the slowing of the rocking motion woke William. Up ahead, a half-dozen men with axes chopped at three trees covering the tracks. A storm must have recently blown through the area. William and a couple of other fellows hopped off the train and ran toward the men. The faster they cleared the tracks, the sooner he would arrive in Sedgemore.

"How bad was the storm? When did it happen?" William asked a black-haired man wearing overalls and a chambray shirt.

"Come yesterday afternoon. It was a bad one. Trees down from here to Knoxville and beyond."

William's stomach plummeted to his toes. The train would never arrive on time if they encountered more delays. He had planned to arrive several hours before the program, so he could explain his mission to Lizzie, and then she would understand his absence.

Repeatedly, the train's brakes squealed as it halted. The male passengers would help clear the tracks and then the locomotive blew its whistle and chugged on. As they crossed an iron bridge towering high over a river, William stared at the brown water rushing below as it carried enormous trees and even a small shed. He hoped the storm had missed Rugby, and that Lizzie was unharmed.

Several hours later, William strode into the Sedgemore station. If he could snag a wagoner heading to the settlement, he could still arrive before the opening of the program. Barrels and crates lined the platform and trunks filled a corner of the station building.

"Is there a driver going to Rugby?" William eyed the bags of mail stacked in the man's office.

"Until they finish clearing the roads, no wagons can get through." The man waved a hand at a stack of crates. "Stuff keeps piling up, waiting for wagons."

"How soon will they finish?" William wiped his forehead with his handkerchief.

"Can't say. Men are working along the pike. But first they had to cut up the trees that landed on their homes and nail up boards to cover holes in their roofs. It's a mess."

"Thank you." William walked to the platform and stared down the muddy and rutted road to Rugby. His father had endured seasickness to follow his dreams. What were mud and fallen trees compared to his love for Lizzie?

• • •

Lizzie dropped an armful of twigs and small branches into a bushel basket and swiped away the hair escaping from her bun. The sounds of saws and men's shouting echoed through Rugby as folks cut up downed trees and large branches. When the settlers finished clearing the roads, the sawmills would have a fresh supply of timber to mill into lumber. Perhaps Lizzie should order enough to rebuild a smaller version of her cottage.

At one time, she would have embraced living in the settlement to stay near William, but like her father, he had run off without a word. He probably wouldn't keep his promise about giving her a job at the Tabard. Mrs. Carroll had entreated Lizzie to continue working at the boardinghouse, but perhaps she should sell her land and build a cottage outside the settlement. Her new female friends would visit her anywhere.

She should be drilling the students to prepare them for tonight, but Mr. Hill had canceled classes so men could saw a large tree that had fallen by the schoolhouse. Lizzie hoped the students would practice their pieces as they worked around their homes. She moved the basket to another section of the lawn, bent over, and resumed clearing the litter.

What did William's cryptic note mean? If a student had written it, William would have quizzed the person on how the lad defined the adverb "soon". She would have understood if one of his parents was sick and his familiar duties required him to return to Cincinnati. But for lesser matters, William could have waited a few more days, unless he had gone to Violet so she could assuage his hurt feelings.

When sweat soaked her dress bodice, Lizzie walked to the springhouse where crocks of milk and butter cooled. She dipped a tin cup and drank the chilly water. She needed a distraction from the heat and the effects of the storm. Wiping her mouth on her apron, Lizzie walked to the Commissary.

No men loitered on the porch, and only one woman stood at the counter purchasing flour and coffee. Lizzie didn't recognize the new settler but nodded at the lady in a simple calico frock and sunbonnet. She strolled to the dry goods section and eyed the display of pillow slips and doilies. Someone had bought the set of slips Deborah had sewn, but everything else remained unsold. Lizzie would talk to Mrs. Hill to learn if the Tabard might decorate the rooms with the local linens. She assumed the Inn would once again buy Viney's coverlets for the beds; maybe she could talk them into purchasing quilts from her friends.

At dinner, Lizzie spooned a tiny serving of chicken potpie onto her plate. Despite her knotted stomach, she had to eat something before heading to the schoolhouse. Fainting would not help her this evening, as she directed the children.

"A mouse eats more than that." Mrs. Carroll nodded her head at Lizzie. "You've skipped too many meals since William left." She placed a dinner roll on Lizzie's plate.

"I'm not hungry." Lizzie forked a bite of chicken and popped it into her mouth.

"That may be, but you need to eat everything before leaving my kitchen, including a helping of rice pudding."

"Yes, ma'am." Lizzie chewed. She shouldn't care if William stayed with Violet or returned to Rugby. But the children would be hurt, and she would be, too.

. . .

After rolling up his pant legs, William held his boots as he forded yet another puddle spreading across the rutted and muddy road. Along the way, he had passed by numerous trees dragged to the roadside. Leaves littered the pike and the floor of the forest. Other timbers had fallen in the woods, and many were wedged in the crooks of tall oaks. The station master had summed up the situation as messy, but such destruction was a tragedy.

Up ahead, men called to each other as they worked. William rounded the curve and spied four oxen hitched to a huge log. The driver shouted at the teams as their muscles strained against the heavy mud and weight of the log. Inch by inch, the oxen dragged the tree from the road, and another fellow unhooked the chain wrapped around the log.

"How badly was Rugby hurt?" William asked the ox driver.

"The winds blew down hundreds of trees and blasted a few barns."

"Anyone hurt?" William's heart drummed. Had Lizzie been injured?

"No, thank God. But the storm made a heap of work."

"Are there more trees to move? Can I help?" William hoped the man would decline his offer so he could continue walking.

"A couple are down about a half-a-mile from here. Bound for Rugby?"

"Yes, I'm their schoolmaster."

The man squinted at him. "You best make haste. Hear there's a recitation tonight."

"Yes. In three hours." William nodded and marched onward. If he didn't run into too many mud holes and trees, he might arrive just as the performance began.

But each time William encountered a group of men hauling a tree off the road, he stopped to assist them. Mud spattered his coat, soaked his trousers, and freckled his face. William held a thick branch and pushed as the leader shouted. He and the other men lifted the tree from the mud and shoved it to the side of the road. At this rate, he wouldn't arrive in Rugby until midnight. William wiped his hands on his pants as the sound of hoofbeats grew closer.

The man reined in his horse. "How's the road between here and Rugby?"

"We've cleared most of it, but the river's still rising. The bridge might be a problem."

William touched the man's leg. "Please, I need to be in Rugby for the school program. It starts in less than an hour. Could I ride with you?"

The man scratched the back of his neck. "I need to fetch the granny woman. My Janie's got the ague. Another passenger would slow me down."

"Please, sir. I'll pay you."

"You're their teacher, aren't you? Come on, then." The man extended his hand.

William climbed up and sat behind the fellow as he urged his horse to trot. A simple farmer had become William's angel as the horse rounded curves and sidestepped mud holes. When they reached the bridge, the man called to his horse.

"Whoa. We best look this over." He dismounted, and William followed.

The brown water raced inches beneath the wooden boards, and a sudden wave spurted through the cracks. If the river continued to rise, soon the flood would smother the bridge and halt travel. William wanted to run across and sprint to Rugby, but they had several miles to ride. When the man led his mare to the edge of the bridge, she flicked her ears and shook her head.

"Come on, Suzie. Just a little water. You can do it." He tugged on the reins, but the horse shied and whinnied.

"Come on, just a short walk." He pulled harder, but the mare reared. The man stared at the river. "You walk ahead, and I'll try one more time. If she won't budge, reckon I'll backtrack. Janie's sister lives not far away. She can help us."

William gripped the railing and set one foot in front of the other as a wave licked his boots. The bridge creaked, and the timbers moaned as the current pushed against them. William's heart hammered against his lungs. He focused on the riverbank, refusing to acknowledge the water slapping his ankles as he inched towards the middle. I'm halfway across, he told himself, think of Lizzie and the children. He had to reach them.

"I'm going back!" The man mounted his horse and dashed off.

William wanted to shout for the fellow to wait until he finished crossing the bridge. If the river swept him away, no one would know of his death. William hauled himself along the railing as the current tugged at his shins. The image of Lizzie's face filled his mind. He would make it back to her. A log rammed into the bridge, and William clutched the railing's rough board as the structure shook. Keep moving. The bridge swayed as William plodded closer to the bank. Bent over, he slogged the last few yards, crawled up the riverbank and collapsed.

The current pushed branches and broken boards across the submerged wooden planking. Another log struck an upright beam supporting the bridge, and the timbers cracked and moaned. A shiver raced down his spine as William emptied his soaked boots. Even after the waters receded, the bridge should be inspected before someone attempted to cross it. He pushed himself up and stumbled towards Rugby. He must prove to Lizzie how he was a man who kept his word.

. . .

"Thank you," Lizzie said as Silas and Josiah placed another bench into place. Thank goodness the little Baptist church had provided the seating. The lads had removed the student's desks to the other room, leaving the lower benches for the smallest students. Next, they carried in a few chairs loaned by the settlers.

"Miss Lizzie, will Mister MacLeod come to watch us?" Silas asked.

The same confusion and pain swirling in Lizzie's heart filled the young man's eyes. William should think about how his absence hurt his students. All afternoon, Lizzie had puzzled what excuse she could provide for William, but she shouldn't be the person to cover for him.

"I don't know. He didn't tell me much before he left." Lizzie rubbed the dust cloth against the polished oak bench. She glanced up at him. "I'm hoping he does. You've worked so hard."

"I hope so, too." Silas touched his cap and walked away with Josiah.

Lizzie finished dusting and sank into William's chair. The children had displayed their penmanship on the chalkboard, and Silas had drawn a bird in the Spencerian style. The dove held a banner with the word, *Welcome.* She had tacked some of their arithmetic papers to the wall so their parents could see their children's work. A bouquet of pink dahlias shimmered on the desk. In thirty minutes, the room would fill with a mixture of mountain folks and settlers. Lizzie prayed they would set aside any prejudices and grudges and view themselves as parents celebrating their children's learning.

William, Lizzie wanted to scream. How dare you miss this important moment. How dare you wound these young hearts and souls! Hadn't Viney struggled for years, blaming herself for her father's rejection? Now, the man Lizzie loved had abandoned these students when they most needed his affirmation and praises.

One-by-one, the parents settled on the benches, holding their babies and toddlers while their older children took their assigned seats. Curiosity swept over the highlanders' faces as they scanned the school room, fragrant with the scent of lemon and beeswax. With its maps, large chalkboard, and even a globe, how different the room must appear from the crude log cabin where the mountain folk had studied for a few months each fall. Their teachers had seldom known more than their older students. Lizzie walked to the center of the room, wishing William could witness the parent's amazed expressions.

"Thank you for coming to hear our students perform their pieces. We will begin by singing the hymn, *I'm Going Home.*" Lizzie hummed a note, raised her hand and the students sang.

"Farewell vain world, I'm going home...."

Tears glistened in a few women's eyes as they recognized the beloved shaped note hymn. A few of the mountain folks sang softly along while the English settlers absorbed the words. As the last notes faded, Lizzie exhaled. Their beginning song had set the tone of the evening, and she prayed the students would remember their parts.

"Charlotte," Lizzie nodded.

The first grader walked to the front of the room. Dressed in a clean pinafore covering a dark blue calico dress with blue ribbons adorning her braids, Charlotte exemplified the status of a settler's offspring.

"'The world is so full of a number of things, I'm sure we should all be as happy as kings,' by Robert Louis Stevenson." Charlotte dashed back to her seat as everyone clapped.

"Very nice. Thank you. Joseph." Lizzie called out the name of each student, and they took their places in the front of the room. Some quoted lines from Shakespeare, while others recited Bible verses or poetry. When younger siblings spied their brothers and sisters, they whispered and nudged their parents. After a half-hour of recitation, Lizzie introduced two songs that the children sang and then continued with their speaking parts. Silas positioned himself up front, and his eyes widened as the door opened.

"'When in the course of human events...'" He fumbled for the words. "Mister MacLeod!"

Lizzie's head jerked towards the door. Water dripped off William's soaked and torn trousers. Brown blotches stained his linen shirt, and one sleeve was ripped at the elbow. His boots oozed muddy water and dirt freckled his weary face. He clutched the doorpost as every pair of eyes stared at him.

"Keep going, Silas. You're doing fine." William sank onto a bench, and a puddle formed at his feet.

Part of Lizzie wanted to hug William, while another part wanted to scold him. How dare he show up at the end of the program and not apologize to his students? But the smiles forming on their faces stilled her tongue. She would postpone her tirade until they were alone.

• • •

William yearned for a hot bath and fresh clothing, but those must wait until he shook every parent's hand and praised their offspring. His boots squished as he circled the room, avoiding Lizzie, who also spoke with the families. The mothers sympathized about his tattered clothing while the fathers praised his courage and determination for crossing the bridge. All the parents thanked him for spending his summer teaching their children. Both settlers and mountain folk begged him to stay in Rugby and teach the next term. Only Mrs. Hill whispered in his ear how Lizzie had been frantic with worry about his whereabouts. He would address those concerns after the hot bath and some food.

With her flushed cheeks and a lavender bow decorating her swept-up hair, Lizzie glowed from an inner beauty that had grown over the summer. William wanted to feel her arms around him, but she hadn't even glanced his way. While he was thankful that the photo of him holding George rested inside his carpetbag at the station, it might be weeks before a wagon could bring everything to Rugby. Without it, he could not prove to Lizzie why he had left. He hoped the photo would be the key to unlock her heart and soothe her resentment.

Instead of strolling back as a couple, Lizzie walked with Mrs. Carroll, and William and Mr. and Mrs. Hill followed them. Mrs. Carroll hadn't pressed him for information but chattered about heating enough water for a good scrubbing while Mrs. Hill scolded William for crossing the bridge in a flood.

"Lizzie, will you please warm up the left-over pot pie cooling in the springhouse? And fetch that half a watermelon," Mrs. Carroll said.

"Yes, ma'am." Lizzie strode to the small stone building.

"Give her time." Mrs. Carroll turned to William. "She's an injured bird. Worried sick about you, while wanting to crack your skull."

"Any suggestions?" William placed the wooden bathtub on the back steps. "I'll set up here, so I won't have to haul everything so far." He doubted that his weary arms could carry hot water to his room. Because of the late hour, no one would come to the back door.

"Leave Lizzie be for tonight. In the morning, try to set things right." Mrs. Carroll grabbed an apron from a hook and tied it on.

William dumped multiple buckets of hot water into the tub, stepped out of his clothes, and sank into the steaming bath. Closing his eyes, he rested his head against the wooden side. Tonight's program had filled him with the sweetness of his students' accomplishments, which reminded him of George. He imagined his son curled up beneath his blue star quilt, sucking his thumb. William mulled over how to win back Lizzie. If he had to crawl through a briar patch, he would, to regain her affections.

CHAPTER TWENTY-ONE

We two have paddled in the stream,
From morning sun till dine,
But seas between us broad have roared,
Since auld lang syne.
–Robert Burns

As lavender, rose, and gold transformed the eastern sky into stained glass, William stretched his arms over his head. After filling his stomach with chicken potpie and watermelon, he had flopped into bed and slept like a hibernating bear. Never again would he take clean, dry clothing and a mattress for granted. Thank goodness he didn't have to teach school today. Somehow, he must retrieve his trunk and parcels. Without the tintype, he couldn't prove to Lizzie why he had left her, and even with it, like the flooded river, she may need several days for her anger to recede.

The river. Had the flood swept away the bridge, or cracked its timbers, making it unsafe for travelers? Certainly, the structure could no longer carry the weight of a loaded wagon, but it might uphold a single horse and rider. William tossed off the bedcovers and opened the doors to his wardrobe.

A few new settlers ate breakfast and nodded at William as he filled his plate with scrambled eggs, bacon, biscuits, and fried potatoes. While his parent's cook created lovely meals, Mrs. Carroll knew how to provide a breakfast for a man who worked with his hands.

"Have you heard anything about the bridge?" William asked Mrs. Carroll as she carried in another platter of eggs.

"Not yet, other than a foolish Scotsman crossed it last night. You could have been swept away. Then what would I say to your mother?"

That a man in love will do anything to restore his beloved's faith in him.

"You would have thought of something." William scooped peach preserves onto his biscuit. "Did Lizzie eat already?"

"Only because I forced her to sit in the kitchen and consume a decent meal. The lass starved herself while you were gone."

"Any idea where she went this morning?" William passed the butter dish to the end of the table.

"No. Other than she visits the Commissary every day." Mrs. Carroll shook her head and strode back into the kitchen.

•　•　•

Lizzie wandered through Rugby's cemetery, pausing at her mother's headstone and then at Aunt Alta's grave. Fresh tree stumps marked where oaks had fallen during the storm. Mrs. Carroll had told her how William had risked his life crossing the bridge, and Lizzie had witnessed enough floods to understand the dangers. Should she fuss at William for his foolishness or allow relief to soothe her heart. But then she would have to forgive him for running off.

Lizzie plopped down by George's grave and waited for the familiar sadness to settle over her, but images of William flashed through her mind. She tried to erase them. After all, George had never abandoned her. The grim reaper had separated them. Lizzie gazed over the many crosses marking men's and women's lives, representing so much pain and sorrow. But also, a reminder of how these folks had not known the number of days they would live. Just as she had not dreamed George would perish a month before their wedding. If William had drowned in the flood, her heart would have shattered once again.

Bereft. Bruised. Overwhelmed. She had allowed love to twine together their hearts. Despite her fury consuming the past few days, Lizzie loved William and wanted to trust him. She wanted him to cherish her. Loving George had taught her to look beyond a man's former actions and to dream of a quiet life together in Rugby. If she wanted to share such happiness with William, she must forget about his impetuous trip and pray that he had spoken the truth about Violet. As Aunt Alta had advised, words laced with honey restored a relationship better than vinegar. Lizzie bowed her head, drinking in the peace of a goldfinch's song.

"Thank you," Lizzie said to George's headstone. Rising, she brushed off her skirt and headed to the Commissary.

. . .

William offered Chestnut a carrot before he brushed him. The horse nudged William's shoulder, and he smiled. At least one person enjoyed his attentions and appreciated his return. He brushed Chestnut until his coat shone, then he saddled the horse and led him out of the stable.

"Have you heard anything about the roads?" William asked Ryan.

"The crews have removed the trees and branches, but we need wind and sun to dry the mud."

"And the bridge?" William mounted Chestnut.

"No word about it. Take care."

"I will."

Chestnut trotted down the pike, avoiding the worst of the puddles and ruts. William paused now and then to allow his horse to rest and drink from a spring. When they reached the bridge, the flood waters churned three inches beneath the planking. He shuddered, remembering the tug of the current snatching at his shins. William dismounted and scanned the timbers for cracks. Although the flood had not swept away any boards, they were slick with silt and littered with twigs and leaves. If he led Chestnut, then the horse should feel safe.

William stroked Chestnut. "It's only a bit of mud and leaves. Trust me. Remember the wonderful rides we've shared. I need your help. So, here we go, lad."

He held the reins, saying soothing words as they inched across the bridge. Once when a gust of wind blew through the trees, Chestnut paused, but followed William when he stepped forward.

"Good job. Halfway across." William continued the monologue until the pair reached the other side of the river. "Thank you, Chestnut. Extra hay for you tonight." William mounted and they trotted away.

By noon, he stood on the Sedgemore platform heaped with trunks, crates of supplies, and barrels waiting to travel to Rugby. The roads would need a week of dry and windy weather before the wagons could haul the baggage to the settlement, and the bridge would need repairing. He might have to search for hours to locate his carpetbag and parcels in this heap.

"Excuse me." William knocked on the stationmaster's office door, and the man opened it.

"Yes?" Dark circles shadowed the fellow's eyes and wrinkles crisscrossed his shirt and trousers.

"Did you organize the items on the dock? Is there a system for searching through that heap?"

The man ran his fingers through his hair. "No. We just stack the next batch on top of the others. We're running out of space. I can only fit the mail bags in my office."

"I see. So, my belongings could be anywhere in that mess?"

"I'm afraid so. When did you arrive?"

"Yesterday." Good gravy, his bags must be at the bottom of that mountain.

The man shrugged his shoulders. "Feel free to dig through it."

"Thank you." William returned to the platform. The mound had measured over a foot high when he had disembarked from the train.

Because of their weight and size, trunks were lined up along the edges of the platform. William spied his and pulled it to one corner. But somewhere in the mess, his carpetbag hid. He picked up a hat box and set it aside as he sifted through parcels, carpetbags, and boxes.

He should have taken the tintype with him. No. During the journey to Rugby, the water and mud he had encountered would have soaked it. At last, William glimpsed his dark blue bag, and pulled it out along with his parcels. Good, he had feared someone might steal it. Looking inside his bag, he found the tintype in an inner pocket. Surely, his son's adorable face would capture Lizzie's heart.

William explained to the clerk about his trunk and the crate of toys before stuffing clean boots and another change of clothing in his saddlebags. He mounted Chestnut and turned towards Rugby. When they reached where Wilson's Creek flowed by the pike, Chestnut could rest while he snacked on the cold biscuits Mrs. Carroll had slipped him. William hoped the good woman could suggest ways to woo Lizzie back to him.

· · ·

"I finished another set of pillow slips," Deborah said as Lizzie opened the back door. "Can we take them to the Commissary?"

Lizzie glanced at Mrs. Carroll. "Can you spare me? I'd like to check if anything sold."

"Ah, surely. We've two hours before supper. Go along with you."

Lizzie and Deborah skirted the worst of the muddy streets as they strolled to the Commissary, stopping to admire the frilly pink hollyhocks edging a settler's fence. They said hello to a girl playing on a front porch of her home and waved at the doctor as he drove by in his rig. For a heartbeat, Lizzie recalled William leaning against her when they sat in the back of Dr. O'Neil's buggy.

"The doctor can't be going far with such mud," Lizzie said, as they climbed the Commissary's porch steps.

"No. The dirt's so soaked that I had to prop up my cornstalks. Waiting for the soil to dry out gave me time to finish these slips."

Lizzie and Deborah checked on their handiwork, but only one pair of pillow slips had sold. A man breezed in, purchased a pound of nails, and departed. No summer visitors or settlers wandered the aisles browsing for a gift or a token to bring back to Cincinnati. A clerk scanned a ledger and glanced up.

"May I help you? Oh, you're the women selling crafts. We haven't sold anymore."

"Then you won't be wanting these?" Deborah held out the slips.

The clerk frowned and cocked her head. "I guess you can place them with the others. Maybe you'll have better luck next week, and if not, then they might sell during the grand opening."

"Thank you." Lizzie stared out a window. If Edith was to have her boots, they couldn't wait for luck. And the opening was a month away. Lizzie would beg Mrs. Hill to buy something, and perhaps her friend could encourage the other English settlers to purchase gifts for their families. After the roads dried, a few visitors would straggle in. But soon schools would soon open for the fall term and families would stay home. Yesterday, she had spied the first goldenrod blooming near Mrs. Carroll's carriage house.

"Are we meeting this week?" Deborah asked when they reached an intersection. "I look forward to sitting with the other women and drinking English tea."

"No, because of the storm, we should wait until next Wednesday." Lizzie touched Deborah's arm. "I will miss everyone, too."

"Do you think Mr. MacLeod will teach the fall term?" Deborah gazed into Lizzie's eyes.

"I don't know. We haven't spoken much since he returned." Lizzie retied her bonnet's ribbons, stiffening her shoulders as she waited for Deborah's lecture.

"I reckoned you would say that. Give him a chance, Lizzie, and listen to him. William's an honest fellow, and he might have a good reason for his trip. And don't forget how you dashed off to your cousin's house and left him wondering. William was frantic about your safety."

"Yes." Lizzie held back a sigh. She hoped William had a good excuse for his behavior.

"See you next week." Deborah bobbed her head.

"Until next week." Lizzie called after her friend.

Instead of heading to the boardinghouse, Lizzie aimed for the trail to the White River. Her boots slid on bits of shale and mud, but the desire to fill her ears with rushing water drove her feet onward. The path twisted around boulders and hemlock trees as the roar of the river grew.

Lizzie climbed onto a large boulder, sat on a flat spot, and hugged her knees. Beneath her, the brown current swept branches, and other debris downstream. Tan froth had gathered where the river had dug out small pockets from the bank. The flood had breached the bridge, but the structure had resisted the force of the water. Yet William had braved the danger, crossed those slippery planks, and hastened on to the performance. Had his desire to please his students driven him onward, or had his motives involved his affections for her?

Deborah's last words tumbled through Lizzie's brain. She missed hearing William's voice, the feel of her hand on his arm, and the mischievous look in his eyes. When George had asked her to marry him, love had nudged her heart to connect her life to a foreigner whose family did not approve of her. Lizzie picked up a stick and tossed it in the river. It spun in the current before racing downstream. Edith had recognized her affections for William, and her voice whispered, "If'n you want his love, let go of your hurt and thinking you're a victim from what he did." Lizzie closed her eyes and exhaled. Her friends spoke the truth and understood her heart.

•   •   •

"I'm famished." William collapsed in a kitchen chair. "Any chance for a bite to eat?" He grinned at Mrs. Carroll.

"There's fresh bread cooling in the pantry and help yourself to the round of cheddar cheese. Mr. Walton ordered it from Boston."

"Thank you." William walked into the pantry, sliced a chunk of bread, and layered cheese upon it. He lifted the steaming kettle off the stove, brewed a cup of tea and carried his snack to the back porch.

How could he convince Lizzie to listen when she wouldn't look him in the eye? He had searched the boardinghouse but couldn't find her. Mrs. Carroll didn't know where she had gone, so he couldn't follow Lizzie. William dusted the crumbs off his hands and pulled open the screen door.

"Do you have a minute or two to talk? And can you keep a secret?" William asked.

"Didn't I keep one for Lizzie?" Mrs. Carroll finished chopping an onion.

"Yes, but this is even more serious. This one could end our relationship or renew it."

"Out with it." Mrs. Carroll put down her knife and faced him.

"I went to Cincinnati to find my son." William pulled the tintype from his waistcoat pocket and handed it to Mrs. Carroll.

"Sweet Joseph, God and Mary, and all the blessed Saints." Mrs. Carroll plopped down in a chair. "Lizzie told me a bit about your situation, but I'd like to hear your side of the story. Start at the beginning."

William explained last year's heartaches, plus what he had told Lizzie, her reaction, and her disapproval of him. "She was right about my negligence, and I needed to accept my responsibilities as his father. Now that I've held George, I understand how much I have missed of his brief life. I love him so much and can't wait to bring him here."

Mrs. Carroll grinned. "You'll be a fine father. Although you wounded her, your actions will assuage Lizzie's anger. Once she feels your son in her arms, he'll steal her heart."

"I hope so. But isn't there something I can do to prove my affections, and my desire to become a husband who will cherish her? Anything that might change her opinion of me?"

Mrs. Carroll rubbed a cheek with one hand. "The lass loves you, and I doubt that bouquets of roses would woo her, but there is something you can do."

William strode to the Commissary, scooped up the women's handiwork, and carried them to the clerk. "I'll take everything. Please wrap them into a parcel."

"Yes, sir. The women who made them will be mighty glad to learn they sold." The clerk wrote the amounts for each item, tallied the sum, and showed William the invoice.

"Please don't tell them who bought everything. If they come to check on their wares, please tell them someone ordered more of their fancy goods." William counted out several bills.

"Yes, sir. I do like a good mystery." She handed him the parcel.

"Thank you." William whistled as he strolled through Rugby.

Soon, the women probably would learn who had bought their fancy work, but he only needed a couple of days to complete his plans. He walked on toward Mr. Hill's farm and found him filling a watering trough.

"William! You look far better than you did last night. I'm thankful you could listen to some of the program. The children were overjoyed when you showed up."

"Yes, sir. I had hoped to arrive early, but the roads were a mess."

"Yes. But they're cleared now, and the water is receding. Have you inspected the Tabard?"

"No, sir. I'm sorry, I had to attend to more personal business. I'll go there next."

"The wind blew away a few shingles from the roof, but we've replaced them. The workers are painting and hanging wallpaper." Mr. Hill leaned on his pitchfork.

"Splendid! We'll finish on time for an October opening." William ran a palm around his neck. "I would like to discuss with you how we will decorate the rooms. I know Lizzie's sister wove many coverlets for the first Tabard. I'd like to buy any she has woven and quilts from the local women. Plus, I thought we could employ the ladies to create more of these." William opened the parcel.

"Very pretty." Mr. Hill eyed a pair of pillow slips. "It's a splendid idea, especially since the storm destroyed much of the highlanders' corn crop. Why don't we see what Mrs. Hill says? She's in the garden."

William carried his bundle and sat with Mrs. Hill beneath the rose arbor. A goldfinch landed on a tall sunflower and pecked at the forming seeds. A climbing red rose spilled its perfume around them as Mrs. Hill ran her fingers over the lace edgings.

"These are lovely! I am so pleased that Lizzie is sharing a skill I taught her. Yes, we should purchase more of these for the Inn. They will add to its rural charm while reminding guest of Rugby's English roots."

"Could you please speak to Lizzie about the order? And make it look as if this were your idea? I don't want her to know that I am involved."

"Certainly. And at the right time, Lizzie will forgive you."

William felt the press of the tintype against his chest, and hoped the right time would be today.

CHAPTER TWENTY-TWO

Ae fond kiss...
–Robert Burns

A new settler, dressed in a crisp muslin shirt and black wool trousers, held open the screen door as Lizzie walked into the Commissary. She scanned the shelves and blinked. All their handiwork had disappeared, and in its place the clerk had created a new display with a tea set dotted with pink roses. Lizzie's skirts swished across the floor, and she stared at the blonde-haired young woman.

"Did you move the pillow slips?" She glanced around the room, searching for a hint of white muslin and lace.

"No, miss, they sold. Here's the money from what you and the ladies earned. Please bring more as soon as you can." The clerk reached across the wooden counter and handed her an envelope.

Lizzie ran her thumbnail over her chin as she walked to the boardinghouse. Something did not feel right about this. While she had faith their work would sell, how odd that *everything* should vanish in one day, especially when nothing had sold for the past week. Lizzie paused beneath a maple tree and counted the bills in the envelope, a tidy sum for each woman. She wanted to twirl and sing at the top of her voice. Like the fluffy cumulus clouds sweeping across the sky, joy soared through her as she dashed into the kitchen.

"Look!" She spread the bills across the kitchen table. "And they want more goods as soon as we can make them. I need to tell everyone."

"What wonderful news." Mrs. Carroll hugged Lizzie. "After that wild storm, what a blessing for those families.

"Something smells wonderful." Mrs. Hill opened the screen door. "Oatmeal raisin?"

"Help yourself." Mrs. Carroll poured steaming water into a teapot and heaped cookies onto a plate. "We're celebrating."

"That's why I came. Amos and I are thrilled with your friends' work. We want to order linens and quilts for the Tabard's rooms. When Viney returns, we would like her to teach some women to spin and weave."

"You bought everything!" Lizzie hugged Mrs. Hill. "Thank you ever so much. You two, have tea. I'm going to tell my friends." Lizzie stuffed the bills into the envelope and raced out the door.

On the outskirts of Rugby, Lizzie strode up the path to Deborah's small homestead. Chickens ran after a rooster who crowed about some tasty bugs. On the porch, a gray and white cat slept near a pot of red blooming geraniums. Wiping her hands on her apron, Deborah walked out.

"I saw you coming. Something amiss in the settlement?"

"No, not at all." Lizzie handed her several bills. "Everything sold, the commissary wants more and even better, Mrs. Hill ordered linens and quilts for the Tabard...."

Deborah grabbed Lizzie by the elbow and swung her around. "Praise God! Edith's going to have her boots, as will every child on the ridge. And their bellies will be full this winter. I'll tell everyone that we need to gather. How about four o'clock?"

. . .

Lizzie stood in the center of the parlor and raised a hand as her friends' questions swirled around her. Deborah handed each woman several bills, and they counted their earnings. Despite their tears, the women's smiles and glowing faces radiated delight. That emotion had eluded Lizzie since George had died, but now it flamed inside her. Together, she and these women would change life on the ridge for their children and families.

"This will pay our taxes and buy coffee and salt." Eliza Jane wept into her hands, and Deborah patted her back.

"I never dreamed we would earn so much. Did you say Viney sells her weaving to folks in Cincinnati?" Missy asked.

"Yes, she does. But first we must fulfill the local orders, then we will think about expanding our markets. Please write in this book how many items you can make in the next month. I saved back a sum to buy another bolt of muslin and thread that everyone will use. Some of us will restock the Commissary, while the rest will make the linens for the Tabard. The Hills also asked for quilts and coverlets. If you have any spare quilts, please bring them to me."

Gratitude flooded Lizzie that these women had become her friends. These ladies showed more gumption than the English girls she had tried to imitate before they departed for their homeland. While Lizzie enjoyed the feel of silk against her skin and how a ruffle skirt whispered across a floor, she wouldn't trade those pleasures for the friendship of these mountain women dressed in faded calico and muslin aprons. After they bought those boots, Lizzie would encourage them to sew a new dress for themselves.

Deborah planted her hands on her waist. "We better stop lollygagging and get to work!"

"Yes. After Viney returns, she can teach you how to weave, and I'll ask my brother to show some of your husbands how to build looms."

"I want to learn, too," Sally said. "My man's handy."

"Yes, he is. And we'll ask the cooper to build spinning wheels," Lizzie said. The ridge would soon hum with the whir of spinning wheels and the clatter of looms. When the guests for the grand opening arrived in October, her friends could revel in how the new inn displayed their talents.

. . .

Mrs. Carroll rounded the corner and raised an eyebrow as William slipped away from his hiding spot near the open parlor door. He followed her into the kitchen and grabbed a fistful of cookies.

"My plan's working. Does Lizzie know who bought their fancy goods?" William bit into an oatmeal raisin cookie. "Yum, my favorite."

"She thinks Mr. and Mrs. Hill purchased them. Should I drop hints?" Mrs. Carroll shoved a split log into the firebox of the cookstove.

"No." William poured a glass of milk and chugged it. "That's a good idea to have her sister teach weaving. Do you know when she will return?"

"Viney wrote their father is fading, so Lizzie wants to visit them soon." Mrs. Carroll dusted a pastry cloth with flour and rolled out pie dough.

"If I can manage it, perhaps I should accompany her."

"From Viney's descriptions of that wild place, Lizzie would be safer if she traveled with you."

William stared out the window, covered with cheesecloth. The fine mesh broke the view into tiny squares. Like the many days he had spent on the ridge, the cloth blurred the overall landscape while the squares framed special moments…meeting Lizzie at the train station, pushing her buggy out of the mud hole, tackling the hours of teaching, and comforting her after her house burned. The summer had healed and challenged them in ways neither of them had foreseen. William hoped they would share many more years that would nurture their love.

"But before you offer to travel with Lizzie, you best be on speaking terms with the lass. Especially if you plan to ask her father for her hand." Mrs. Carroll layered peaches into the pie crust and sprinkled them with nutmeg and sugar.

"Yes. You're right about that." William walked to his room, flopped onto his bed, and pulled the tintype from his waistcoat pocket. In the image, dark circles shadowed his eyes and his son's expression showed confusion. He missed holding George and smelling his special sweetness. William longed to teach his son to drink from a two handled mug and hold his hand when George took his first steps. The sooner he brought his son to Rugby, the sooner little George would transform him into a real father. With the help of Kate, William would become a decent parent, a role he longed to share with Lizzie.

During dinner, William chatted with the two new settlers as Lizzie cut her fried fish into small bites and ate it. When he passed her a basket of rolls, she nodded, and thanked him. Lizzie simply engaged in the general conversation and answered the few questions the settlers asked her. How could he propose marriage if she wouldn't look at him?

After he and Lizzie cleared the dinner dishes and carried them into the kitchen, William touched her shoulder. She froze. Her lips pressed into a thin line and her eyes glinted.

"Would you please go for a stroll with me? It's a lovely evening."

"I'm sorry, but it will be dark by the time I finish these dishes and cleaning the kitchen." Lizzie turned away.

"I'll help." William picked up a towel. He would stand on his head if that would convince Lizzie to listen to him. "Or I can wash them if you like."

"No need. Plus, I have a headache."

"Then a walk and fresh air will do your head good," Mrs. Carroll said. "And I'd appreciate your help, William. A little dishwashing music while I rest my feet." Mrs. Carroll reached for her fiddle.

Although Mrs. Carroll started with a beautiful slow air that pulled at William's soul, she soon bowed a spate of reels and jigs that hastened the washing. While Lizzie scrubbed, William dried, stacked, and carried the dishes to their shelf. At last, every pot and bowl sparkled, and William poured the dish water onto a lilac bush.

"Off with you. I'll see you in the morning." Mrs. Carroll yawned and shooed them away.

Bats fluttered high above their heads, and tree frogs trilled as William offered Lizzie his arm. She shook her head, pressing her hands against her skirt. Now what should he do? *Walk, simply walk.*

They wandered the gravel paths meandering through Rugby, pausing at the Inn.

"Congratulations on the Inn ordering more of your handiwork." William stared at the moon rising above the tree line.

"You know?" Lizzie cocked her head.

"The village is buzzing with the news. I think this development will please my father. He likes those old crafts."

.   .   .

"I hope he approves." Lizzie hadn't considered how William's father was the biggest investor and might not accept the Hill's decision. Like a snail's slimy trail, apprehension oozed over her. If he canceled the order, what would she say to her friends? Perhaps she should write to William's father and plead with him.

Clouds of fireflies danced along the edge of the woods near the library, and its windows reflected the moonlight sifting through the trees. The day's heat lifted the rich scent of warm, damp earth, and it mingled with the cool fog descending into the hollows. She loved this time of the evening and the soft look of the mist. Lizzie couldn't imagine living anywhere else than in this beloved settlement. She wished William could once again be the man she had cherished so they could share a life in Rugby.

"Lizzie, please may I explain about my absence?" William touched her arm.

The look that had haunted William had vanished. Lizzie recalled Deborah's advice and the roar of a river sweeping away her pessimistic thoughts. She nodded her head and her shoulders relaxed.

"I think this will show you why I left." From his waistcoat pocket, William pulled out an envelope and handed it to Lizzie.

Her fingers trembled as she slid out a tintype of William holding an older baby. The child's eyes and nose looked like William's, as did the mop of hair. Sadness lingered on the boy's face as he clutched a stuffed animal. Her heart thawed in the wonder of what William was showing her.

"My son." William looked down the pike, where fog twisted around the curves. "I brought him to my parents' house."

"When you told me that story about a cousin, I knew you were the man." Lizzie glanced at William's eyes, warm with a certain peace she had never witnessed. "What's your son's name?"

"George. The orphanage director chose it."

Lizzie slumped against a tree, wishing the man had called this boy John or Patrick, or some other common name. What slight of God's hand had prompted this? Yet perhaps this was a prod from heaven to create fresh memories for that name.

"Are you faint? Do you need to sit down?" William gripped her shoulder.

"I'll be fine." Lizzie gazed up at the moon. She would not dwell on the past but would embrace this young child who deserved love and nurturing. "Tell me what happened."

As William related his tale, he paced in a circle. Lizzie watched fear and heartache flit across his face, but when he described George, a softness lit his expression. William had bonded with his child and embraced the immensity of those responsibilities.

"Do you think your mother will ever acknowledge him?" Lizzie recalled how his mother's cutting words had bruised her spirit. What sorrow little George would endure if his grandmother rejected him.

"I don't know, but I hope so. I plan to bring him to Rugby, where folks will love him, and he will learn that social classes don't matter. Where he can become a man who respects women as his equal."

As if she were sucking on honeycomb, a sweetness for this man and for his son flowed through Lizzie. She wanted to hold George, look into his eyes, and tell him how precious he was to her. She would help the lad grow into a brilliant future.

Lizzie slid her fingers into William's. "Every child should have a mother."

"Oh, Elizabeth." Tears glittered in the corners of William's eyes. "I dearly love you. You are the wife of my dreams."

"Then invite me into your dreams." Lizzie could hear Deborah fussing about how some men needed things spelled out for them.

"I need to get down on bended knees and show you the ring." William fumbled in his other waistcoat pocket.

"Yes, as if I were one of those society girls." A comet soared through her as Lizzie held out her hands to capture William's words and love. She would hold dear this moment that would knit her life with William's.

"I've never wanted one of those society girls." He sank to one knee. "Will you please marry me? Every day, I will cherish and honor you. Please become my wife and the mother of my son." He lifted the lid of a small box. Circled by flaming rubies, a diamond sparkled against a band of gold.

"Yes. And I promise to bring you joy every morning and night." Lizzie cupped William's cheek as he slid the ring on her finger. Her women friends would swoon when they saw her ring and tease her about marrying a wealthy flat lander.

Lizzie slipped her arms around William's waist, covering his mouth with hers. His breath tasted of butter and sugar. A stirring to give William many sons and daughters quickened her heartbeat. Even if she had to wash heaps of diapers, she wanted to hold their children's soft hands as they discovered the richness of the ridge. She deepened her kiss as his fingers ran up and down her ribs.

"I want to be careful, my love." William stepped back and pointed toward the Tabard. "See those windows? I will have the carpenters turn that wing into a suite where we can live while we rebuild your cottage."

"Our family will need more rooms than a cottage can offer." Lizzie kissed William's hands and held them to her cheek.

"Then we will build a house in the village with a parlor, where your friends can gather and knit." William wrapped an arm around her waist. "When you're ready, we'll draw up the plans. But first our wedding."

"Yes, a wedding shared with everyone we love." Like the fireflies flashing their lights, joy and hope sparkled inside Lizzie as they strolled back home to the faint music of Mrs. Carroll's fiddle.

EPILOGUE

Viney handed her sister a stack of linens, and Lizzie placed them in the bottom drawer of a chifforobe that graced a corner of her quarters in the Tabard. The scent of beeswax and lemons floated through the room with cream-colored wallpaper dotted with small pink roses.

"The edging on this pillow slip is beautiful." Viney ran a finger over the lace.

"Deborah knit it and Edith created the doily sitting on that table. I love how the mountain women's talents shine in every room of the Tabard, as do yours." Lizzie gazed at Viney. How wonderful to share this last day as a single woman with her newly married sister.

Viney plopped on to a large four-poster bed built from oak. She bounced a bit on the mattress. "Looks like William wants plenty of room. Charlie and I need one of these for the addition he's building onto Aunt Alta's cabin."

"Well, you can't have it, but William can tell you who made it." Lizzie's cheeks blazed, and she stuck her head into the chifforobe. Tomorrow night, she and William would share this bed and their love.

"Your friends are here, Lizzie." Mrs. Carroll ushered Deborah and Edith into her boardinghouse room. Edith lifted one foot, showing off her black kid boots.

"It tickles me that I can wear these here boots to your wedding. And with a new dress, too!" Edith grinned.

Lizzie hugged the two women, and Deborah kissed Lizzie's cheek.

"Let me brush your hair," Deborah said. "Seeing as how you don't have a mother; I'll share about my wedding night." She picked up a hairbrush and stroked Lizzie's hair while whispering details that made Lizzie blush.

"I'll help you, Viney." Edith eased Lizzie's sister into a pale pink gown sprigged with blue flowers. The gold wedding band on Viney's hand glimmered as she wrapped her braids like a crown on her head and pinned on a garland of white snow asters.

Standing in her chemise and drawers, Lizzie inhaled and held onto the bedpost while Deborah tugged on her corset laces and knotted the ribbons. Lizzie slid on three petticoats before her friend straightened a bustle and Lizzie fastened the ties. While William would love her in a simple calico frock, for this special day, Lizzie wanted to present herself as a refined lady adorned and prepared to entertain society. She sprinkled rosewater over her undergarments and on her hair.

"William will relish burying his nose in your hair, and elsewhere," Viney said.

"You hush," Lizzie said. Viney glowed from the love of her sweet Charlie. A warmth spread over Lizzie. Tonight, she and William would delight in the same pleasures.

Deborah and Edith guided the cream-colored gown over Lizzie's head. The satin whispered as the dress slid into place. The bodice hugged her bosom, and the tiny lace-edged sleeves rode the tops of her shoulders. Rows of ruffles billowed across the skirt. Lizzie had formed dozens of small silk roses and stitched them along the top ruffle that began just below her knees. From the doorway, Mrs. Carroll wiped away tears.

"Perfect. Like a white Christmas rose," Mrs. Carroll said. "And here is my gift. I didn't want you to see it until today." She lifted the lid off a pasteboard box, unfolding a veil of Irish lace. "My aunt Eileen, bless her soul, was a nun. She and the other sisters crocheted it for my wedding day."

Hundreds of tiny lace flowers kissed Lizzie's cheeks as her friends draped the veil over her head. Lizzie gazed out through the delicate lace at the amazement sweeping across her friends' faces.

"It's as if someone stitched together dozens of Queen Anne's Lace blossoms," Deborah said.

"The lace you knit is just as lovely. Thank you for the linens you sewed for me. For opening your hearts. Your faith and friendship carried William and me to this day." Lizzie gazed upon the faces of her dear friends.

"When you feel like fussing about him, we will be here for you," Deborah said.

"Now, let's haste to the wedding," Mrs. Carroll said.

A settler had swept the dusting of snow off the path leading to Christ Church. Pine wreaths decorated the doors of homes and pine boughs edged the tops of picket fences. A scattering of snowflakes sifted from the few clouds drifting over the ridge. Lizzie's heartbeat quickened when they reached the church. Deborah's husband opened the door.

The perfume from scores of pink roses surrounded her. Enormous bouquets glowed at the front of the church and clusters of roses and pine branches adorned the pews. Rose petals sparkled on the long white cloth covering the aisle. Lizzie blinked back tears. The roses were not just for her, but for William's sister, who had loved the pink blossoms. Mrs. Carroll handed Lizzie a bouquet of red roses, gardenias, and ivy.

Dressed in a kilt, Mr. MacLeod approached Lizzie. A thick black beard speckled with gray framed his square face as his intense blue eyes, so like William's, stared into hers. He had arrived on last night's train, and much to William's sorrow, without Mrs. MacLeod. Lizzie hoped one day his mother would accept her and George.

"I meant to say this during the Grand Opening, but I couldn't find a spare moment. Thank you for giving William the courage to be a father. I never agreed with what my wife did to his child, but I was so deep in my grief that I could barely breathe." Mr. MacLeod patted Lizzie's shoulder. "William was right to say that your beauty is like a red, red rose."

Lizzie dabbed at her tears. "Thank you. I loved your grandson from the moment I saw the tintype. And he's charmed everyone in Rugby."

Near the door, another man in a kilt, holding an odd, shaped bag attached to narrow horns, puffed his cheeks; he fingered a long flute-like thing, and a caterwauling began. Every head in the church turned, and a couple of babies cried.

"I didn't tell William that I brought a piper. Please allow this old Scot to honor a family tradition." Mr. MacLeod offered Lizzie his arm.

The hymn *Amazing Grace* vibrated through the floorboards as Viney and Charlie led the procession. The clouds broke and sunshine flowed through the stained-glass windows and over the glowing wood paneling. At the front of the church, dressed in a tartan waistcoat, frock coat and black trousers, William held George, who wore a light blue suit with short pants and waved when he spied his new mother. As Lizzie stepped upon the rose petals, their perfume swirled around her. Friends and their families, along with Mrs. Carroll and dozens of settlers, rose from their seats. When Mr. MacLeod presented Lizzie to William at the altar, the minister in his white robe placed Lizzie's hands on William's. They repeated the sacred words to bind them together. *With all my heart*, Lizzie wanted to add after she repeated, "I do."

William handed George to his father and lifted Lizzie's veil. Their lips lingered as the bells of Christ Church rang out across the ridge. Tonight, they could kiss and caress each other until the sun rose. And if she led William to a laurel thicket, they would feel no shame.

Near the doorway, Mrs. Carroll drew her bow and played *Ae Fond Kiss* as George babbled and Lizzie's women friends clapped. Lizzie reached for her new son, and he rubbed his cheek against hers. William wrapped an arm around her waist, and they gazed at the joy flowing from the folks who cherished them. Throughout the upcoming years, sweetness and sorrow would mingle in their lives, but their courage and love would brave the challenges and welcome the blessings.

THE END

AUTHOR'S NOTE

Like Lizzie and William, all of us wish for second chances to undo decisions we have made. Some of those choices might resemble William's situation with an unplanned child. Others are less serious, like why didn't I take trigonometry in high school, so I wouldn't have cried my way through my college calculus class? Yet from making unwise choices, we grow and learn not to repeat those mistakes.

Grief is another bond that draws together folks who are healing from the death of a loved one. The pain of grieving has no timeline, yet as days and years pass, hope inches into people's hearts. In 2015, my son, who had served in Afghanistan and suffered from PTSD took his life. Just as Lizzie struggled with moments that triggered deep heartache, I have experienced how a bugle playing Taps snatches away my breath. For those of you who are grieving, find some small way to commemorate your loved one. Every year, my husband plants a four-acre field of poppies in honor of our son and thousands of visitors stroll around the memorial, drinking in the peace and beauty of the flowers.

To view our poppies, look at this link: https://www.youtube.com/watch?v=5lejWMNmO3o.

Also, for military survivors seeking comfort, please contact: https://www.taps.org/. The Tragedy Assistance Program for Survivors offers numerous services and support for grieving families.

Today, Historic Rugby thrives in the Cumberland Mountains of Tennessee. Located about an hour west of Knoxville, the restored village offers tours, special events such as Halloween ghost stories in the cemetery, elegant Christmas teas, and Irish Road Bowling. Visitors can stay in various types of lodgings, and hike trails in the Big South Fork of the Cumberland River National Park. Or they can splash in the Gentlemen's Swimming hole and wander through Beacon Hill where new residents have built homes. Many couples choose to marry in Christ Church, especially at Christmas time. If you would like a tour: https://historicrugby.org/

Ae Fond Kiss is my favorite Robbie Burns song. As a child, my parents often played bagpipe records and recordings of folk artists singing the songs of Robbie Burns (1759-1796). In Scotland, Burns is revered as their national poet who wrote his verses in the Scot's dialect, and *Auld Lang Syne* is his most famous song, commonly sung on New Year's Eve.

You can hear *Ae Fond Kiss* at this link:
https://www.youtube.com/watch?v=bWzXTebD5X0

For years, I have knitted lace doilies and edgings from fine cotton thread. If you are interested in this tradition, there are many books and online sources for lace patterns and supplies.

Also, a guild offers a newsletter and is a source for patterns and inspiration: https://www.lacyknittersguild.org/

Just as Lizzie's friends encouraged her, a community of folks helped me create this novel. Many thanks to my first readers, Lisa Lenzo, John Van Voorhees, Kay Hubbard, Robin Heald and Kathy Gilbert Warren. Numerous thanks to Sally Martin, Rita King, and Sue Guigar for their expert advice on how William could lead Chestnut across the bridge. Thank you to my patient and loving agent, Terrie Wolf of AKA Literary Management. Thank you to Reagan Rothe and the fine folks at Black Rose Writing for publishing this next novel in the series about Historical Rugby. Thank you to David King for the splendid cover design and to Ginny Shilliday for singing *Ae Fond Kiss* on the book trailer. Thank you to a wonderful group of women known as The Quilters who *always* are there for each other, including me, and are the role models for Lizzie's women friends. Many thanks to Liz Carroll whose music and creativity inspire me. And most of all, thanks be to God for giving me a gift of storytelling.

ABOUT THE AUTHOR

Joan Donaldson is the author of two other novels set in Historic Rugby, *On Viney's Mountain* and *Hearts of Mercy*. *The Christian Science Monitor* has published her essays, and they air on Michigan Public Radio. Accompanied by her cats, Turnip and Puca, she writes from her yellow house nestled on an organic blueberry farm in Michigan. Every year to honor their deceased son, her husband plants four acres of poppies that draw hundreds of visitors who find comfort, beauty, and peace in the waving red flowers. In her free time, Joan sews quilts, gardens, plays a small harp, and pretends with her grandchildren.

HEARTS
of
MERCY
INDIE APPROVED READER
"Shocking, intriguing and poignant. Joan captures a moment
in time few are aware of. Beautifully written and researched."
-Viola Shipman, International Best-Selling Author of The Recipe Box
JOAN DONALDSON

NOTE FROM JOAN DONALDSON

Word-of-mouth is crucial for any author to succeed. If you enjoyed *Ae Fond Kiss*, please leave a review online—anywhere you are able. Even if it's just a sentence or two. It would make all the difference and would be very much appreciated.

Thanks!
Joan Donaldson

We hope you enjoyed reading this title from:

BLACK ROSE writing™

www.blackrosewriting.com

Subscribe to our mailing list – *The Rosevine* – and receive **FREE** books, daily deals, and stay current with news about upcoming releases and our hottest authors.
Scan the QR code below to sign up.

Already a subscriber? Please accept a sincere thank you for being a fan of Black Rose Writing authors.

View other Black Rose Writing titles at www.blackrosewriting.com/books and use promo code **PRINT** to receive a **20% discount** when purchasing.